Breakthrough

Breakthrough

John C. Robinson

Winchester, UK
Washington, USA

First published by Roundfire Books, 2015
Roundfire Books is an imprint of John Hunt Publishing Ltd., Laurel House, Station Approach,
Alresford, Hants, SO24 9JH, UK
office1@jhpbooks.net
www.johnhuntpublishing.com
www.roundfire-books.com

For distributor details and how to order please visit the 'Ordering' section on our website.

ISBN: 978 1 78535 092 4
Library of Congress Control Number: 2015935818

A CIP catalogue record for this book is available from the British Library.

Design: Stuart Davies

Printed in the USA by Edwards Brothers Malloy

We operate a distinctive and ethical publishing philosophy in all
areas of our business, from our global network of authors to
production and worldwide distribution.

Although a work of fiction, the events, experiences and processes in this story can and do happen all the time. In this regard, it is a true story. And, while it has been described as a novel of ideas, its purpose is to transcend ideas altogether.

Part I

Chapter 1

"The modern world is a Godless snake pit of evil, temptation and eternal damnation. Where will you turn for deliverance when *you* are the sinner!?"

Thirty-two-year-old Emma Jensen sat attentively on the hard wooden pew, her thin, angular frame rigidly upright, bravely determined to grasp the sermon's fiery message. Old Testament words burned through her worn overcoat and threadbare dress, branding her heart with terror. As Pastor Hoeller's feverish diatribe intensified, every member of the small but loyal congregation stiffened to attention, desperately trying to avoid their preacher's accusing glare and the punishment of Hell it promised.

The First Christian Church of Mayhew was a small, unpretentious, whitewashed wooden structure in the rural Central Valley of California. Meeting hall, office, small kitchen, and unpaved parking lot, it was a model of religious austerity five miles off Interstate 80 heading south from Sacramento. Every day the tentacles of sin city crept further into field and stream of this vast farming region, once proudly hailed as the salad bowl of the country. Rural attitudes, however, run deeper than strip malls and fast-food restaurants in these parts, defying the superficial glitter of progress. What Pastor Hoeller's church lacked in modern architecture it made up for in stern interpretation of scripture, as unforgiving as the pews, rough as the wood floors, and bleak as the growing dustbowl of climate change ravaging the Central Valley. This was no nonsense, hardpan fundamentalism.

No one and nothing moved, not even the dank cold air seeping through cracks in the barren walls.

A cruel February day crushed all life outside. Its slate-gray sky had merged this morning with dense tule fog, intent on

1

freezing to death whatever life winter's long infertility hadn't already taken. Seasonal Affective Disorder, SAD for short, was not in short supply during Sacramento's cold rainy months. But even the gloomy weather knew its supporting role behind Pastor Hoeller's scathing oration. Man was born with a fallen nature, inherently, hopelessly and eternally lost without redemption in Christ. Only the one true religion and repentance from sinful ways can save a man's soul.

For five years, Emma – a thin, pale, wisp of a woman with dishwater-blonde hair and an enduring determination not to be blown away in the sweeping valley winds – had been trying to start a family. Children, of course, were a sign of God's favor. Adding to the public humiliation of her missing fecundity was her husband Paul, a faithless ne'er-do-well who eked out a marginal living as a mechanic and occasional church handyman, forcing her to work at the old five-and-dime instead of being home baking bread and instructing children in the ways of the Lord. Emma worried that God was punishing her for Paul's lack of faith, and in the privacy of their dilapidated one-bedroom rented house, she berated his lack of industry and ambition. Maybe her mother had been right before she died in saying that Paul was the Devil's lazy stepson. Emma hung on Pastor Hoeller's every word searching for a way to restore God's blessing on her home.

As if carved from hard Yosemite granite, Paul sat heavy and motionless on Emma's right. He was two years younger and two inches shorter than his wife, biblically plagued with a nervous twitch in his right eye and a limp caused when a car fell off the blocks onto his right hip. A loyal if uncomplicated husband with a chronic windblown expression, Paul had learned his various roles in the fundamentalist script and played each one properly: husband, worker, believer, sinner, failure. His rough hands were no longer allowed to caress Emma's thin body for pleasure or comfort; she now scheduled sex for procreation only. Though he appeared as grimly pious as Hoeller's sermons, Paul was miles away, in some wasteland beyond depression. No longer looking to Hoeller's God for answers, he had forgotten how to pray. He had forgotten what it was that he ever prayed for in the first place.

Paul's life ended at the age of seven when his mother died of cancer. An aged aunt, permanently embalmed in her sickly-sweet drugstore perfume, whose faded mourning garments and lack of human warmth blended into a flat shade of bleak, told him that his "Mama" had gone on a long trip. It took Paul a year to realize she wasn't coming back. After that, he was a shell: a "good boy" on the outside but shriveled, empty, and dead inside – a mute testament to an impoverished childhood. People occasionally talked at him, but never with him. Life settled into a droning engine of chores and expectations no longer organized around an emotional core.

Paul's father, a quiet dustbowl survivor long ago defeated by his own childhood depression, slid steadily into an alcoholic haze. Helplessly shepherding his three sad children, the man said little, did little, and died one day on the old family divan. No one realized he was gone until the next day when his aroma announced the end of a spectacularly meaningless life. Seventeen at the time, and the oldest child, Paul was left to raise himself and look after his little brother and sister until they could run the house on their own. In this kind of family you grow up like tumbleweed, don't ask for much, and the dust-filled restless wind eventually blows you on your way.

Undistinguished socially and academically, and lost in a world that had long ago forgotten him, Paul drifted out of school unnoticed in the tenth grade and, on the advice of a disinterested uncle, found work in small automotive garage near the center of this small sparse farming town. Spark plugs, engine grease, and mechanical small talk became strangely comforting for a life no longer lived. Marriage, he was told, was the next logical thing to do, so when Paul was judged as good marriage material by Emma who lived down the road, his fate was sealed.

In the early years of their marriage, Paul and Emma had seemed almost normal. There was talk of the future and a brief spark of playful passion that came close to touching his buried soul. Emma, of course, directed their lives. Still, Paul enjoyed the attention and tried to do his part. But like old thrift-store doilies, the linen of their relationship had aged gray and musty, losing its sheen to the unwitnessed passage of time and Emma's stern guidance. One day, without realizing it, Paul returned to his lonely inner cell, closed its door, and resumed dying, far removed from the antiseptic void of his wife's judgmental heart.

Paul knew there was something wrong inside. Too much emptiness. Then came the bad dreams of dead bodies, mirrors without reflection, and terrifying killing machines. He considered consulting a doctor. Maybe his constant heaviness and fatigue were symptoms of an illness like cancer. Somebody in town, he recalled, had died from a disease named after an old-time baseball player. Did he have it too? Turning briefly to religion for answers, he once asked Pastor Hoeller whether it was possible for a man's soul to die while he was still alive – for surely his had – but immediately regretted it, enduring a five-minute harangue on the sin of absent faith. The idea of medical treatment for depression, he knew, would meet with equally scathing censure. According to Emma and Pastor Hoeller, God brought healing, not medicine. And so far as "therapists" were concerned, all those foul-mouthed talk show "know-it-alls" were already on the Devil's payroll, waiting to steal your mind, your money, and then your soul. Perhaps because his soul was already gone, Paul no longer listened.

As the sermon moved relentlessly toward its familiar conclu-sions – descriptions of damnation and prescriptions for penance – Paul pulled himself back to reality. It would soon be time to stand up, sing a hymn or two, act appropriately saved, and demonstrate his determination to carry Paster Hoeller's message to a world of sinners. He would drive Emma home, where she would begin her relentless Sunday cleaning and he would "busy" himself with the chores she appointed: sweep the garage, fix the dripping faucet and take fresh-baked muffins to some lady across town.

When the service finally ended, Paul and Emma, along with the other thirty or so parishioners, said their goodbyes and hurried out to the cold parking lot. The darkening sky now promised rain, and kept its pledge before they reached the desolation of home and one more dismal Sunday night. Later in the evening, after Emma found solace in Bible study followed by a descent into fitful sleep, Paul found himself walking outside with his painful limping gait down muddy country roads beneath an uncaring and critical moon, as he did so often these days. What was the purpose of this tortured life? Paul wanted to die, he just didn't know how.

Chapter 2

April. Spring had come early this year, the Sacramento valley bursting into bloom as water-soaked fields gave way to green grasses, wild flowers, baseball, tractors, hay fever and, most of all, soul-warming sunshine. With the balm of lengthening daylight, the water-soaked spirits of the citizenry were steadily restored. Life once again held all the promises of a new year.

Tom smelled the garlic bread in the oven and noticed the water on the stove had begun to boil. His wife Veronica, who preferred "Ronnie", was still on the phone scheduling appointments for tomorrow's hospice visits. An attractive, cheerful and energetic redhead with lightning-quick humor, she multitasked her family into a verisimilitude of order, like a captain skillfully steering his sailing vessel through a world of gales and shoals. Brushing a strand of copper hair from Irish green eyes as she wrote in her appointment book, Ronnie happily juggled the details of phone conversations, meal preparation, and family supervision all at the same time – a feat Tom admired but was constitutionally incapable of emulating.

Charlie, their daughter's insane two-year-old beagle, had just come in from her daily sentence to backyard Siberia and raced wildly around the kitchen as if she had never seen human beings before. Laura, her 15-year-old owner, seemed entirely oblivious to the dog's irritating frenzy, choosing instead to nibble peckishly at salad croutons and watch reruns of *Mash* on the kitchen TV. Depending on whether the topic was adult privileges or household chores, she was either very mature – her own opinion, or fecklessly undependable – her father's frustrated assessment. Tom knew that adolescents were usually both but this one seemed to require constant reminders to feed and walk her dog, pick up her magazines, get off the phone, do her homework, and get to bed at a reasonable hour. Still he marveled at her keen intelligence, bubbling personality, and bold opinions expressed in school essays and dinner-table discussions. For better or worse, she had also earned the nickname "Mini-Mom" for the similarity of temperament and stature with her mother, a resemblance Laura prized and disparaged equally. Like any teenager, she was a challenge but a wonderful one.

Disdainful of (or perhaps simply oblivious to) dinnertime chaos, Laura's 19-year-old brother Erik had retreated to the adjoining family room where he read the sports page in front of a televised preseason Giants game. A star baseball player at the local junior college, where he was also purported to be attending classes, Erik had emotionally left the family two seasons ago but was kind enough to continue living and dining with them. Lanky, darkly handsome, a heartthrob to Laura's girlfriends, and at ease on any couch, Erik made young adulthood seem like a breeze.

It was Monday night in the McLaughlin family.

"Put in the noodles and turn down the heat!" shouted Ronnie over the din to no one in particular. The look on her face said, "Now!" Charlie's interest in playing fetch with a decapitated stuffed animal had totally absorbed Laura and Erik rarely heard anything at this time of evening except the magic words, "Dinner's on." As usual, Tom automatically performed the requested action. He knew Ronnie had little time to get the next day's hospice visits scheduled before taking off for the "Death and Dying" course she taught Monday nights at the state college. It would be death and dying for the dinner if someone didn't step in.

Hospice social worker and evening college instructor had been Ronnie's career solutions to the midlife vocational lament of "Why am I here?" Her fourth and fifth careers respectively (preceded by dental assistant, elementary-school teacher, and substance-abuse educator), Ronnie had finally found what she did and loved best. Her patients and students agreed. On her graduation from the social-work program, Tom had humorously given Ronnie a professional-looking nameplate for her desk which read, "Veronica McLaughlin, A.A., B.A., B.A., M.S.W. (no Ph.D.!)" in recognition of her many accomplishments and his determination that she cease going to school and get a real job.

Ronnie was also a woman of convictions, especially where family was concerned. "Family first" comprised her principle mantra, a non-negotiable value she learned from her mother, and everyone knew that a fierce "Mama Bear" rose up when anyone threatened her loved ones. Close friends also became family, acquiring the traditional surnames and statuses of Uncle and Aunt regardless of biological relationships. Ronnie just knew what was "right" and Tom trusted her instincts. Marital conflict emerged whenever Tom "forgot" about family while pursuing his miscellaneous distractions, like reading Eastern religions, lunching with friends, or leaving on short notice for professional workshops to acquire the requisite continuing-education units to renew his psychology license. Tom knew when to give in, and it was mostly always.

Finally the kitchen ruckus got to Tom, as it usually did, and he abruptly entered the fray with his customary exasperation, "Laura! Feed your dog and set the table. Let's get organized. Erik, we're eating...NOW!" As Ronnie finished scheduling the last of her appointments, the family located their accustomed places around the table and went to work on their steaming plates: Erik systematically devouring "his" half of the entire bowl of spaghetti, Tom soothing his rattled nerves with a glass of wine, and Ronnie and Laura, more concerned with figures than their appetites, eating slowly and chattering on about "really cool" shoes in a recent catalogue. Waiting beneath the table for stray peas or bread crusts, of course, was "you-know-who."

The McLaughlin dinner-table conversation usually included Laura's homework, Erik's baseball schedule, and various snippets of the day's news. Increasingly impatient with small talk, Erik had recently commenced espousing rather remarkable views on life, society, and religion. Tonight the subject was whether Jesus and Buddha had the same revelation. Who would have guessed that this taciturn athlete would suddenly transform into a religious philosopher? *How long will this stage last?* Tom wondered. *Who even knows what it means?* There was never enough time to grasp such imponderables.

Interrupting Tom's reverie, Ronnie asked, "Do you have a full day tomorrow?"

"Yes, ten hours," Tom replied.

"That's too much! When are you going to start turning people away and have a decent workload? You come home tired and cranky when you work so hard."

A clinical psychologist in private practice for over two decades, Tom had learned to peer deeply into people's souls searching for the gifts hidden within their struggles, and rarely turned anyone away. This is what he did best. At fifty, he was still trim and athletic, squeezing in vigorous thrice-weekly bike rides along the Sacramento bike trail for exercise. Sandy-brown hair and twinkling eyes overlooked a poorly-trimmed beard and ready smile. Paul began taking off Wednesdays a year ago (with the grand idea of writing a book about men at midlife). Unfortunately, he made up for the lost hours by dispersing Wednesdays' psychotherapy clients across the rest of the week, and soon became addicted to writing, an addiction now leading to even longer days. One evening, Tom ended up in the emergency room with a racing heartbeat – atrial fibrillation – too much coffee and too many patients. He still hadn't gotten the message. Determined to put off any personal encounters with death and dying until they were both old and gray, Ronnie did not let Tom forget his close call.

After nearly twenty years of marriage, Tom and Ronnie were still a good match. Warm-hearted by nature, Ronnie naturally assumed her predestined role as the family's emotional center, though Tom, silently watchful, stepped in when the proverbial pot boiled over. With two working parents, the family's nerves frazzled occasionally, particularly since Ronnie's days were often harder than Tom's – helping people die was no easy job. But together, they made a mostly consistent and compatible parenting team. And they still knew how to laugh, how to love, and when to leave each other alone.

As the evening wound down, dishes, homework, and the Giants game were completed with the usual aplomb, Ronnie returned from her class and the McLaughlin family fell gratefully into their beds for the night. For the three minutes it took him to fall asleep, Tom wondered where this remarkable and busy life was heading.

Chapter 3

Emma liked to see things done properly, and she directed her lust for order into household chores, her work at the five-and-dime, and *her* marriage. Paul, she reasoned, needed scrupulous oversight due to his persistently slothful character. Always ready to inventory the moral turpitude of others, Emma enjoyed exposing character flaws under the unforgiving magnifying glass of strict Christian scripture. She fancied herself a sort of moral enforcer for mankind at large. Someday, Emma hoped, she would earn the opportunity to instruct others on how things *should* be done and imagined herself teaching Bible-study classes for Pastor Hoeller.

Emma's life plan had formed early in a bleak and violent childhood. Her father, an occasionally-employed truck driver who could "charm the skin off a snake," considered her mother to be his personal property and someone who "needed" to be taught to respect and obey the Christian hierarchy of God, HUSBAND, wife, and children. Too many children, too many beatings, too much alcohol, and too many screams in the night led Emma to construct her own version of Christian life, and she knew exactly what she wanted: compliant husband, three clean and respectful children, and a position of moral authority in the church. And never, late at night when the house was asleep, would she be used as his "little wife" again. When her mother lost interest in living and gave in to prescription-drug abuse, dying a year later from an "unintended" overdose of opioids and alcohol, Emma moved out. Her siblings would have to fend for themselves. In search of a safe and docile husband to provide social respect and economic stability, she found Paul.

Drawn to Paul's polite, unquestioning obedience, Emma reckoned him a diligent workhorse and proper pupil for her brand of spiritual direction. Not only was he agreeable, he seemed to feel personally responsible for her happiness. Her requests were frequent and simple, "Paul, will you paint the church kitchen?" and "Can you hang these shelves in Pastor Hoeller's office for his books. He will be so grateful." In the beginning, Paul's only "plan" was to please Emma, asking nothing for himself. As emotional numbness spread like Novocain over his tortured soul, he was unaware that he had any needs. Eventually he actually took refuge in his depression.

Despite her very best efforts – and she fancied herself a formidable field marshal in God's army – Emma's life plan was slipping away. Paul's disinclination for hard work, let alone ambition, and her own barren womb, meant that no one of significance in the church respected her. The women considered her a "wanna-be" with a "no account" husband and marriage. God was not shining on her. Unlike her spineless husband, however, Emma refused to indulge in depression. In the face of such adversity, she would strive even harder, with piety and determined service, to please God and Pastor Hoeller – figures frequently confused with one another in Emma's unconscious. Pastor Hoeller had become the incarnation of her brutal yet charmingly seductive father, and his violent words held her like a terrified deer in a semi's headlights. If she could only earn his love, or at least his approval of her good works...

Paul's life, on the other hand, had already ended. Feeling neither self nor soul, neither love nor the hope of love, he was steadily drowning in a dark and cancerous emptiness. Numbness had given way to deadness. He woke up at night in feverish sweats, cringing at the sound of Emma's angry snoring, and wondered how his life had become this waking nightmare. He was disappearing.

One night, Paul dreamed he saw Jesus slowly emerging from the bottom a coal-black lake carrying a heavy wooden cross on his shoulder. As Jesus approached, Paul was profoundly moved by the sadness in his eyes, as if He were bearing Paul's own sorrow. Jesus laid the cross at Paul's feet, silently took his hand, and began to walk back down into the lake. When the water reached his neck, Paul awoke in terror.

Chapter 4

Morning in the McLaughlin household was no less hectic than its evenings, marked by the supersonic blur – and corresponding cacophony – of showers, dressing, make-up, breakfast, and shotgun departures.

Tom always drove the same route to work. Glancing absent-mindedly at the five or six horses boarded at his neighbor's corral across the road from home, he moved onto a series of residential streets shadowed by a high canopy of mature elm and oak. There were few sidewalks in this residential area, which blended small farmhouses on acre lots with 1950s California ranch-style homes and an occasional subdivision of modern, high-density dwellings. Commuters, mothers with school-age children, high school and college students sped in every direction as Tom navigated his regular maze, soon entering the two-lane, rapidly moving artery that led onto the Highway 50 corridor heading downtown. Once off the freeway, however, the beauty of downtown Sacramento healed the tense freeway warrior with its ancient oaks and distinctive Victorians. Sacramento cherished its trees for their natural protection from its hot and punishing summers, and who didn't love those stately old homes? While Dutch Elm disease had systematically eradicated some of its mighty denizens, Sacramento was in no short supply of gnarly oaks, wide-spreading maples, and a vast assortment of imported trees, showcasing the largest arboreal variety of any city in the country – all growing happily in this garden-valley climate abundantly fed by the Sacramento and American Rivers.

On the commute this morning, Tom's thoughts wandered back to the surprise party Ronnie had thrown for his fiftieth birthday six weeks earlier. Organized with military precision and wartime secrecy, it was perfect. The excuse: a dull gathering, attendance mandated, for her hospice staff put on by hospital administration ("suits" as they were less than affectionately called). Cleverly scheduled the week *after* the family celebrated his birthday, Tom had no idea this train was barreling his way. The moment he recalled most vividly that evening was when he suddenly realized that these "strangers" were his friends – dozens of them! For the first time in his life, he experienced "tunnel vision," as if the world was observed from the wrong end of a telescope – small and far away. The rest of the evening dissolved into a glorious and happy haze, fortunately captured on video by Erik so Tom could later see and remember what happened.

The party had been fabulous. But the lingering pleasure of being lovingly feted by family and friends could not erase the fact of turning fifty with its nagging reminder of age. "Have I accomplished all I set out to do with my life?" he wondered, waiting at a stoplight. "Does my life have any purpose beyond what I am doing now? What happens when we – no, I – die?" Unanswerable questions, perhaps, but deeply important to Tom who, by nature, pondered the meaning of life at every turn. He wondered, too, whether these were ultimately religious questions, as the great psychoanalyst Carl Jung believed.

The signal changed to green before he received any answers but he did recall a dream from his first spiritual retreat last year. Tom had gone to a retreat center in the Sierra Nevada foothills for a weekend of meditation and contemplation in hopes of understanding what it meant to live a spiritual life. In the dream, the retreat leader came into his room the first night and urgently extoled, "Tom. Wake up! You're late. There is something you must know." He never figured out what the dream meant but turning fifty seemed to evoke the same startled response.

Tom had little clarity on matters of religion. His parents had left the fold in favor of scientific explanations of life. His own education was equally bereft of spiritual guidance: a B.A. in psychology and five years of graduate-school training in clinical psychology had left little room for spirituality. Indeed, the field of psychology at that time had little interest in religious or spiritual matters, trying desperately instead to be a "hard science" like physics and chemistry. Psychology's attitude toward ultimate questions ranged from disinterest to skepticism, and Freud's disdain for religious belief had left a long shadow of disapproval. Religious experiences, like those described by the father of psychology, William James, were equated with hysteria, psychosis, drug abuse, or disordered brain function. Interestingly, a new generation of spiritually oriented psychologists had recently begun to appear on the scene, and their desire to apply the scientific method to religious experience was slowly growing. Still, the general population was far more religious than most psychiatrists and psychologists.

Tom suspended his philosophic broodings as he pulled into the office parking lot at 7:30. He locked the car and carried his briefcase – an overly expensive birthday gift from Ronnie – up the back steps, opened the back door, and punched in the code disarming the security system. Three years ago, Tom and his partner, Mark, moved their practices from a fancy medical office building with glass walls and elevator "muzac" to this recently restored Victorian home. Painted cream with green trim, it rested happily on a shady downtown street. Rooms with high molded ceilings, rounded windows, and fireplaces, provided a relaxed and elegant ambiance for the sharing of personal and often painful feelings unlocked in psychotherapy.

Buying the building had been the exciting part. The "For Sale" sign claimed that it met code for commercial office use. It turned out that the land was approved for commercial use, but not the Victorian itself. Six months after they purchased it, a building inspector walked into the waiting room and informed Maggie, their secretary, that the offices were in violation of codes and had to be vacated within thirty days. It turned out the contractor who restored the house neglected little things – like legally mandated handicap access. Because 80-year-old Victorians downtown were built a half level off the ground (due to the yearly flood risk from the Sacramento and American Rivers before the levees), there was no way for disabled people to get up the front stairs. There was also no elevator to the second floor, insufficient parking spaces, and no firewall protecting the Victorian next door. Naturally the original contractor had moved to Hawaii, whereabouts unknown.

Nearly three years later, Tom could laugh at this nightmare, and the sweat and ingenuity that saved their real-estate investment. The city's Historical Preservation Board, they learned, could certify the building as a "restored national landmark" and waive certain code requirements. Reason eventually prevailed, however the politically sensitive requirement of handicap access could not be waived, forcing Tom and Mark to build an accessible room in the basement (below flood level, of course).

As if all this were insufficient introduction to the joys of office management, Tom and Mark one morning discovered an electrical cord snaking out from under that back porch into the "unused" one car garage. A Ripple-drinking transient had moved in with his radio, single-bulb-hanging light fixture, hot plate, and mattress, and needed electrical juice to run the joint. What a mess he left when the police finally ousted him. To prevent further freeloaders, the entire garage was torn down, making room for two more precious parking spaces. But all that was history now.

After switching on lights, opening the front door, plugging in the coffee maker, and turning on the classical-music station, Tom unlocked his file cabinet and began to review his charts for the day, a ritual he performed every morning. Maggie would appear at 8:30, a concession Tom and Mark had made to her fear of rush-hour traffic.

Maggie was another story. After several flighty or undependable young secretaries (one ended up in a psych ward for unknown reasons after only two days on the job, another especially buxom gal was charmed from her duties by the beer-drinking guy rehabbing another Victorian nearby, and a third – I kid you not! – had taken to doing live radio broadcasts over the telephone every morning as a substitute DJ), they had decided an older, more settled woman would be ideal.

Maggie was that. She had worked thirty years for her last employer, a general practice physician, and promised thirty years more for them. But she was also a bit eccentric in ways inconceivable in her initial interview. For one thing, she adopted an increasing menagerie of scruffy neighborhood cats (which caused havoc for allergy sufferers and Tom's one cat phobic client). For another, she wrote with such a tremor that she used her left hand to keep the right hand steady (they guessed she was alcoholic but never caught her drinking on the job). Lastly, Maggie talked a mile a minute (one day, Mark got so angry that he actually shouted, "SHUT UP, MAGGIE!" which produced only the briefest hesitation before she had to explain why she talked so much).

But on the plus side, Maggie was devoted. She considered Tom and Mark "her boys," took work home against their instructions, and endeared herself to every patient that came through the front door. In some strange and charming way, perhaps because she was so eccentric, Maggie made this old Victorian a family and a home.

Despite this comfortable and cozy ambiance, psychotherapy was a challenging occupation. Every day Tom worked systematically to help patients understand and resolve a wide range of psychological conditions, interpersonal conflicts, long-term personality problems, and painful early traumas, all the while coping with the unconscious projection of their original parental experiences onto him as therapist, technically known as "transference." But the work was invariably interesting, challenging, and rewarding, and Tom loved it.

In the remaining minutes before his first patient, Tom leafed through yesterday's mail. It was the usual assortment of junk and professional advertisements, psychological journals, letters, and payments. One ad caught his eye. It was for a nine-day "Vision Quest" in the Nevada desert. He remembered from a college anthropology class that a Vision Quest had something to do with a religious rite practiced by Native Americans. The quester, usually a young man, would travel far out into the wilderness to pray and fast alone for many days until receiving a vision for his life and the life of the tribe. "I bet that would force me to look at my meaning-of-life questions," Tom joked to himself, and tossed the flyer in an inbox humorously labeled: "Look at when you have nothing else to do." The contents of this inbox were ritually discarded every six months due to its outdated contents.

At 8:00, Tom opened his office door, invited in his first client, and began his day.

Chapter 5

Still pondering the revelations of his last client, Tom absent-mindedly punched the lit intercom button and said, "Yes?"

Maggie chirped back, "Line 2."

Tom switched to the caller's line, announcing himself. "Dr. McLaughlin."

"Tom. This is Clarence Kelly. How are you?"

Tom met Father Kelly, a priest his age and director of a local Catholic retreat center, six months earlier at a conference on psychology and religion. A tall, thin, thoughtful man, he impressed Tom immediately with his natural kindness, wide grasp of world religions, and genuine modesty. They had shared a table for the day and found much in common as individuals, seekers of life's meaning, and helping professionals.

"I'm good!" Tom replied. "How wonderful to hear from you. What's up?"

"Tom, a man walked into the retreat center the other day muttering something about Jesus and a lake. He normally attends a small fundamentalist church in the south area but I guess he came to me for a second opinion. He thought he had lost his soul and feared Jesus was coming to take him to Hell as punishment for his sins. His pastor had apparently confirmed the likelihood of this terrifying fate."

"What did you tell him?"

"Not much of value, I fear. I tried to reassure him and learn more about his religious beliefs. His fear of Hell was apparently magnified by a recent dream about Jesus emerging from a black lake and then leading him back down. Anyway, the man was very disturbed. Embarrassed for having come at all, he also refused my invitation to return. I wrote your name and telephone number on a piece of paper and asked him to consider calling you. You'll probably never hear from him."

"I doubt he'll call," agreed Tom. "You know as well as I do that very conservative Christians rarely consult secular mental-health professionals. If he does, I'll certainly let you know, assuming he agrees to sign a release. Still, it's an interesting dream. Jesus may symbolize a desperate religious longing for some kind of salvation. Salvation from what, we don't know. Bodies of water often represent the unconscious and its blackness in the dream suggests a seriously depressed mood. I would guess that he's dying emotionally. I hope he gets help somewhere."

Clarence agreed and added, "There was also something else about him, something innocent and sweet. I don't know what that means."

"Neither do I, so let's do that lunch we talked about six months ago and discuss more about cases like this. I've been thinking of calling you for weeks."

Tom and Clarence consulted their crowded calendars, miraculously found a day they could meet, and said their goodbyes. Each wondered momentarily why it had taken this strange character to bring them together again.

Chapter 6

Paul did not call Dr. McLaughlin. He carried his business card in his wallet for several weeks. One scalding hot day in summer, Paul limped up the front stairs, walked into Tom's waiting room and, as the sign suggested, waited.

What Tom saw when he stepped into the waiting room was startling: a thin, rather unkempt, almost emaciated thirtysomething man with sunken yet searching eyes, and, for want of a better description, a strange kind of presence. The aura around this sad reluctant man, however, seemed ever so slightly brighter and more peaceful, a subtle nimbus of stillness and calm.

"Are you Dr. McLaughlin?"

"Yes. And you?"

"I am Paul Jensen. Your number was given to me by a priest. I can't remember his name. But he said you knew about depression and the soul."

"I know about depression. And I know it can affect us deeply, right down to our soul. Reverend Kelly said you might call."

"Can I talk to you?"

"Unfortunately, I have another appointment this hour, but I do have a cancellation today at three o'clock. Would you be willing to come back?"

"Yes. Thank you."

With that, the man left the office.

Paul re-appeared at 3:00 and stood patiently by the magazine rack. Entering Tom's office, their conversation resumed as if no time had lapsed. Speaking in a steady monotone as if he didn't really expect anyone to listen, as if he were talking to himself, Paul began describing the barrenness of his life. Tom mentally checked off the typical signs of Major Depression: depressed mood, loss of interest and pleasure in customary life activities, feelings of worthlessness, diminished concentration and memory, and recurrent thoughts of death. Paul repeated his nightmare of Jesus taking him into the lake, which had become a recurring dream, and described his lonely wanderings through empty streets at night. His childhood history cried out for its emotional austerity and deprivation, and Tom felt a pang of empathy for the profound grief and depression this man had endured as a boy. Paul's next comments, however, were entirely unexpected.

"Dr. McLaughlin, there is more to the dream. Now when Jesus takes my hand, a peace surrounds me and I feel like God is present. It fills me with joy. For days afterwards I don't care what happens around me. I am happy. I notice wonderful things, like the beauty in nature or radiant light shining everywhere in the world. And then it slips away and my depression returns. I cannot work. I can barely talk to my wife. She is certain my condition is the Devil's handiwork. I can't go on like this. I don't know where else to turn."

Knocked momentarily off balance by these unusual remarks, Tom asked, "What do you think this dream means?"

"That's just it," Paul replied. "I no longer think of it as a dream. I think it's real. I think Jesus has come for me. I just don't know why and I don't think I'm ready to go."

As if to steady himself, Tom conducted the rest of the interview in a proper professional manner, asking questions, performing an informal "mental status exam," seeking additional history. When the hour was almost up, he felt compelled to discuss the customary range of treatment approaches for depression (medication, psychotherapy, hospitalization if necessary) and make sure that Paul was not an immediate suicide risk. They scheduled a second appointment for later in the week and said goodbye. Looking out of his office window, Tom watched Paul leave the building, hobble down the street, turn the corner, and disappear from sight. *What a strange character*, Tom thought.

Chapter 7

Dinner that night at the McLaughlin house was only slightly more chaotic than normal. Fifteen-year-old Laura had been invited to the prom by an 18-year-old boy. A full round of parental inquiries met that announcement, with unsolicited older-brother advice thrown in for free. Contributing to the chaos, Erik wanted to host a party at the house for the whole baseball team the same night as the prom, and hoped not to be disturbed by his "parental units." Charlie had chewed off a huge patch of hair just above her tail, but no one seemed very motivated at the moment to examine her for ticks or fleas. The Giants were losing again, dishes needed to be done, homework started, and "someone" had thrown a huge pile of clean laundry on the floor in the hallway for "someone else" to fold. All the while Laura juggled a steady stream of impassioned telephone calls about who was wearing what and going with whom to the prom.

Bedtime couldn't come fast enough for Tom, who sometimes fell asleep before his children (a behavior he had detested in his own parents). At 9:30, however, Ronnie was still typing chart notes from her patient visits that day, and pleaded with him to wait up for "just half an hour more...please." Lying in bed, Tom opened a soporific tomb of required reading for an advanced course on psychotherapy. He was barely awake when Ronnie tumbled into bed.

"Tom. Sit up. I gotta tell you this incredible thing that happened today with one of my patients," Ronnie began.

Rousing himself, Tom pulled himself upright, straightened his pillow, and forced his mind to focus.

"I was with a family who knew their father would die very soon, perhaps within hours. They were gathered around his bed. We had talked a lot about saying goodbye and each member had

24

done their best to express their love over the last few days. The father had slipped into a coma and there was little left to do but wait for the end."

"It must be hard just to sit there in that terrible grief and wait," Tom reflected out loud.

"Yes, but that's not the important part of this story. Pay attention. So the hours dragged on and the family resumed their habit of having the TV on for noise and distraction. It was on nearly every time I visited. The next part's the key. I could tell death was near. The father had lapsed in chain-stokes breathing. Everyone was just standing around his bed. Suddenly, the TV picture changed to static. Everyone looked at it kind of dumbfounded. Then, through the static, I swear we all heard Amazing Grace, and exactly when it ended, the man took his last breath and died. The TV station came back on and everyone froze for what seemed like an eternity, looking at each other, as if asking, 'Did this just happen?' I get tingles just telling you this!"

Tom scratched his beard. "Does that kind of thing happen often?"

"Actually, yes. Well, not exactly that but things just as remarkable, spiritual things. Every hospice worker who has been around long enough can tell you the same kind of incredible stories."

"Really?"

"Like terminal patients seeing departed loved ones just before they die and holding their arms outstretched as if being received into Heaven. Or family members seeing the just-deceased person a day or so later telling them everything is alright now and not to worry."

"This happens all the time?"

"Not always, but every week or so something like that will happen. Often the dying person will know his or her time has come even when everyone else, including the doctor, is in denial or way off base in their estimate of the time of death. And other times, the patient stays beyond the expected point of death because the family cannot emotionally let them go. Then it's my job to help people release the loved one. Within minutes of the family saying 'You can go now, we'll be okay,' the patient dies. You see, it's not as mechanistic as we all used to think. It's a spiritual process."

"But these experiences can also be explained by impaired brain function, traumatic grief, or simply miscalculation," Tom rebutted.

"From a distance, you can reduce anything to scientific explanations. But when you're there, you just know it's something sacred or extraordinary. You just know it."

"Well, I'm not sure I buy all that New Age philosophy you social workers dabble in, but it reminds me of something odd that happened to me today."

More alert now, Tom's mind turned back to Paul's appearance in his office. He continued, "Father Kelly – remember, I met him at that conference on psychology and religion – referred this guy who just stopped by the office today without even making an appointment. He looked terribly depressed and seemed to have no idea why. But more to the point, he kept talking about a recurring dream he has of Jesus walking out of a lake and touching him, after which he feels completely at peace. For days afterward, this peace seems to surround him, and then wears off."

"Wow," Ronnie exhaled. "What do you think the dream means?"

"To tell you the truth, I'm not sure. I've never analyzed a dream quite like this. Its religious imagery worries me a little. Does it suggest psychosis or a death wish? Fortunately, I'm scheduled to present a case in one of my consultation groups tomorrow. I wasn't sure who I wanted to discuss until now."

Tom and Ronnie lay still in each other's arms for several

minutes. Finally the weight of the day began pulling them down into sleep. Little more was said beyond the usual "Goodnight," "I love you," and "See you in the morning." Tom dropped into a deep and dreamless void.

Chapter 8

Tom regularly attended two separate consultation groups that alternated biweekly. Their focus was on long-term, depth-oriented psychotherapy – the kind of therapy that might go on for months or even years and address the emotional conditions responsible for serious relationship or career problems, like anxiety, depression, addiction, or longstanding personality problems. Consultation groups like these were important sources of clinical insight, peer review and continued learning. The identity of the client, of course, was withheld or disguised to ensure confidentiality. When he had a difficult case, talking it out, asking for others' clinical impressions or advice, and exploring his own emotional reactions to the patient (a process psychotherapists called counter-transference) always seemed to help. Tom had participated in both groups for many years.

This noon's group was composed of two male and two female therapists, now longstanding friends, plus Tom. They met over lunch in the presenter's office, so the group changed location each time. As people arrived at Tom's office on this day, friendly greetings and small talk were exchanged about vacations, professional conferences, and recent events. Eventually the conversation quieted and all eyes turned to Tom.

"What 'cha got?" Frank asked, glancing at the file Tom held in his hands. A short, thin and intense man with an impatient and restless manner of speaking, Frank was often the confrontational member of the group, a role that seemed an essential part of his character.

"Well," Tom began, "this is a thirty-five-year-old married white male and under-employed mechanic and handyman complaining of severe depression. A priest friend of mine referred him. His presenting complaint is depression but it's focused around a peculiar and recurring dream of Jesus ascending from a lake to take him away. You should also know that he comes from a fundamentalist church, so it is not surprising that he believes this dream presages some kind of terrible punishment for a sinful life. Apparently his own pastor has confirmed that conclusion."

"Interesting beginning," opened Carol, who was a particularly kind and compassionate voice in the group. An older, well-dressed therapist with grown children, she often served as the emotional "caretaker" in the group. "How many times have you seen him?"

"Just once. I explored his complaint, took a history, and did some informal mental-status assessment. He's coming back again tomorrow."

"What's your question or concern in presenting this man?" continued Carol.

"Well, first of all, this kind of complaint is highly unusual in my practice. Not the depression, of course, or its impact on his ability to work, but the religious focus. What do you make of it?"

Perry leaped in first. The most "by-the-book" therapist in the group, he imagined himself the group's teacher or consultant, as if conducting a seminar on psychopathology and psychotherapy. "I would certainly want to consider a psychotic depression, one with religious delusions of sin and unworthiness. You see them more frequently on in-patient psychiatry units. These guys hear voices, think God is talking to them, or sometimes even believe they *are* Jesus. You know, the 'Jesus Complex?' They rant and rave about their delusions until you hit them with antipsychotic meds, then they settle down."

Frank added, "Biological psychiatrists typically argue that these symptoms reflect a genetic or biochemical disposition to developing mental illness. The treatment of choice, of course, is still medication to correct the chemical imbalance."

"You might also investigate drug abuse or neurological disease," Carol added thoughtfully. "Chronic methamphetamine or cocaine abusers can develop toxic psychoses, alcoholics in withdrawal can become very religious, and altered brain function from disease or chemical deficiency can also show psychotic features."

"But he's not psychotic in the usual sense," responded Tom. "He manifests no auditory hallucinations, grandiosity, or delusions. He reports no family history of mental illness. There is no recent evidence of physical illness and he is fully oriented to time, place, and person. It's not so simple."

"In any case," Perry advised, "you should probably get him a physical exam and, if nothing shows up, start antipsychotic medications and see if that helps. He may still have an encapsulated delusion or well-defended psychotic core, and if it gets out of control, he could decompensate rapidly."

"He doesn't want medication," Tom responded. "He was adamant about that. And I don't think he meets the legal criteria for involuntary hospitalization. He's not crazy in the usual sense and, despite his depression, he is not so gravely disabled that he cannot care for himself."

Barbara had been listening quietly. She was the Jungian therapist in the group, which meant that she viewed psychological problems with the highly symbolic orientation espoused by Carl Jung. She liked to talk about personality "complexes" and the "archetypes of the collective unconscious." Tentatively she began, "Some personality types, those that rely exclusively on understanding the world through their senses, ignore the intuitive and symbolic functioning of the unconscious. While we talk easily about the symbolic meaning of an event or dream, they experience the dream's symbolism literally. This kind of personality believes the dream figure *is* Jesus."

"Yes. That seems closer to what I'm experiencing with this man," Tom reflected. "He can't see that Jesus is just a dream symbol. How would you approach this confusion?"

"It's difficult. You must proceed cautiously. If you challenge the patient, he'll immediately feel you don't believe the most important thing in his life and drop out of therapy. You must go slowly, carefully, gradually testing his beliefs against objective reality, helping him see that they are in fact symbols for some emotional issue in his life. Perhaps, in his depression, he feels his life is meaningless, which can easily become a religious question to believers, hence the religious dream imagery."

"Thank you, Barbara," Tom said. "That helps. I realize this man's symptoms could be any of the conditions we discussed, but this symbolic approach matches my personal experience with him at the moment. His Jesus image is symbolic of something very important to him. I'll let you know what happens next."

"Wait," interrupted Barbara, "There is one more piece. How does this patient make you feel?"

After a long pause, Tom stumbled... "I know it's irrational, but I feel kind of anxious, like there's something bigger here that I don't understand. Even at this early stage, this case disturbs me. I don't have a handle on it. I don't know what's going to happen."

"Anything else?" asked Barbara.

"Well, yes. Religion bothers me. I had no childhood exposure to organized religion. From the outside, it always seemed irrational and controlling...like how religion tells you what to think and how to behave. And I know that cults and brain-washing exist and can be extremely dangerous. For me, personally, it all adds up to something uncomfortable and unfamiliar. Since I'm not even sure what I believe, how can I work with a man so certain of his delusional beliefs? Maybe I should refer him back to the priest."

"I don't think so," inserted Perry. "Your priest friend knew this man's problem was not simply a matter of religious belief. The likelihood of serious psychopathology here argues for clinical over clerical intervention." Perry laughed. "You can't get out of it that easily."

The group thanked Tom for presenting such a "fascinating case" and discussed who was on next. Plans were made, lunches cleaned up, and the group disbanded for their own offices. As they vacated his office, Tom's anxiety felt closer to dread. He wondered why but stuffed his feelings beneath a well-practiced professional demeanor.

Chapter 9

The small office was dark and dusty, smelling vaguely of mildew. A vintage coat rack stood in one corner littered with musty drab sweaters and jackets, weapons against the cold drafts that moved through barely insulated wooden walls on angry winter days. A dirty, fading rug that had obviously seen many better lifetimes, lay forlornly on the floor, supporting a couple old wooden bank chairs. Pastor Hoeller sat at his ancient roll-top desk staring mutely at the clutter of handwritten sermon notes, reference books, a well-worn Bible, and the ubiquitous stacks of church calendars, newsletters, and telephone messages – all weapons in his crusade against sin and the ravages of the modern world. A heavyset man in his early sixties with a sparse comb-over hairstyle – if you could call it a style – he had lost none of his youthful vigor and still loved the power of the bully pulpit. The war against spiritual corruption was never won, he thought, and quickly wrote this little gem into Sunday's sermon.

Jimmy Hoeller fashioned himself an Old Testament prophet. The strength of his convictions, however, was barely equal to the cabal of demons inside whispering enticements to alcohol, women, fury, greed and doubt; demons he mostly kept in the dark through the force of his religious zeal; demons birthed from an insane childhood. Beginning at the age of ten, his Bible-salesman father would take him on "business trips," which always eventuated in pass-out-drunk evenings and occasional late-night "soirees" with loud and obnoxious women, behavior rationalized to Jimmy in the name of a "hard knocks" educational curriculum on the sins of the world. While Jimmy's mother, a timid and fearful soul, was relieved to be free of her husband's disgusting attentions, Jimmy was not so merry – his father's snoring alone ruined his sleep, and the beatings were not so great either. Ironically, the Bible pulled him through, but not in the usual way. Jimmy could see how important it was to his father's customers, but more to the point, he saw the power of its beliefs and prescriptions to control others, power he wanted. He began practicing sermons in his bedroom when he was alone at home. Discovering a natural talent for oratorical grandiosity in a nearby fringe fire-and-brimstone seminary, Jimmy soon constructed "Pastor Hoeller" – a convincing model of ministerial authority. Three churches later, he found his home in a congregation he could control with merely a raised eyebrow; raising his voice turned parishioners into a perfect chorus of sycophants.

Noticing a telephone message from Emma Jensen, Pastor Hoeller's self-congratulatory reverie evaporated into the explosive inner tension and rage always threatening to undermine his demeanor. Why had she called? Her message, poorly scribbled out by an aged church volunteer, had apparently drowned in the ocean of mess on his desk, now rose again like a dead and bloated fish. No way he could decipher it. The volunteer had mumbled something about Mrs. Jensen coming in this morning. Well surely Emma knew why she had made this appointment!

At the scheduled time, no sooner and no later, and fearful as a church mouse, Emma arrived outside Pastor Hoeller's office and quietly knocked on his door. She thought she heard some shuffling of papers before his deep stern voice called out "Come in." Once inside, Emma quickly surveyed the clutter and imagined how wonderfully her talent for cleanliness and organization would benefit this hardworking man. In deference to his serious, impatient countenance, Emma chose to say nothing for the time being. Maybe soon, if she could inch her way into his confidence…

Pastor Hoeller broke into Emma's reverie: "Good Day, Mrs. Jensen. What business of the Lord brings you here today?"

After an imperceptible pause to find the first words of her rehearsed speech, Emma responded, "It is my husband, Paul. I fear for his soul. I believe he is under Satan's spell."

Pastor Hoeller's dark eyes brightened with interest. "Yes, go on."

"We have been married five years. During that time, he has given me no children. He no longer even tries. He barely brings in a living. And night spells possess him. He wakes up with fevers in the dark of the night and wanders outside when he thinks I'm sleeping."

"Has he taken to drink or other women?" asked Pastor Hoeller.

"Not to my knowledge. But he has done something worse. I believe he is talking to a psychologist. About us. About religion. I saw a note he had written with things he wanted to ask this doctor, questions about depression, whether a man can lose his soul, and why Jesus visits him at night."

"Yes," responded Pastor Hoeller. "He came to me last week with the same cockamamie questions. The Devil's beckoning, I said. I told him to pray for his soul and cease immediately this faithless distraction. And now he is seeing a psychologist?"

"Yes. I think this man is trying to take my husband away from me and the Lord. Paul said the doctor told him that Jesus is only a symbol of his unhappiness and that they should talk more about it. God knows Paul is unhappy because he has drifted away from the Word, but now I can't reach him. It seems no one can reach him. What am I to do?"

With a sudden, scathing anger that shook Emma and quaked the office walls, Pastor Hoeller spat out, "Spiritual warfare! *Your* husband has fallen under the satanic influence of demons and ungodly people. He is in imminent danger of losing his soul. Paul Jensen shall receive his Maker's attention this Sunday. God will reveal him to be an example of the Devil's wily charm and then, before all the assembled, display His power in this sinner's conversion. The Spirit will rid Paul of this demonic alliance and its pestiferous stank. You have done correctly bringing this matter to me, Emma. Your righteousness will be rewarded."

Emma smiled inwardly. Whatever was in store for Paul, Pastor Hoeller had approvingly noticed her Christian piety. If Paul could be also healed, all the better. If not, her long martyrdom might at least yield a special role in the church. Pastor Hoeller might even let her clean his office, or God willing, help run the church or even teach Bible study, and her life would be complete. Eyes averted, twinkling with possibilities, Emma turned to go and closed the door without a sound.

Chapter 10

Three a.m. The phone seemed to ring indefinitely before Tom climbed out of sleep and stumbled downstairs to his professional line. The answering machine stopped recording before Tom could see who it was. He pushed "Play." A call from Paul! Tom was startled to hear a confused and mumbled message about "revelation" and "eternity," words repeated incoherently over and over. *Oh God*, thought Tom, *is this guy decompensating on me already? I wonder if I should call the psych unit and be sure they have a bed.*

Paul ended his rambling message saying he had to see Dr. McLaughlin in the morning. He'd be waiting at the office at seven a.m., an hour before Tom's first regularly scheduled appointment. Tom looked at the wall clock. "Jeez I hope I can get back to sleep," he whined to an empty room. "What a way to start the day."

Tom's remaining sleep was fitful and his early-morning routine a sleep-deprived blur: shower, dress, hair, cereal, teeth, and out the door – all before the family was even up.

Tom pulled into the empty parking lot. There he was, standing on the front landing, looking strangely upwards. "Toward Heaven?" Tom joked cynically to himself. There was no outward sign of agitation or emotion, though Paul did look as if he had been waiting a long time. "All night?" Tom wondered out loud. Yet there was no pacing, no signs of impatience, paranoia or agitation. *What on Earth is this about?*

Tom greeted Paul and quickly disarmed the security system and let them into the building and into his office. Paul quietly took his seat.

"Paul, what's happening? Are you ok?"

"Dr. McLaughlin, everything's changed," Paul began softly. "It started around midnight. Jesus came to me again in my dream. I couldn't go back to sleep so I walked outside into the starry night. The first thing I noticed was the light – soft, but bright. It was everywhere, even in the dark. I know that sounds crazy. There was no moon and the streetlight by our house is broken. But still everything I saw – each leaf, pebble, bush and tree – was lit up, like Christmas lights. It was so beautiful, like I was in a whole other world. I thought I was still dreaming but this was way too clear and vivid for a dream.

"And there's more. You know how you can sense another person or an animal before you see them. There was no one around, but I felt surrounded by something alive. At first I was scared. It felt like the presence of something huge but I sensed it was completely safe and full of love. It was around and *in* everything. Then I realized it was the light. The light was conscious and alive, and its presence was everywhere…EVERYWHERE.

"Things kept changing. Suddenly there was no future and no past. Time had stopped! My mind opened up like a huge book – whatever questions I had were instantly answered by this presence. And all that mattered was this light around me. It knew me. Knew everything I had gone through. Knew every day of my life. All my pain, questions, and troubles. And none of that had any bearing. It loved me anyway. My whole life made perfect sense in a way I can't explain now. But I knew that no matter what happened, I had nothing to fear, not even death. I was surrounded by this love. I was going to be OK.

"Then it went even further. I melted into this presence. It was the greatest peace I have ever known. Maybe a minute; maybe eternity. For that instant, there just wasn't any "me" anymore. It's impossible to explain.

"The next thing I knew it was over. I looked around, dazed. The light had returned to normal but everything still looked so beautiful. I know it sounds crazy, but I was so happy that all I could do was fall on my knees and cry. I kept saying 'Thank you, thank you, thank you' over and over. When my emotions finally settled, I lay down on the street and looked up at the heavens. I was so happy. Anyway, that's what happened. I had to tell someone. I had to tell you."

Tom could not think of a single word to say. He could not even move. Mesmerized by Paul's astonishing account, he sat in the chair like a dead weight. It was as if his mind, too, had stopped. None of this was even remotely familiar from his clinical training. Was he still asleep? He had to rouse himself. Trying at last to act like a psychologist, Tom cleared his throat, but still no words came.

Sensing Dr. McLaughlin's struggle, Paul resumed his soliloquy, filling in more details and repeating his wonderment and gratitude. Finally, as the morning sun poured through the office's mahogany shutters, Paul concluded, "When I called you, I was still high. I was beyond myself. Even now, it has not really left me. This feeling of Presence is like an ocean of love holding me and everything in its deep peace. I can sense it. I am in it. Don't you see? God never left the world, God is the world. Do you understand what I'm saying? There is no ugliness or sin. Heaven is here! We're in it. I'm no longer afraid of death, for I know now that death is just the doorway into to this total love."

Tom sat speechless, motionless, dumbstruck. He had not a single reasonable thing to say. He tried again to talk. Nothing. Nothing. There were no words. He was mute.

Paul's response was merely to sit silently in his strangely altered state. He observed Tom's immobilization but did not try to help him. Though Paul felt genuine compassion for his doctor's bewilderment, it didn't really matter. It was enough now just to be alive. "I've returned to Eden," Paul mused aloud to himself. "I have been given a new life."

The session ended anticlimactically. Paul simply got up, said goodbye, and started to leave. His movement broke Tom's transfixed state enough for him to ask, "Will you come back? Do you want another appointment? I think we should discuss this some more." *God, those were lame statements!* Tom thought. But he couldn't let Paul go without some follow-up.

"If you like, I'll be back next week, same time." With that simple promise, Paul walked quietly from the office, leaving behind some of the peace he had found in the night. Tom did not move again until his next client, who had now been waiting nearly twenty minutes, knocked impatiently on the office door.

Chapter 11

Situated in the heart of California's central valley, Sacramento often sees 105-110 degree temperatures during its rainless summer months. Today was the first really hot spell of the year. Already sweltering inside, the First Christian Church of Mayhew had filled to capacity with upwards of forty devout souls. Emma had made sure it would be. Anguished descriptions of Paul's fall from grace had been rehearsed and delivered to all who would listen, well-placed rumors were circulated to the curious and meddling, and official calls had been placed at Pastor Hoeller's direction. Together these well-planned tactics ensured that all but the most disabled or shut-in of the congregation were at services today in spite of the heat. Dripping profusely with sweat, fanning themselves desperately, the audience waited for the call of their prophet.

By delaying services until the very last straggler had found a seat and the room fell silent, Pastor Hoeller let the suffering and irritability of the assembled faithful build. He wanted anger and frustration to fill the small, tightly packed sanctuary. Though it would be aimed first at him for holding them hostage, the pastor knew from years of audience manipulation that this emotional pressure-cooker would also cause the congregation to ride on his every thundering word, looking for a suitable place to explode when the time came, and today Paul would be his lightning rod. A diffuse but palpable tension was rapidly mounting.

Seated in the third pew from the front, Emma and Paul waited with the others for services to begin. To Emma, Paul had seemed especially "out-to-lunch" since one night last week when she had found him twirling ecstatically in the starry black night. More than inattentive, he acted plain crazy! He hardly slept, walked for miles each day, talked to neighbors about the beauty of the world. One day she found him sitting at the base of the single old tree in their desolate back yard examining a trail of ants. He was completely absorbed in this simple study, as if there could not possibly be anything in the entire world more interesting or more fulfilling than these stupid insects. Had she been less godly, Emma might have called the paramedics, but she knew better. Like an alcoholic or drug user, Paul's spiritual will had grown lax, allowing Satan's worldly temptations to seduce and possess his soul. She was truly grateful for Pastor Hoeller's promised assistance.

Paul, on the other hand, was oblivious to all this. Like a docile child, he let Emma lead him up the front stairs and into church with no particular thoughts at all. The world was so incredibly alive and interesting, so saturated with holiness, that no place was removed from grace. Church? Sure, why not? The number of people packed into this sauna was a little surprising, but far less surprising than the miracle of his own breath, the wonder of eyesight, the bead of sweat trickling down his neck, and the joy he felt in the steady Presence of God. Resting in this invisible peace and astonished by nearly everything around him, Paul was content to sit here the whole day.

Then it began. Pastor Hoeller walked slowly to the pulpit. The assembled were immediately hushed by his powerful presence. He stood erect, firm, resolute, quiet, holding his ancient Bible open in his left hand, eyes closed, head slightly lifted upward, until he felt the familiar rush of the Holy Ghost filling him with authority and inspiration. Like a lion confined in too small a cage, he began pacing back and forth across the small stage. Belying his burning eyes, Pastor Hoeller's first words were soft and gentle, stroking the fearful silence. His quiet, barely audible voice pulled people close as they strained to hear. Once inside his vortex, however, the winds of righteous fury would circle and roar around these captive souls. There was no escape and no hiding. In that awful moment, the congregation understood that they were sinners in the hands of an angry, vengeful God – and that

God was now personified in Pastor Hoeller.

As he had a thousand times before, Pastor Hoeller reminded his audience of the enormous battle that had raged between God and Satan since the time of Creation. Satan opposed the Holy Spirit with every power of Hell – deception, charm, lust, greed, and lies – and even now was winning as the world plunged headlong toward the apocalypse. Demon spirits dwelled in the multitudes that turned their backs on the Holy Spirit. Jesus had come down to this Hell-bound cesspool to give his life to save mankind from Adam and Eve's original sin. Only in his relationship with Christ can man can gain salvation. But time is running out. When the trumpet blows, the predictions of the prophets and apostles will come to pass: Jesus will return in person to remove his faithful from the Earth and God's army will defeat the forces of Satan at Armageddon. All who have not been saved will be condemned to an eternity in hell. And when this holy purge is over, Christ and his faithful will establish the perfect order of Heaven on Earth.

Swelling with the power he recognized as the Holy Ghost, Pastor Hoeller ominously shifted his gaze and his sermon toward its target in the third pew. People stray from God, he warned. Even those who had once given their hearts to Jesus forget. Even those baptized of original sin in the name of the Spirit can fall from grace, for they become weak and unable to resist the Devil's whisper. The gate to Heaven is narrow, he warned, and the righteous path demands absolute obedience to the literal word of God as revealed in the Bible. Then he looked at Paul.

"There is one among us who has slipped. Who has been lulled into Satan's army by weakness and wrong belief. He has been lost for a long time, his wife tells me, and he needs our help. Brother Jensen. Please come forward."

The congregation gasped in unison and then froze. You could hear a pin drop if anyone had the temerity to drop one. Emma turned to stone. Awed by the play of dust particles in a shaft of sunlight pouring through the cracked stained-glass window, Paul heard nothing.

"Come to God," Pastor Hoeler intoned. "Jesus is waiting for you to repent now, this very moment. Cry to God to save your soul and send Satan on his way. Brother Jensen, what say you? Come forward and give your testimony."

No one moved. Paul startled when he heard his name called. What was happening? Was he supposed to do something? He looked to Pastor Hoeller for direction.

"Come forward, Brother Jensen. Confess you sins and call for the Holy Spirit to wash you of Satan's evil and corruption. Come forward, NOW! Time is running out. Only your testament will bring forth God's salvation."

With a sharp jab from Emma's elbow, Paul rose unsteadily to his feet and stumbled toward the pulpit. What was he supposed to do? A testament? He dimly recalled similar services in the past. Some errant soul would be called forward to confess things everyone knew he was doing – drinking, whoring, gambling – and promise to give them up whereupon Pastor Hoeller would touch his forehead and say "You are forgiven in the name of the Holy Spirit. Go and sin no more."

Paul stood dumbly. Audience tension mounted. But what was he supposed to confess? He could think of nothing to say.

With a dark, menacing rage full of impatience, Pastor Hoeller tried to move things along. "Brother Jensen, have you not been forgetful of your duties as head of your family? To provide, to tithe, to set an example for your wife of godly behavior? Worse, have you not left the church to consort with the enemy of God? Have you not sought counsel from Satan himself? Have you not brought your spiritual burdens to a *mental-health counselor*," he twisted his face in disgust as he pronounced these words, "instead of the Lord? ... Brother Jensen, WHAT IS YOUR TESTIMONY?"

Now Paul thought he understood: *The pastor believes I've lost my faith in God. Is that what this is all about? What a relief! Wait until he hears the truth.* With that, Paul readied himself to speak.

He began slowly, tentatively. "It is true that I have suffered deeply. I had lost my soul in a dark pit of depression and damnation. It is true that I abandoned my work. I was too sick to function. My torment was unbearable. But now it is over. My suffering ended last week when I felt God's Presence surround me in the night. I have been living in grace ever since."

"What are you talking about?" Pastor Hoeller asked suspiciously.

Warming to the topic and its profound meaning in his life, Paul could not stop himself. He had wanted to share his vision with everyone he met since that night. He wanted desperately to help others see the lit world as he did. He took this opportunity now to unburden himself.

"The universe is alive. I know that now. It is alive and conscious. Everything! The world is filled with God. It is made of God. It is the very consciousness of God. Reality is God. The divine Presence is in everything, including us, and it makes everything perfect. There is no sin, there is only God."

Pastor Hoeller was stunned. What kind of demonic blasphemy was this? Before he could collect himself, Paul innocently continued.

"Heaven is not some future time or place. Heaven is here now, all around us. This is the Garden! We haven't left. God never kicked us out! And you don't have to be good enough. There is nothing to fix, no problem to solve, nothing to pray for. God is not some vengeful tyrant demanding perfect obedience. You are already perfect because God is your being. You and me and this world are infinitely beautiful and infinitely precious because it is all divine. Worship the beauty that you are and that is all around you. There is no more to understand than this." Paul's eloquence surprised even himself.

Paul was radiant. He was complete. He felt one with divinity. He felt a depth of love toward every shining person in the room that transcended anything he had ever known. He was so happy. No one responded. Something was wrong. What was it?

Now the storm broke. Pastor Hoeller's fury, unleashed by this heinous display of sin and depravity, erupted. "The universe is alive? There is no sin? This is the Garden of Eden? You have nothing to pray for? God is your being? Have you not totally lost your mind and your soul to Satan?" Turning to the audience, he raged, "This man's testimony is false! It is all lies. You see before you not a man but Satan himself. The Devil is here."

The congregation gasped aloud this time. Emma felt herself shrivel up inside. Turning back to Paul, Hoeller screamed, "Repent this evil, Brother Jensen, or you will twist and burn in Hell forever! The Devil has your soul. Beg God for forgiveness. You are at the gates of Hell."

There was nothing Paul could do. They didn't get it. Instead of joy his words had somehow released a torrent of misunderstanding and vitriol. Faces in the congregation were now contorting into masks of hatred. Their words shocked his calm:

"Sinner!"

"Devil worshipper!"

"Satan."

Exploding with maniacal rage, Pastor Hoeller pronounced his verdict: "Leave this House of God, Paul Jensen, and never return. You are the worst of Satan's spawn. As of this moment, this man has no fellowship with us. He is dead in our eyes. We pray that God have mercy on his soul. You are expelled. Leave us."

Loathing and disgust bit viciously at Paul's back as he stepped out from the church's dark anteroom into the hot sun. The peace he felt inside and in the world around him, however, was strangely untouched. Invisible, infinite, eternal, conscious and wondrous, this loving unity seemed to hold everything in a timeless grace. Paul had no idea what he would do next. He did not know how Emma would feel tonight. He had no plans beyond his meeting the next day with Dr. McLaughlin.

Emma left the church in shock. Shame and embarrassment scorched her soul on the walk to her car; no one wanted to talk to this fallen woman. Some felt sorry for her, others viewed her disgrace as deserved, coming directly from God, and no one wanted to risk any association with Emma Jensen.

Paul was not waiting for her at the car. He was nowhere in sight. It didn't matter. All Emma wanted was to go home, sit in her humiliation, and cry alone. And plot her revenge. This was the blackest day of her life, and somebody was going to pay for it.

When Paul returned home that night, he found the house dark and Emma in bed. If there were such a process as cold fusion, Emma had achieved it. Paul hoped she would be willing to talk with him about what happened. He realized then how ignorant he was. No one really wanted to know God. They only wanted the security of familiar rules and beliefs. Paul felt more alone than ever before in his life. The only question Emma asked the following day was whether he was going back to that psychologist and what the man's name was. After his reply, she wrapped the shroud of hatred around her and became impenetrable.

Chapter 12

Determined to recover his professional grasp in this bizarre new case, Tom planned to use his third session with Paul to gather more in-depth information about his childhood, developmental history, and marriage. He might even do some psychological testing to assess the nature and degree of his depression and screen for other clinical syndromes – perhaps a thought disorder or intellectual impairment. Then he would formulate a diagnosis and treatment plan. Once this diagnostic phase was completed, Tom thought, then his old feeling of control and mastery would return and he could proceed with confidence.

Paul's mental state on his arrival at the office immediately dislodged Tom's well-intentioned clinical plan. Once again, Tom was struck – perhaps a better word would be "stunned" – by Paul's strange behavior. Unhurried. Peaceful. Calm. And most curiously, conscious of the "here-and-now" with such keen awareness that he seemed both distracted and awestruck by the simplest things – early-morning light enlivening the bookcase; the magically changing numbers of Tom's digital clock; the sound of his pants brushing the chair as he shifted position;…and most of all, the absolute beauty, perfection and preciousness of every thing, every experience, every piece of creation. Paul was no longer gripped by any personal angst or struggle; instead, he radiated peace, ease, happiness and gratitude.

While Tom observed Paul quietly, his mind was whirling. *What a remarkable state of consciousness*, he thought. *So peaceful. No disturbing thoughts, no problems, no worries, and more puzzling, almost no self at all. Indeed he seems empty, no, spacious is a better word, as if his mind were silent yet open to infinity, whatever that meant. Can this be? Look! See how he observes the world with such rapture, like an infant, marveling at every new perception and sensation. Instead of dismissing objects in the room as something he's seen countless times, like a chair or table, each object appears, in one respect or another, entirely new to him, as if he'd never seen it before. Is he psychotic? Delirious? Brain damaged? Sometimes people with frontal-lobe pathology can't form abstractions. Is this neurological? Is he dissociating or dreaming? And why isn't he alarmed by his strange experience, because he's not living in the normal world of everyday perceptions and concerns. God, this is so disorienting!*

On impulse, Tom pulled out a Rorschach card, one of the standard series of inkblots psychologists sometimes use to assess an individual's perception and thought processes, and handed it to Paul, who took the card, held it delicately, almost lovingly, and appeared fascinated and delighted.

"Tell me what you see," Tom instructed.

"It's beautiful. The cardboard is so light and shiny and rectangular. I love its whiteness and blackness. It's perfect."

"But what do you see? What does the inkblot look like?"

"I see the universe. Everything is here. I feel its energy. It's like me, alive, pulsing with the infinite. Same as my body. My physical being feels sacred, beautiful, miraculous. When I feel this energy, ecstasy shoots through me like fireworks in my soul. I can barely stand the joy."

The inkblot itself hardly matters at all to him, thought Tom. *He only seems to perceive physical properties of the card, and with such intense and altered awareness. God, that's weird!*

Paul looked up at Tom and said, "You are like that, too, you know. Can you feel the life force flowing through your hands and eyes, your mind and body? Can you feel God's Presence as your own? Have you ever noticed how exquisitely beautiful your face is? Look in the mirror. It's shining, like the face of an angel. The divine is everywhere. It's all love: the walls, the ceiling, your books, space itself, you and me. I dwell in oneness with this amazing force, I just want to dance and twirl and shout. I almost can't sit still! I am in love with this world."

Tom was astonished. And once again speechless. He

wondered inside, *What do you say to a guy like this? Is he manic? He doesn't seem to sleep well at night but doesn't appear hyper.*

"What about your depression?" Tom said aloud.

"I discovered last week that my 'depression,' as you call it, was as remarkable and full of 'God' as your inkblot. Not the God every one thinks of – some scary big guy you have to pray to – but just consciousness. Everything is conscious, even this shiny card." Paul lovingly placed the inkblot on the table between them and continued. "So when I stopped fighting my depression and experienced its essence, I discovered it was simply a contracted state of perfect being. I was holding myself so tight it was causing emotional pain, but even this pain was filled at its core with divine energy. It's all part of the miracle of existence. When I understood this, I just relaxed into the warm joyous energy of my body." As if to illustrate this, Paul settled back quietly into his chair like a luxuriously soft feather bed.

Again Tom was dumbstruck. No thought. No sense of time. He was awake, he was sure of that. The clock ticked loudly like a metronome. Birds sang outside his window. Light streamed into the room. It suddenly struck Tom that he had begun to enter this same state of "divine" consciousness. Tom jerked back violently, trying to shake off this altered perceptual state. Had someone slipped LSD into his coffee? Was he going crazy? Was the air poisoned? Panic rose up inside him. He caught his breath, stood up, and began to move around the room trying desperately to re-establish the normal reality of body and mind. Pretending to look purposeful, he pulled out more notepaper and sat down again.

Then Paul spoke kindly. "It scares you, doesn't it, this feeling? Don't be frightened. There is a consciousness beyond all the terrible and confusing delusions of the world. We are always in its grace."

Tom didn't want to hear any more. These were crazy feelings and words, and their escalating, terrifying, unfathomable implications arrested his mind like a frozen computer. He'd had enough. He had to finish the hour and get his act together. Even that phrase – getting one's act together – disturbed him, implying that it was all an act. *Forget it,* he lectured himself. *Put on your professional hat and tie things up.*

Regaining his well-practiced clinical voice, Tom said, "I am not sure what to say, Paul. I'd like to think more about what you've been telling me and discuss it with colleagues. Let's stop for today and reschedule next week."

After Paul left, Tom sat at his desk trying to make notes. The page remained white and empty. Nothing.

Chapter 13

At home that night, during dinner and throughout the evening, Tom appeared distracted and preoccupied but no one asked him what was wrong until bedtime, when Ronnie closed the bedroom door and said, "Tom. What's with you? You hardly talked at dinner; you've been wandering around aimlessly. You haven't heard a word anyone has said. Is something bothering you?"

Tom sighed. "It's that case I told you about, Ronnie. The guy who dreams of Jesus. He's driving me nuts. I can't make heads or tails out of him."

"So what?" Ronnie asked. "Some clients take longer to figure out than others."

"This is different. This guy is like no one I have ever seen. Every time I try to take charge of the session, his words unglue me. I can't explain it. Being with him is like being on a mind-altering drug and the effects last for hours. I just don't get it."

"That's heavy. Maybe you should get additional consultation."

"I plan to," said Tom. "In fact, I've called my consultation group and asked if I can switch with Carol and present tomorrow. I just don't know what else to do. This guy is dismantling my reality with his strange religious talk. What's even scarier, I almost think I'm beginning to see what he's talking about, to actually see what he sees, and that really freaks me out. What if I became like him? What if I lost my familiar self?"

"What are you talking about?" Ronnie asked, with mounting apprehension.

"Everything. The world seems brighter, more vivid, more arresting, more enchanting. Regular things don't matter in the same way. Like doing the dishes. Before, it was a chore to get done as quickly as possible. Tonight, it felt like playing in a watery wonderland of soap and bubbles, warmth and slippery wetness. I almost regretted rinsing the water away. I'm afraid I could get stuck in this man's dimension, like the Twilight Zone. What if going to work didn't matter because everything around you was so completely perfect, fascinating and fulfilling? What if I just started loving everyone, found amazing beauty in every face and blade of grass, and no longer viewed the world through the lens of problems, goals, or responsibilities? What if I stopped being the person I'm so used to being?"

"Wow! He's having quite an effect on you," Ronnie said slowly, her mouth still open, her mind disarmed.

"I can get rid of him," Tom said with sudden determination. "And maybe that's the answer. I know that if I never saw him again, the world would click back into place and everything would be normal again."

"And are you going to do that?" Ronnie asked.

"I'll decide after my consultation group tomorrow."

"He scares me," Ronnie said. "I don't like what's happening to you."

"I don't know how I feel," Tom said. "My customary self starts disintegrating around him." Tom tried to choose his next words carefully. "Yet, there is something right and true about Paul's state of consciousness. I just don't know where it leads."

"Now you're scaring me, Tom. Put yourself back together. Either get a psychological grasp of this screwball or let him go. We don't need you becoming some kind of psycho-flake. Family is real. Reality is real. I am real. Get it together."

"You're right. This is crazy. I'll get it straightened out during group tomorrow. What a weird day. Let's hit the sack."

Tom forced himself to lie still, pretending sleep. When the first rays of light came across the horizon, he was not sure he had slept at all.

Chapter 14

The major activity of the Board of Psychology is the enforcement of the licensing law contained in the California Business and Professions code. The Board's mandate – to evaluate consumer complaints against psychologists – involves handling approximately 700 complaints a year against California's 22,000 psychologists. While the majority of these complaints are closed for lack of merit, roughly 20% proceed to formal investigations conducted by the Medical Board. Half of these are referred to the Attorney General's office where formal charges are filed.

Under "Laws Governing Professional Behavior" in the Business and Professions Code, a psychologist's license to practice can be denied, suspended, or revoked for numerous reasons including personal, business or sexual involvement with clients, criminal convictions, drug or alcohol abuse, or gross negligence. A negligent act is one that departs from the standard of care in the professional community. If a psychologist is convicted of violating the Business and Professions Code, punishment may consist of a fine, imprisonment, or both. Civil suits may also be brought against the psychologist for any damages caused by his malpractice. Finally, ethical principles enumerated by the American Psychological Association also apply. If a member is found to have acted unethically, the APA can sanction him with a warning, reprimand, censure, stipulated resignation, or expulsion from the organization.

The Board's automated phone system picked up Emma's call. She was instantly annoyed with the mechanical voice. She wanted satisfaction NOW. After listening to all the options, she punched the number of the one she wanted for "The Enforcement Department." Its automated message then instructed her to file a complaint in writing or online at the board's website, which irritated Emma even more. "Where are the real people?" she spat out. She didn't even own a computer. Punching the final option to reach an operator, Emma heard a real human being answer.

"May I help you?"

"Yes," Emma said firmly. "I don't have a computer and I don't write very well but I want to report a psychologist for practicing religion without a license."

"What do you mean, practicing religion without a license?" asked the clerk.

"I mean that this man has been telling my husband to turn away from God, our pastor, and our church. Since my husband has been seeing him, he no longer cares about anything. The pastor says this psychologist is practicing religion. Isn't it wrong for a psychologist to practice religion?" Emma demanded.

"A psychologist must practice within the scope of the psychology license as well as his formal training and professional experience. Some psychologists do work with emotional problems involving religion. What you have told me so far would not necessarily imply any wrongdoing. You would have to give me more information about specific misconduct."

Emma's thoughts spun urgently. What would be a good charge?

"But is it legal for a psychologist to act like a pastor?" she pressed.

"Well, a psychologist is ethically forbidden to engage in dual relationships with clients. That means having two different kinds of relationship at once, one professional and another personal, sexual, or business-related."

"What if he is seeing the client professionally and also gives religious advice that only a pastor can do?"

"If he is conducting religious rites and ceremonies in the therapeutic hour, which may be both professionally and scientifically inappropriate, and especially if he is doing so without the requisite religious training and certification, then the psychologist could be in violation of several ethical provisions, including

Multiple or 'Dual' Relationships, Misuse of Psychologist's Influence, and exceeding Boundaries of Competence. Such ethical violations would have to be investigated to determine the extent to which they violate the law."

Excited by her progress, Emma pronounced with exaggerated gravity, "I wish to make formal charges of ethical misconduct involving Multiple Relationships, Misuse of Psychologist's Influence, and Boundaries of Competence violations."

"It is usually the client who makes brings the complaints," clarified the clerk.

"My husband is under this man's influence and too confused to make a complaint. Don't you see? This man has brainwashed my husband!"

"OK. From what you have told me, we can open a preliminary investigation. Who is the psychologist?"

"Dr. Thomas McLaughlin," Emma said proudly.

The next five minutes were spent detailing her accusations, obtaining specific information: dates, addresses, things said. Emma embellished her account liberally. The worst that could happen was that one or more of the charges would be dismissed. So what? At least the guy would think twice about continuing with Paul. And at best, who knows...maybe he'd lose his license.

Emma hung up the phone feeling smug and revenged. One down and one to go. Her next call was to Pastor Hoeller.

"First Christian Church of Mayhew," answered the elderly but *real* person.

"Is Pastor Hoeller in please? This is Emma Jensen calling. He is expecting me."

"Just a minute."

His voice was unmistakable: gruff, short, and impatient. But did he seem a little friendlier than usual? Emma wondered.

"This is Emma Jensen. I have spoken to the women from the church advisory council. Everyone is prepared to be at Dr. McLaughlin's office at one o'clock sharp tomorrow. We have also contacted our three sister churches. It turns out there's a lot of anger in the Christian community toward 'psycho' therapists talking weak and confused people out of their faith. It's high time the Christian community spoke up. And by the way," she mentioned in her most conspiratorial tone, "we anonymously called all the news stations in town to alert them to this demonstration. That Dr. McLaughlin will never defy God again."

Pastor Hoeller liked Emma's plan for many reasons. It gave him a public soapbox to preach scripture, additional notoriety, and a cause that might bring attention to their little church.

Pulling himself out of fantasy, he replied, "Sister Jensen, you have shown the courage of the righteous. Tomorrow the Lord will be on our side and I will sermonize to our brave Christian brothers and sisters about the satanic abomination of the mental-health establishment. We will pray that this man's punishment will be quick and severe."

Emma politely thanked Pastor Hoeller and hung up. She liked this special relationship with him. If this worked out, maybe she could do more special things in the church. And anyway, by this time tomorrow, that lying doctor would be out of her husband's life forever. Then she would tearfully ask Paul to repent his ways and return to the church with her to ask God's forgiveness. How could he deny her?

Chapter 15

Tom's consultation group arrived promptly at noon at his office. The day was already into the 90s and everyone brought water bottles. Construction noises leaked into the room from a new office building going up down the street, an annoying distraction. But they focused quickly – all were curious about this latest turn of events and what kind of crisis would cause Tom to request a change in their rotation schedule, a rare event. They were also eager to help a colleague in whatever way they could. Greetings were brief, lunch bags opened, and the group got down to business without delay.

"Thank you all for changing our schedule on such short notice. This is about that patient I presented last week. I really need some help here. I don't know if this case is more about this patient or me. It's kind of embarrassing. Maybe you can help me sort it out."

Tom succinctly reviewed the clinical details he had presented at their previous meeting and tried his best to describe the "weirdness" of Paul's last session. It was even harder to explain the peculiar way Paul's altered consciousness had "rubbed off" on him. When Tom was done, the group sat quietly.

This time Barbara, the Jungian, began. "There is something frankly mystical about this man. His emotional condition has apparently opened him to the religious layer of the psyche, releasing all sorts of metaphysical perceptions and intuitions. He is truly in an altered state."

"The guy is psychotic!" Frank countered, saying each word with equal clarity and emphasis to make his point. "I don't care what layer this stuff is coming from, he needs meds. He needs them now. You don't even know where this guy is sleeping? The guy's wandering around at night in a haze. He may need psychiatric admission for his own protection."

"But he's not classically psychotic. He's not talking about voices or paranoid delusions or irrational guilt. He's not agitated or depressed. He's not unhappy at all. And he's too calm to be in the manic phase of bipolar illness. What would medication be for?"

"Still, he may still be delirious," Carol cautioned. "That Rorschach response was very concrete, very organic. You're lucky the guy didn't eat the card! He needs to be seen neurologically...CAT Scan, MRI, physical exam, close observation. Only then do you have the luxury to theorize about mystical states."

"OK, I get that. And from the objective side of me, I agree. But how do you explain my response? I'm not organic! I'm not psychotic! But something happens to me in his presence. I begin to experience Paul's altered consciousness. It freaks me out!"

"Yes, that is peculiar," mused Carol. "That's never happened to me."

"And as crazy as it sounds, there's something in what he says that is real," Tom ventured. "I sense the reality he is describing, though I don't want to, and it pulls me further in. I don't know what to think about that."

"Don't go there," Perry said firmly. "Your perspective will slip away if you start talking about 'far out' metaphysical possibilities like contagious mystical states. No one has ever written about that in the clinical literature, unless you want to talk about hysteria. You know, there is a rare syndrome called *folie-a-deux*, a French term describing the situation where two people share the same delusions. You don't look psychotic to me yet," Perry joked, "but don't get pulled into his craziness. Inexperienced therapists, especially those with spiritual leanings, often make the mistake of believing their patient's religious delusions. You're too smart for that. Get him a physical, get him a neurological consult, and then if he's clean, get him on meds."

It all seems so obvious, Tom thought. *I could have said all this myself. I should have!* Where was his head these days?

"Yeah, OK, you're right. I don't know how I got so flaked out on this guy. I'll set up the medical consultations this afternoon. I don't know what got into me."

"Everyone loses perspective once in a while," Carol reassured Tom. "That's why we have consultation groups, to keep each other in line. Do the conservative thing and let's see what you learn."

Barbara quietly chimed in, "It's still interesting, this mystical stuff. Don't throw it all out. Wait and see."

Just at that moment, Maggie opened the office door. Her face was white.

"Tom, come out here. You have to see this. Maybe you all should come."

Startled by her intrusion, Tom asked, "What is it, Maggie?"

"Look for yourself."

All five members of the group moved quickly to look out the waiting-room window onto the street. There on the sidewalk were at least thirty people marching in a long narrow loop. Every third or fourth protester carried a placard with slogans like, "Leave Our Religion Alone," "Stop Practicing Religion Without a License," "Dr. McLaughlin Is A God-less Charlatan," "The Christian Churches of Mayhew Condemn Dr. McLaughlin." In the center of the loop stood a thick, swarthy man dressed in the dark clothes of an old-time preacher, hoisting a Bible like a weapon. He moved restlessly and used a bullhorn to quote scriptural passages supposedly condemning psychotherapists. Even more disturbing, however, was the sight of three local news channels. *What the hell is going on?* Tom wondered.

By bedtime, after watching the 6:00 and 10:00 o'clock news programs, Tom had his answer. This was all about Paul's church! Tom had unknowingly struck a hornets' nest, and the hornets were furious. Where would this go? The next morning, Tom found out.

At 8:00 a.m. sharp his quiet preparation time was interrupted by a call from someone named Larry Bennett with the Board of Psychology. They were investigating several charges of professional misconduct and wanted to meet with him. Perhaps he should consult his attorney, the investigator suggested, and be prepared to talk about that demonstration outside your office. An unbelievable nightmare was tightening like a noose around his neck. The meeting with Mr. Bennett was scheduled for the following Monday at Tom's office.

Chapter 16

The next day, Tom could barely keep his mind on therapy. The anxiety symptoms he was used to treating were now his: sudden, gripping, nameless dread; cold, clammy hands; difficulty swallowing; not enough air in the room; heart palpitations, nausea and gut gripes. Panic had taken charge of his body. No, this was more than panic – this was terror. *Am I going crazy?* he asked himself. *What the hell am I going to do?*

When the lunch hour arrived, he found himself calling Father Kelly.

"Hi, Tom. Good to hear from you. What's cooking?"

"Clarence, are you busy tonight? I really need some help. It's sort of a religious crisis, I think. I need to talk to someone out of my field. I can't explain it now."

Clarence heard the uncharacteristic urgency in Tom's voice. "Certainly – nothing I can't change tonight. Let's meet at that coffee shop on 10th and K Streets. It's large and usually quiet on weeknights. 7:30 okay with you?"

"Done!" Tom exclaimed with some relief. "Thank you so much. I'll see you then."

Having dispelled some of his anxiety arranging this meeting, Tom's afternoon became more focused and for a while he was back in the groove. Panic swelled again in his final therapy hour and he could not leave the office soon enough. Cars, lights, darkness, pedestrians, storefronts, fear...his hands trembled on the wheel as he drove down K Street.

Clarence was waiting inside the coffee shop, sitting calmly with two cups of coffee at a table in the rear of the restaurant.

Thank God! Tom exhaled, as he rushed to greet him.

"Hi, Tom. Sit down. I got you decaf. Didn't think you needed to be any more wired," joked Clarence, who rarely took offence at others' beliefs or questions – the spiritual journey was difficult enough without imposed conflicts. And he loved that journey, loved exploring its meaning and challenges, especially with bright, genuinely interested seekers. Dressed casually in street clothes, he welcomed Tom with his warm smile and heartfelt handshake. Grateful for this safe and supportive friend, Tom babbled nearly incoherently at first.

"Clarence, I'm in deep shit – excuse the language. Man, am I glad to see you! I've got so much to tell you."

"Slow down, Tom. We've got lots of time. I can stay all night if you need. It's one of the benefits of the Vow of Celibacy. So take a deep breath and tell me the whole story."

"It's about that guy you referred me. He's having some kind of continuous religious experience. My colleagues think he's psychotic and that I'm just as crazy for believing him. His church picketed my office last night and threatens to return – did you see my name on the news last night? Worse, the Board of Psychology is suddenly investigating me for a complaint of practicing beyond my training, and my wife thinks I'm flaking out."

"Jesus, Mary and Joseph!" laughed Clarence. "Excuse my language – I use it in place of swearing. Let's take one piece at a time. What's this about a continuous religious experience?"

With none of the clinical distance that characterized his consultation-group presentation, Tom poured out the whole story. He described Paul's words, his behavior, and his extraordinary state of consciousness.

"It's not like anything I've ever seen," concluded Tom. "I don't know what to think or do. I am stumped."

Clarence listened intently, and when Tom finished, he said, "Tom, it sounds like Paul is having a mystical experience. It may be new to you, but it's not new to religion. People have been having mystical experiences since the beginning of time. In fact, that's how most of the major religions developed. Someone has a profound, first-hand experience of the divine and is so moved by its power and illumination that he teaches others. Jesus, Buddha, Muhammad, Moses, all had mystical experiences. In time, the teacher's disciples organize his or her teachings into scripture, theology, and related devotional practices, and a formal religion is born."

"You mean this guy is going to start a religion?"

"That would be very unlikely," Clarence replied. "You see, what people don't realize is that this experience still happens, and not infrequently, and it happens to everyday people. You don't have to be a prophet or religious founder. You don't even have to be religious. The mystical experience can occur without warning, sometimes when the individual has hit rock bottom emotionally. In fact, one of the founders of Alcoholics Anonymous described his own mystical experience, influencing the spirituality component of the Twelve-Step program."

"I never knew that! Tell me more about the mystical experience."

"OK. Ask anyone who has had this experience – and I have talked to many – and they will tell you it is the most beautiful, reassuring, and unforgettable experience they have ever had. For them, it constitutes the direct experience of the divine, but not the divine you think of, some guy with a white beard sitting up in the sky and judging us when we die, but rather a divine consciousness that feels unconditionally loving, accepting and kind."

"Yeah, that's exactly how he described it too," Tom interjected. "What else?" he asked in amazement.

"Though the experience may vary some from one person to another, it is often characterized by subtle light shining through creation like a stained-glass window. The light is felt to be alive, conscious and omnipresent, an actual divine Presence that surrounds or engulfs the person in a warm blanket of love. The mystical experience is beyond human control – though some seek it through drugs or extreme practices – but most view it as a gift of grace. The experience is one of unbounded joy and rapture that exceeds anything known to ordinary human life. Lastly, it may also involve some form of revelation or illumination – as if one is given knowledge about the ultimate nature or purpose of the universe or human life."

"So what *is* the purpose of life? I've been wondering about that myself!"

"Well," Clarence continued, "each of us has to find that for our self. But the sense the mystical experience gives people is that the universe, and everything in it, is perfect, whole, and holy even if we can't see that from our limited human vantage point. It's inherently life-affirming. Even the polarity of good and evil is transcended in the realization that nothing can ultimately be evil in God. I believe this experience is one of the most important experiences of life because it changes everything, shifting us to a much higher state of awareness, understanding and love."

"Does the person having the mystical experience lose touch with conventional reality?" Tom asked.

"During the experience," Clarence replied, "the world is seen afresh as radiant, perfect, precious, and saturated with the sacred. Things seem clearer, more vibrant and colorful...perhaps it's more accurate to say that rather than losing touch with reality, people experience a heightened awareness of it. The person is awestruck by the smallest things and may feel as if the everyday world has been transformed into a personal Heaven."

"So what happens next?"

"For most, the experience is brief – a matter of minutes. For some, it can go on for several days, intensifying and receding. Usually it ceases sooner or later, though some are able to move back into that altered state voluntarily. In any case, the individual returns to his everyday life full of gratitude and humility, knowing for the first time that the world itself is a miraculous, generous, and holy gift. The fear of death disappears, for the person having a mystical experience realizes that there is no death; only a reunion with this divine reality. Can you see how dramatic this experience would be for people? Imagine having this encounter: even if you went back to your normal activities, your life would be altered forever."

Once more Tom was dumbfounded. He finally asked, "Clarence, are you saying that the mystical experience is not abnormal or psychotic?"

"Yes. Even the research on mystical experiences indicates that they happen to normal people and are not related to any kind of psychopathology. In fact, Tom, if you think about it, the mystical experience also happens in small ways to all of us. Haven't you ever felt spellbound by birdsong in the woods, or awed by the miracle of childbirth? Sometimes people sense this Presence in great cathedrals. It is a natural human experience. Depending on one's tradition, it may be called Satori, enlightenment, Christ Consciousness, or a hundred other names."

Niggling at the corners of his mind, something had been bothering Tom, something about Paul and his church. Now he knew what it was. "So why doesn't Paul's church welcome his experience?"

"Ah, now we arrive at the not-so-holy problem of religious politics. There are fundamental differences between religion and mysticism. The institutions that form around an individual's mystical experience are eventually corrupted in one degree or another by human nature – you know – the ego's desire for power, control, wealth, or fame. It's happened to every religion under the sun. Those who have not had the experience but hold the institutional power distrust the mystic. To them, he looks like a heretic, like someone trying undermine their authority."

"How does spirituality differ from religion and mysticism?" Tom asked, as if he were in class.

"Religion is the formal organization of faith and practice derived from the divine revelations of a specific person's mystical experience. Spirituality is our personal relationship to the divine, however we conceive or experience it. So, in a church of 300 believers, there will be one religion but 300 different spiritual takes on it. And lastly, mysticism is the direct and unmediated contact with the divine. It's not about beliefs at all; it's about pure and ecstatic experience.

"You should also know that mystical experiences can be described on a continuum. At one end are little ones, like being awed by a spectacular sunset, the perfection of your new baby's hands, or the miracle and mystery of love. We all have experiences like that. At the other end of the continuum are the big mystical experiences like the ones we've just been discussing. Finally, there is something else we might call mystical consciousness. It's a kind of intentional, thought-free and heightened awareness. Some call it 'mindfulness.' All the same mystical qualities I've been describing can be discerned in mystical consciousness when you learn the skill, though at a lesser intensity."

"It also sounds like you can be spiritual and not religious?"

"Yes. You can have spiritual beliefs formed from a mix of religious, spiritual, philosophical, and even scientific ideas. You can also be religious but not spiritual, like when someone holds firmly to a prescribed religious doctrine without a sense of its personal significance. And you can be religious and spiritual without any grasp of the mystical dimension at all."

"One more thing, Tom. Mystical experiences change you, even your personality. They can awaken new spiritual energies, motivations, insights, and abilities in some people, threatening established relationships or religious authority."

"Wow! That helps a lot," exhaled Tom. "I see that religion also can be a form of social control that has nothing to do with spirituality or mystical experience. In this case, it appears that Paul's wife and his church want to suppress his mystical experience and control him instead."

"Yes. In fact, as you know, all manner of cruelty, wars, intolerance, and bigotry have been justified in the name of religion. And, as two of your most famous psychologists – Jung and Maslow – observed, religious authorities can actually be motivated to suppress mystical experiences among their followers in order to their retain institutional power."

"I want to get back to Paul's mystical experience," Tom interjected. "He continues to view reality – even himself and others – as a living, sacred, conscious Presence. What is that about?"

"That perception is central to the mystical experience and to highly mystical religions. In fact, every religion has a mystical wing that embraces this revelation. Some in Christianity call it 'Christ Consciousness' and in Buddhism it might be called 'Buddha mind.' You disconnect from your everyday self, dissolving your separate awareness to a lesser or greater extent into divine consciousness, the Presence Paul is describing. Then you live in a state of ecstasy, grace, unity, wonder, and gratitude, at least for the duration of the experience. Everything becomes a divine revelation. And in this experience our perception of the world is radically altered. This mystical shift in consciousness even convinces the individual that the original Garden of Eden is still here."

"So where is God in this vision?"

"The Presence that Paul feels is a direct experience of God, but not the Western version humans invented. Western culture tends to distrust these direct experiences of God and prefers to imagine a divine human-like figure in charge of everything, like a King or Father. It's literally a projection of our man's egocentric and sometimes violent nature; that's why God has been described as terrifying, judgmental and punitive. The God Paul experiences is really the cosmos itself as an infinitely conscious, intelligent and loving Being that is everywhere and in everything."

"I never realized how much interplay there was between psychology, religion, spirituality and mysticism," mused Tom. "And from the mystical perspective, life itself is a sacred experience, just as Paul seems to be saying."

"Yes. All religions speak of the sacred nature of life. Keep in mind also that these ideas are neither new nor exclusively religious. They can also be found in the history of philosophy through the writings of teachers like Plato, Plotinus, Spinoza, and countless others, as well as in poetry, the arts, mythology, and even scientists, from Copernicus to Einstein and modern theoretical physics."

"I'm amazed," Tom said. "I feel so much better about this case. I don't think Paul is psychotic. I don't think my colleagues are correct. I think this is really a conflict between the world-views of religion, psychology, science, and mysticism."

"One more thing, Tom. Anyone can have a mystical experience. And that includes people who also have real and significant psychological problems. In other words, a psychotic can also have a mystical encounter that gets tangled up in his delusions or grandiosity. An experience of mystical identification or union with God can wrongly lead a highly disordered person to believe he alone is God. So you have to keep your diagnostic skills sharp and watch how the individual's experience is integrated into his personality and his life. The healthy mystic is happy and well-adjusted and they don't need treatment; the psychiatric patient is never truly happy and content."

"One additional problem. It is so difficult to describe Paul's mystical state of consciousness. Words don't seem to do it justice and end up sounding crazy."

"Yes, that is a real problem. The awesome power and beauty of the mystical experience makes it very difficult to reduce to words. In fact, many argue that the human mind cannot really grasp the experience, cannot capture it with concepts or language. 'Ineffable' is often a word often used to describe it."

They sat in silence for a few minutes. Clarence watched Tom patiently, respecting Tom's need to digest all this new information. Finally Tom resumed, "That helps, Clarence. I see now that my job is to help Paul understand all this, and especially the kinds of problems it will cause in his marriage and community. In fact, we both need to sort it out. Now I can't wait for our next session."

Tom could have stayed all night. He was nearly ecstatic with his newly expanded perspective. Clarence, on the other hand, was ready for bed. Goodbyes were said and Tom gave Clarence an enormous parting hug in gratitude. On the drive home, Tom marveled at simply being alive. His anxiety was gone, replaced now by the beauty of the night sky, wonder at the simple miracle of existence, and happiness in believing for the first time in his life that perhaps the world was purposeful and holy.

Chapter 17

Remarkably, the rest of Tom's week fell nicely into place all by itself. Pastor Hoeller had lost interest in the street theater as soon as the television cameras left – his arthritic hip was acting up anyway. With his departure, the picketers' enthusiasm rapidly dwindled and they too disappeared. Tom's friends and colleagues called to joke about Tom's 15 minutes of fame, which thankfully ended as quickly as it had begun. And, with what he had learned from Clarence, Tom felt confident that the Board of Psychology would also go away.

Friday night at last. The air was cooling with those delicious Delta breezes, allergy season was behind him and all was finally right with the world. In strict accordance with the McLaughlin family's Friday routine, it was time to go out for pizza. This evening promised to be especially interesting: Laura had asked if she could invite the prom boy out to pizza with them! Josh was 17, drove his own car, and she obviously had a crush on him. Her final instructions to her parents and brother, presented with a stern and no-nonsense tenor, warned, "Do not make a big deal out of this, especially in front of Josh."

And the evening had been great fun. Josh turned out to be a neat kid, the kind parents like. Polite, a little shy, not the type to move too quickly. Laura was so cute, teasing him, showing him the house and yard after they got home. Even more fun was Erik's reaction: He stayed home! Said he had things to do in his room. Then, when Laura and Josh were quietly nestled on the couch watching television, Erik appeared on this suspicious scene and promptly plopped down between them. He started talking with Josh about baseball and flipping the channels looking for a game. Erik was working his charm (and, he believed, protecting his little sister). Josh, a junior varsity baseball player, moved comfortably into this familiar ground probably hoping that Erik would eventually go to bed. He didn't. Laura grumbled to herself as the evening wore down but avoided making a scene. Payback would be hers.

Meanwhile, at the other end of the house, Tom and Ronnie settled into the living room for an evening of peace, quiet, and good reading. Unable to pass by a used bookstore without stopping in, Tom's home study overflowed with books now double- and even triple-stacked on the shelves. He liked ebooks well enough, but loved the feel and smell of the real thing. Tonight he cracked open a new novel about the history of philosophy, a subject he had always wanted to understand. Ronnie's literary obsession ran to mystery books written by women about female PIs. She had collected hundreds of them, kept an updated, alphabetized record on her computer, and fantasized about opening a chain of mystery bookstores in airports, coffee houses, and department stores. In his typically psychological (and facetious) turn of mind, Tom speculated aloud about Ronnie's unconscious feminist motives. Not easily intimidated, she responded with her own psychoanalytic interpretation of his chronically messy study, positing deep Freudian conflicts between anal-retentive and anal-expulsive tendencies. This embarrassing (and possibly too close to true) observation convinced Tom to change the topic.

They had not talked about Paul, or Tom's strange mental state, since the prior week's uncomfortable discussion. Though Tom seemed ready to disappear happily into his novel, Ronnie's lingering apprehension compelled her to interrupt his disappearing act to ask about Paul. She listened attentively as Tom patiently recited Clarence's comments, and was tremendously relieved by their clarity and the obvious return of Tom's professional objectivity – and sanity. So that was the conclusion of this strange case, she thought, it was just a client having a religious experience. Tom had his head on straight again and that's all she really wanted. With a silent sigh of relief, Ronnie returned to the latest adventures of her favorite heroine.

Before any of them realized it, the evening was over. Erik had fallen asleep on the couch, ruining his sister's romantic adventures and Josh had an 11:30 curfew. Whether a kiss was stolen on his way out was no one's business. With life back to normal and another exhausting week behind them, Ronnie led Tom upstairs by the hand and locked the bedroom door.

The weekend ran its usual course. Laura spent Saturday night at a friend's and Tom and Ronnie partook of their usual movie date. Chores, grocery shopping, homework, Ronnie's class prep, and Tom's bicycle ride up the American River Parkway chewed up most of Sunday. Dinner that night was simple, "every man for himself" – whatever and whenever they wanted. A little TV watching and off to bed. Perfect.

The message on Tom's office voicemail the next morning, however, was a surprise. "Dr. McLaughlin. This is Dr. Spence from Sacramento Psychiatric Hospital. Your patient, Paul Jensen, was brought in yesterday afternoon by his wife. Their family doctor made the referral and insisted he be admitted despite the wife's reluctance – she apparently doesn't like mental-health professionals. Though the patient didn't want to stay, he clearly evidenced religious delusions and was admitted on a 5250 involuntary hold. We'll keep him here until his psychosis clears. Don't bother coming over. Mrs. Jensen advised us that you were no longer his doctor. Given his current psychiatric incompetence, we must respect his wife's request. If this provision should change, we'll let you know."

Before he could even begin to react, a second message came on.

"Dr. McLaughlin, this is Paul. I'm at Sacramento Psychiatric Hospital on a patient phone I'm not supposed to use. Emma brought me in Saturday. Our family doctor made her take me in, saying I might be a danger to myself or others. Emma was upset and crying so hard that I just couldn't refuse her. She's afraid I'm going crazy because of my relationship with God. The psychiatrist met with her for half an hour and told me I was severely depressed. He said I needed electrical treatment. Said it wouldn't hurt and I'd feel better almost immediately. If it makes her happy, I don't mind. I'm happy wherever I am. The treatments begin tomorrow early. Anyway, I don't know if I'll be seeing you again. It's OK. I just wanted to thank you for listening. Goodbye."

Tom reeled in stunned disbelief. Paul was in a psychiatric unit? Shock treatment? Tomorrow? And now Paul was no longer his patient. How had all this happened? Emma probably bought into the idea of shock treatment when she learned it would erase his newfound mental state. She had won! And there was nothing Tom could do. Then he remembered the meeting scheduled this morning with Larry Bennett from the Board of Psychology. Oh God, he was in no mood to explain all this to a Board investigator – in one hour.

Chapter 18

The BOP investigator was prompt and all business. Even Maggie refrained from extraneous monologue while showing him into Tom's office. After obtaining written permission to tape record the meeting, Mr. Bennett carefully reviewed Emma Jensen's charges against Tom and then sat back expectantly. Well-built, muscular, dark suit and crew-cut – a former military policeman? – with an ominously large briefcase, he was serious with a capital "S."

Bolstered by his meeting with Clarence Kelly, Tom pulled himself together and for the next forty-five minutes reiterated the details of Paul's referral, presenting complaints, his initial clinical assessment, subsequent consultation feedback, follow-up session, and consultation with Clarence. Tom omitted his own strange reaction – the guy didn't need any more ammunition. The demonstration in front of his office, he hypothesized, must have been planned by the patient's wife and their fundamentalist pastor, both of whom vehemently opposed psychological treatment on religious grounds. Beginning to feel more confident, Tom finally related last night's telephone messages and the patient's transfer of care.

"Did you try to influence Mr. Jensen's religious beliefs in any way during your treatment?" Mr. Bennett queried.

"No. I only saw him twice and we were in a diagnostic phase. Treatment per se had not really begun."

"What was your diagnosis?"

"So far, I had only considered his presenting complaints to reflect a non-pathological 'Religious or Spiritual Problem.'" Tom assumed Mr. Bennett understood this "V Code" category in the *Diagnostic and Statistical Manual of Mental Disorders* of the American Psychiatric Association – the official rulebook for making psychiatric diagnoses. It referred to problems an individual might want to discuss that are not related to any mental illness or disorder. Examples could include normal grief after the death of a spouse, career or job dissatisfaction, or an immigrant's difficulties adjusting to their new culture...normal stress or life problems in the absence of diagnosable psychopathology. More to the point, it could also include spiritual concerns that the client did not wish to discuss with his clergy.

Tom continued. "After talking with Reverend Kelly, it was my impression that Mr. Jensen had undergone a mystical experience. Though he may have been depressed by history, probably qualifying for an earlier diagnosis of Dysthymic Disorder or Major Depression, there was no current evidence for a mood disorder. He actually seemed pretty happy without any signs of mania."

"Does that mean that you disagree with Dr. Spence's decision to admit Mr. Jensen for psychiatric treatment, including electroconvulsive therapy?"

"Actually, yes. In my opinion, this patient is not psychotic, hence shock treatments are contraindicated and could possibly be dangerous to him."

"Dr. McLaughlin, I spoke with Dr. Spence on the phone last night. The psychiatric indications he gave for his diagnosis and decision to admit were logical, solid, and irrefutable. The man was depressed by history, delusional by his own account, and too impaired even to go to work. The Board of Psychology has never encountered a diagnosis of mystical experience, and certainly such a diagnosis makes no sense here. In fact, that particular term cannot be found anywhere in the *Diagnostic and Statistical Manual*. I think, Dr. McLaughlin, you should be prepared to defend your license against several charges of negligence. That is my opinion and will be my recommendation to the Board. You may also have to answer to a civil law suit from the patient's wife asking for damages for misdiagnosis and failure to provide proper and timely medical intervention. You will be hearing from us."

Mr. Bennett turned off the tape recorder, put away his notes and files, and exited the office with little more than a nod. Tom could not move. Tears welled up in his eyes. He felt catastrophically helpless and began to sob. He couldn't defend himself any better than he just had. The Board of Psychology and a prominent local psychiatrist were joining ranks to discredit him, perhaps even destroy his career. Worse yet, Paul might at this very moment be undergoing electric-shock treatments designed to eradicate his sacred joy and put him back in the hellfire world of Pastor Hoeller. But what could he do? Wiping his tears with a tissue from the ever-present box of Kleenex, Tom thought, *I have lost my patient, my license is now in jeopardy, and the ending of my career would be a financial nightmare for my family.* He could not stop crying long enough to call Ronnie. Maggie peeped around the corner. Her face went white and she disappeared to find Tom's partner, Mark, and to call Tom's wife.

Finally, after several cathartic minutes, a profound stillness came over Tom. Staring blankly at the mess of papers on his desk, his eyes drifted to his "Look into someday when you have nothing else to do" inbox. A flyer proposed, "Come on a Vision Quest and search for the sacred meaning of your life." Almost absentmindedly, Tom read the brochure. *Is this for real?* he wondered. *Why am I reading this?* Then it began to grab him. *It would be so good to get away from this nightmare, get out of here, try to figure out what all this means. I've got nothing to lose,* he thought. *It's probably totally crazy. Am I flaking out like Ronnie fears? When is this Vision Quest? Tomorrow?!*

Tom hurriedly dialed the number on the brochure. The leader picked up. Yes, there was one more space. There had been a cancellation. You needed a sleeping bag, backpack, warm clothes, and nine uninterrupted days. No one, not even your family, will know where you are. You'll need to catch a plane to Las Vegas tonight. The group leaves before dawn in the morning.

What do you say?

Without further thought, Tom gave a bewildered Maggie instructions to cancel the day's remaining patients as well as his appointments for the next two weeks. "Tell them it's a family emergency," he said, for surely it was. He arranged for coverage, made airline reservations, and sat back. Telling Ronnie would not be so easy. Just as she entered his mind, she likewise burst into his office with tears in her eyes. After a very truncated explanation of his legal problems to his befuddled partner, Tom hurried home with Ronnie.

Chapter 19

Sitting in the United Airlines terminal at LAX on a layover from Sacramento to Las Vegas, Tom barely noticed the thinning crowds of tired passengers. It had been raining all day – a surprise this time of year – and people lugged bags, umbrellas and overcoats to and from their flights. Many sat huddled around cell phones, iPads, and Kindles trying to stay awake and pass the time. Tom allowed the steam from a cup of coffee to massage his weary and reddened eyes.

The rush out of Sacramento had been insane. He and Ronnie had talked and cried, shouted and argued, and gone round and round all afternoon about this hair-brained, impulsive Vision Quest idea. How the hell could he just up and leave? Did he really think he would solve these problems by running away? What if the family needed him? No phone access or even knowledge of his whereabouts for nine days! What about his responsibility to the family? Tom was on the verge of giving in and fell apart again. As he cried, Ronnie softened. She could see how shattered Tom felt and she knew from past experiences that his introverted nature called him to solitude and introspection when he was in pain. It was nothing personal, he wasn't leaving her, he just needed to find himself. And he would be a pill at home – pacing, moping and lamenting his troubles. And there was one more thing. As a social worker, Ronnie understood that real character is revealed and defined by crisis; Tom's reaction came from a very deep part of his nature that even he did not anticipate. As if driven by the force of a psychological imperative, he had to pursue this quest. He would later find out why.

Having made her side of the decision, Ronnie took charge. She told him to go, that she understood, and helped round up the required camping equipment while he packed. After re-composing themselves, Tom and Ronnie "explained" Dad's sudden camping trip to Laura and Erik – Ronnie would help them understand it later – and raced to the airport for a six o'clock flight. There was no time for goodbyes – just a hug, a wave from the boarding ramp, blinked-back tears, and a silent prayer.

So here he sat, broken, slumped in a hard airport seat, waiting to board the last flight to Las Vegas. Weary, depleted, sad, Tom had no idea what to expect. The leader promised someone would pick him up to join the others. The assembled group would camp the first night on the outskirts of Las Vegas before driving, and then hiking, far out into the desert. God, was he up for this? With all that had happened so quickly, his reality was coming apart. He felt buffeted like a kite in a hurricane. Just then, he heard his flight announced and rose to board the plane.

Chapter 20

Tom's plane landed in the expensively remodeled Las Vegas International Airport. Billboards everywhere enticed the adventurous traveler with extravagant shows, glitzy nightlife, fancy hotels, thrilling theme parks, and most of all, gambling. Fun for everyone in the family, 24 hours a day. There were no signs for arduous, dirty, fasting, lonely, high desert Vision Quests. What a surprise.

Tom was greeted by a blonde woman, mid-forties, solidly compacted physique, and dressed like something out of the old west: jeans, leather leggings, boots, flannel shirt, vest, and cowboy hat. Her name was Mel. Friendly but obviously on a timetable, she whisked him into a van where he met three other "questers" – Mary, a 22-year-old artist, Canon, a 40-year-old former rock musician, and Jim, a 60-year-old physician from Maryland. They drove south in darkness and silence for over an hour, winding their way out of Las Vegas on Highway 15 and into the desert night. Eventually Mel pulled off the road into a campground outside of Baker where they met the quest organizer, a 59-year-old woman named Sam who looked as weathered as the surrounding desert, and four additional questers: Steve, a 35-year-old divorcing accountant; Jean, a 72-year-old widowed teacher; Sherry, a 46-year-old metaphysical book store owner; and Laurence, a 40-year-old corporate attorney.

By 8:30, the group assembled to eat a cold meal of rice and bean burritos, chips, and iced tea, unroll their sleeping bags, and gather around a campfire to get acquainted and discuss their journey. Sam asked each person to say a few words about why they had come on this journey. Awkward at first, the group began to share their stories: career crossroads, recent or impending divorces, spiritual interests, family deaths, career burnout, chronic health problems, the typical assortment of life challenges that cause people to reflect deeply on their lives. Tom had difficulty explaining his reasons for coming; his situation seemed so complex and unusual, and in ways he could not grasp, embarrassing. Was this a professional matter, a crisis of faith, a personal failure? What did it all mean?

When they were done sharing, Sam explained the structure of the Vision Quest. They would leave the next day to find a base camp. They would then spend three days in preparation, which included examining their personal goals, asking the spirits for support, and finding their own site. After that, each person camped alone, with only water and no food, for three days. On the third night, the "quester" was instructed to remain awake in a mandala-shaped medicine wheel constructed during the day. The purpose: stay up all night, face your life and call forth a vision. The next day, the group would re-assemble at base camp and share their experiences in sacred circle. There would be more, of course, but this was all they needed to know to start.

As the evening grew late, Sam, steeped in American Indian tradition, called in a variety of spirits and each "quester" was asked to make a blessing and a prayer. With little experience in religious matters, Tom waited for some kind of inspiration. All he could offer was a tepid, "May we each find the answers we seek." They slept on the hard desert ground under a half moon's pale disinterested light while a soft wind blew through the night.

The next day, after a hardy breakfast of oatmeal, cold cereal with soymilk, muffins, fruit, and apple juice, the band packed up their two vans and turned north on 127 driving further into the desert. Campers and truckers owned most of the highway. As they drove, Sam carefully watched the terrain looking for – or intuitively sensing – the right place to leave the known world. The landscape on both sides of the road was barren and uninviting – flat for miles, carelessly strewn with rocks and lonely sagebrush. Mountains rose in the distance, hewn by impersonal gods millions of years ago: Earth-shattering volcanoes, jolting tectonic plates, and ceaseless cycles of wind, rain, floods, sun, and time. Despite its inhospitable appearance, Sam assured the group that wildlife thrived in this wild landscape: rattlesnakes, rabbits, spiders, hawks, wildflowers, and desert foxes. She also reminded them that Indians, pioneers, prospectors, minors, and scientists had all come and gone from this vast land – none staying long but all changed by its elemental power.

"There. Turn left. Pull off the road. We'll head up through those canyons." Now Sam knew exactly what she wanted though she had never been off the road here before.

The two vans drove as far as they could, moving slowly like an early wagon train between boulders, dry washes, and rock outcroppings. Whenever necessary, the men got out to push aside small obstructing boulders or to scout alternate routes. When they could go no further, the vans were unloaded and backpacking began. For the next five hours, the small group carried in their provisions of food, water, and camping equipment. In this hot, dry desert climate, it was easy (and critical) to drink at least a gallon of water a day in addition to what was needed for cooking. They packed in 50 gallons of water, making trip after trip between the vans and base camp. Tom was surprised at just how much work this trek required.

The group set up camp on a relatively flat rocky terrace overlooking numerous dry arroyos. Evidence of recurring winter flashfloods was everywhere. Following others' examples, Tom tied his plastic tarp onto a creosote bush, anchoring the other end with rocks, and placed his writing pad, sleeping bag, and backpack beneath it. Shade was critical in this treeless wasteland, and this was the only shade you would find. In the unlikely event of rain, you also needed the plastic tarp to keep dry.

The wind blew non-stop the entire day. Tarps were torn away from their moorings, chased across the desert floor, and reattached. The wind flapped the plastic constantly, so loud and persistent that you couldn't hear your neighbor talking ten feet away. Hanging motionless in the sky, the sun beat down relentlessly on the thin plastic. It quickly became apparent that there was no escape from the harsh physical reality of the desert. As the day wore on, Tom felt increasingly torn and shredded by its fierce and punishing forces and wondered, *How am I ever going to focus on my life in such insufferable desolation where nothing matters but what the desert wants?* He began to feel sad, missing Ronnie and the kids terribly. *Have I merely complicated my already screwed-up life with this crazy journey into hell? And why does this "quest" require so much struggle and hardship?* The monotonous drone of the wind beneath the pitiless sun was the only answer he received.

Tom dreamed that night that his consciousness left his body. His awareness rose high over the desert and he found himself looking down on the site he would pick for his three-day solo fast. Looking up at him was a wolf. What impressed Tom most was the extraordinary clarity of this scene and the feeling that he had somehow glimpsed a sacred dimension of existence. This was not like any dream he'd ever had.

The wind stopped sometime during the night and the group awoke with the rising sun to a crisp and stunning day. Vistas stretched to the horizon in all directions – crystal clear mountains, birdsong sharp in your ears, the dirt smell of desert arroyos. No signs of civilization, no other people, nothing but this desert, now transformed into a peaceful wilderness of rock, brush, and breakfast preparations. What a relief!

The next two days were spent acclimating to life in the desert. Glowing sunrises bleeding over the horizon followed cycles of day and night, heat and cold, wind and silence, shedding and replacing layers of clothes, repairing shredded tarps. People visited, hiked, shared stories over meals, and noticed a wide assortment of wildlife that had been hiding the first day.

The night before their solo experience, the group ate a solemn and introspective dinner. After dinner Sam ceremonially passed around a peace pipe, prayers were said to the spirits, and each quester shared again his or her hopes and fears for the time alone. By now, Tom had further described his crisis to the group. "I am so lost," he confessed. No one tried to fix his problem. No one offered answers. They were to be found "out there."

As the desert air cooled sharply and shadows turned day into night, each member of the group quietly retreated to his or her sleeping bag. They would begin the next day in silence, immediately hiking out to their selected campsite in the vast and impersonal desert in search of a healing life-vision.

It was at this point that Tom understood the power of the Vision Quest and its recipe of personal distress, unfamiliar surroundings, loss of civilized comforts (like TV, newspapers, radio, books), social isolation, profound solitude, overpowering and uncontrollable physical conditions, prolonged fasting, ceremony and prayer, and a commitment to stay awake for the final vision. These elements stripped the psyche of human pretense and psychological defense, exposing core emotional issues in the awesome – and spiritual – sovereignty of the desert. Tom's only tools were patience, prayer, meditation, and journal writing. He did not know if he could fast three days. He did not know if he could stay up all night. He did not know what, if anything, was going to happen. He did not know much of anything.

Chapter 21

They arose with the sun, received a cup of tea and silent blessing with a smoking smudge stick, turned in their watches and cell phones, and journeyed out into the desert dawn, alone.

The early morning was still cold. Tom hiked carefully, his backpack heavy with bedroll, sleeping bag, warm clothes, his personal journal, and three one-gallon water jugs tied to the frame. Trekking over loose rocks and dry riverbeds, Tom stumbled frequently, unaccustomed to the top-heavy weight of his pack. His legs grew wobbly as he traversed the nearly three miles to the site he had picked at the base of a rocky butte. Tom was now truly alone. The solo quest had begun.

When he reached his campsite, Tom blessed it with an offering of tobacco and cornmeal, as Sam had instructed, sprinkling it in the four directions: east to the beginning of life, south to the body and emotions, north to the elders, ancestors, and their wisdom, and west to the end of life's journey. He wasn't sure how he felt about these Native American rituals, and didn't really know much about prayer, but performed them with sincerity.

Tying his tarp between a large boulder and his backpack, Tom set up camp and waited. The sun climbed into the sky with infinite slowness, finally stopping to glare down at him from directly above. Now Tom could not be sure that the sun was moving at all. Boredom, heat, wind, insects, hunger, wind, loneliness, boredom, thirst, water, hunger, wind, frustration, heat, heat, heat. He meditated and prayed. Wrote in his journal. Sipped water to quell hunger pangs. Walked around. Unexpectedly, he stripped off his clothes and stood naked in the elements, the wind, sun, and air bathing his naked body, baptizing him. Time stretched until it seemed to break and there was no time left at all. Had he entered some other dimension of time and reality? He dressed and sat quietly on his sleeping bag.

The first day finally ended. Tom didn't think much had been accomplished. The sun, which had stared down at him with little personal interest, now sank rapidly over the mountains to the west. Tom moved his sleeping bag from his tarp shelter out under the night sky. Fear crept into the bag with him. Were there predatory animals at night? Night spirits? Nightmares? He had never been so alone and isolated in his life. Curling into a ball, Tom prayed to whoever God was for protection, insight, and comfort. Watching shooting stars and satellites play through the Milky Way, he eventually fell asleep.

Dawn. He was learning to love the sunrise. It began with the barest hint of light over the dark eastern ridge and then gradually spread its glow across a perfectly azure sky to awaken the world. He greeted the sun as a friend now, welcoming its warmth and light. Reflecting on these thoughts, Tom noticed how his consciousness was changing. It felt like the first day of Creation. And he was beginning to relate to the Earth and sky, sun and moon, to weather, plants, and animals as if they were alive, sentient beings in communication with each other. He spoke to them, asked them questions, shared his feelings, and prayed for their blessings on his day. Everything had a kind of meaning and message, though he couldn't tell if it came from them or him. The wind said, "Be still and watch." The birds said, "Wake up. Pay attention." The ground said, "You are resting on the Mother." It was comforting, puzzling, intriguing. *Wow,* he thought, *this different consciousness is just below the surface in us, hidden by the distractions of modern life; it comes out like stars at night when the glaring lights of civilization are absent. Where is this going?*

The second day grew hotter and Tom's hunger pangs more insistent. For a moment, he realized he was drinking water too fast. It would not last if he continued at this rate. For over an hour, all he could think about was eating, remembering the tastes of all the foods he loved, and some that surprised him. French toast, diet coke, scrambled eggs, Thanksgiving stuffing, coffee, BLTs. Finally he had to stop himself – this was torture and the second day was only just beginning! Worse, time had not only stopped, it was taking forever, which was one of the strangest thoughts he'd had so far.

Needing to *do* something, Tom began to build the prescribed medicine wheel. Picking rocks of all sizes, he made a large circle with an opening to enter and exit. In it, he used other rocks to symbolize the important people in his life, past and present – his parents, grandparents, ancestors, children, and future unborn grandchildren. He started thinking then about his entire life: childhood disappointments, the death of his father, all the things he hadn't said to his father and grandmother, how much he loved Ronnie, what he wanted for each child, regrets that he hadn't done enough for his family, and contemplation of his own shortening future. As the sun set each day, so his life would set someday, and he would leave his children and this world. This was the autumn of his life. The wind picked up, as it often did in the afternoon, seeming to know and express his mood. Tom began to cry and was surprised to hear himself sobbing for his father. *Where are you, Dad? I need you. You would understand what I'm going through.*

Then it was over. The sorrow left, the wind died down, and there was only the present, barren landscape, timeless, forever, impersonal...mystical? None of this made sense. It didn't need to. Thoughts came and went in disordered sequences, sucked away by the vast desert vacuum. More strange thoughts. *Why am I alive? Why are we here? Where is God?* In this emptying, Tom realized that what he thought he knew consisted merely of beliefs overlaid on the timelessness of this new consciousness. But beliefs were not innocent, they carried the power to start wars, create poverty, maintain prejudice. Even religious beliefs. Why were we so invested in beliefs that cause so much pain?

No longer hungry, and with more energy than he would have expected on a fast, Tom hiked to the top of the butte behind his campsite. Vigorous movement felt good, purposeful, alive, and the summit, perhaps only 60 feet high, provided a panoramic vision of the area. But there was something closer: perfect, tiny, delicate, colorful wildflowers hidden from the wind in crevices everywhere. Tom thought, *Look how they grow in such beauty and joyous profusion with no hope of ever being seen. No ego at all. They grow for the love of God. Now that's an unusual thought. We, too, grow for the love of God.* That thought felt even stranger. Somehow Tom knew he was no longer himself. He had entered an altered state of consciousness. Feeling braver, he asked aloud, "What is consciousness? Where is it? Who is it?" The answer moved into his awareness as easily as water into a sponge: *It is God. Consciousness is God. Personal consciousness is simply a limited state of this consciousness. is simply a limited state of this consciousness.* With this realization, the landscape around Tom filled with consciousness. He sensed it directly, sensed it was awake and aware, aware of him and aware of him sensing it. He thought, *The world is alive. This is what Paul has been talking about. Consciousness is not just in me, I am in it, and it is everywhere.*

Tom sat down on a rock and let the implications multiply. *I have been blinded by the culture's belief that God is somewhere else, appearing to man only in some radical, scary or otherworldly Hollywood-like form. I am experiencing God right now*, he thought. *And God is conscious of me.* Tom was stunned. *And if all of this is the consciousness and being of the divine, then I must be made of that, too, filled with God's being.* Suddenly joy began to spread inside him like an inner sun. *There is nothing I have to do or be, no place I have to go, to find God. This is it. I am in God, God is in me; we are one consciousness.*

On the top of this windy, ragged butte, Tom opened his arms to the Earth and sky and laughed. "Thank you, God," he shouted. Even louder, "THANK YOU, THANK YOU, THANK YOU." Again, with no hesitancy, Tom lay face down on the hot and holy ground, making as much contact between the Earth and his body as possible, and loved her. There were no boundaries now. For a moment, he was complete.

Eventually Tom climbed slowly to his feet and made his way back to his campsite. The wind blew through his body as if it were a thin, porous fabric. As the evening cooled and the sun's fiery chariot rushed below the horizon, Tom sat quietly. It was enough, he understood, simply to be, for divinity was found in simply being. Words sounding like the ranting of a crazed prophet had come from him! What a surprise. Tom sipped his water – luxuriating in its soft velvet flow across parched lips and crystal-clear taste, unrolled his sleeping bag, and lay contentedly under a canopy of starlight. He went to sleep in the arms of God.

Chapter 22

Day three began with the same sunrise. Last night's mood, however, was not the same. Gone were amazing thoughts and feelings from the top of the butte. Tom could recover the words but not the mystical consciousness accompanying them. Time was going too slowly again. Sixteen hours is a long day when you have nothing to do, nowhere to go, nothing to eat, nothing to read, and no one to talk to. By the height of the sun, Tom judged that it must only be about 11:00 am. It seemed like a full day had already passed and it wasn't even noon. It was too hot to just sit and too hot to venture far from the tarp's limited shade. There was no escape from this suffocating heat. *I don't think I can do this all day and then stay up all night*, thought Tom. Fear gripped his heart. *Is it supposed to get harder as the time goes by?* Trapped in a grueling, wretched, endless, boring, hot, hungry, empty inferno, he asked out loud, "Am I in Hell? How can this be spiritual?"

Then, as if he were having a conversation in his mind with someone else, came a response that he recorded in his journal, "It is the hell known to the all addicts, whether the addiction is heroin, alcohol, gambling, work, money, sex, power, things, beliefs, security, perfection, even the idea of a future. Addictions are attachments that separate you from the divine. This separation is hell, psychologically and literally. It is the outcome of choosing ego over soul."

Tom felt awful. His muscles, sore from sleeping on the ground, screamed their unhappiness as he sat uncomfortably on his miserable ground cloth. His hair felt oily and dirty. He hadn't even brushed his teeth this morning. The monochrome desert didn't care a whit about his great revelations. Tom's stomach tightened with the hopelessness of it all. *This Vision Quest has been a terrible decision*, he thought. *All I've done is run away from my problems.* Picking the dirt from under his fingernails, he started to cry.

"What do I do?"

The "conversation" continued, the "other" voice inside saying, "Hell has to be faced for what it is, that's all. It's a transitional state, like the body's withdrawal from a chemical dependency. You have to go through it and be willing to give up your dependency, layer by layer by layer."

"But where is God in this suffering? What happened to my experience last night of everything being sacred?"

"This is the other face of God, the dark face, the void, the absence of light. God is behind the darkness, like the sun behind the moon during a solar eclipse." The voice continued, "Las Vegas is an example of that darkness: false images of glamour, grandiosity, security, and never-ending gratification. But it is a lie, inherently empty, a collective fabrication with no ultimate reality and no greater meaning, purpose or permanence. Hell is the inevitable and terrible grief of knowing that who you think you are is a lie created in the hopes of reversing your original loss of the divine world."

"So where is God in this hell and where is the divine world?"

"God?! Look at around you. Really look. Look as if you have never seen the world so clearly and intensely before. This is the divine world, more beautiful, miraculous, and indescribable than anything you could imagine. Seeing reality as it really is opens you to the mystical. The 'reality' you have seen is the one you've been taught to think about, full of problems, dangers, beliefs, expectations and disappointment. It's time to wake up from thought."

Tom reflected on this peculiar dialogue. He wasn't sure he believed or even understood it. And where had it come from? Tom would never have invented these ideas on his own. Then he noticed something else: Hell had disappeared! The same physical conditions still surrounded him, but the hellish mental state that started the dialogue was gone, replaced by crystal-clear perception of the surrounding desert. His senses – sight, hearing, smell, touch, taste – had become intense again, connecting him to everything. Now the heat, dust and timelessness were part of a vast array of amazing stimuli. No longer boring at all. Time, too, had disappeared.

Tom wandered through a wonderland of fresh sensory experience. There was no one to be and nothing to achieve. He felt unabashedly happy and free for the first time in years. *This world is so awesome, so present, so remarkably alive, and this is enough! What more could you want? A wonderland of holiness and Presence.*

Contemplating these peculiar reveries, Tom realized something else – that his heightened awareness of sacred reality waxed and waned. More accurately, he saw that mystical reality didn't change, but his awareness of it was easily displaced by worries, thoughts, fears, goals, ambitions, needs, future, problems...on and on and on. When he intentionally returned his attention to the non-conceptual and highly sensory here-and-now, his mystical consciousness resumed – color, clarity, beauty, wonder, consciousness, life, holiness. In the hot desert sun, Tom sat in radical awe and reflected, *This must be why native peoples speak of everything as spiritual, as full of spirits, even inanimate things like rocks or wind, because in the freshness of mystical experience, everything is one with the Presence. In mystical consciousness, a tree is the divine, evoking reverence, communion, and teaching.*

Awakening to one's own spiritual nature, Tom realized, no matter what path you take, always leads to this consciousness. For God is here. In the end, it's not so much about beliefs or techniques, it's about a deceptively simple shift in awareness that reveals "the other world." Heaven is here on Earth! Hidden behind layers of thought and belief, people simply don't see it. *This awakened consciousness is the purpose and destiny of life,* Tom thought, *seeing, knowing, and celebrating the divine in all things!*

Then the ultimate question arose in Tom: *If I truly believed all this, how would I live my life differently?"*

Tom suddenly noticed that the sun was setting. There was little time to get ready. Tonight would be the culmination of the whole Vision Quest, the stay-up-all-night ritual. Tom dismantled his tarp, rolled up his sleeping bag, put on several layers of extra clothes, and stored the remainder of his meager possessions in his backpack, and sat on his bedroll in the center of his mandala. Could there still be more?

The wind had been picking up steadily for the past hour. To the north, a dust storm was building – an awesome and terrifying spectacle. One of the questers had gone far in that direction. Tom feared for him, and for another who had climbed high into the crevice of the mountain behind base camp. *The winds must be ferocious up there,* he thought. Time was running out. He felt gritty with dirt after six bathless days in the desert. Now the sun was nearly gone. It felt like death, like the planet was being torn apart by savage winds. There was no place to hide. He was alone. It had all been leading here, to this.

The dust storm raged across the desert, a huge rapidly approaching cloud with a grotesque face and two extended arms reaching toward his tiny camp. It was the end of the world, the apocalypse. *No one can help me now,* thought Tom. Entering the medicine wheel he had created earlier was all the protection he had. It was his sacred space. It felt like nothing against the howling wind.

Tom was terrified as he sat upright in the circle, bearing the wind's spectacular assaults against his back. *Nobody in his right mind would be outside unprotected on a night like this. I am going to die. Whatever happens is now in God's hands.* Several days later, Tom would learn the winds exceeded 60 miles an hour that night.

Tom shivered alone in his medicine wheel, freezing. He pulled his ski cap down over his head and tied the hood of his parka over that. Still the wind blew through him. Mentally, he went to each place in his medicine wheel to express his feelings, apologies, and prayers to those he loved. Tears came to his eyes, drying almost immediately in the ferocious wind and invasive sand. Then, quite unexpectedly, Tom stood up and began chanting indecipherable syllables and dancing unknown steps as if he were part of some larger world ritual. He shouted praises to the moon, the night sky, the monstrous cloud, and the wind. He sang out his love to the divine while the storm grew ever wilder and the night colder. His body trembled uncontrollably. He was not going to survive in these conditions.

Finally, with no other choice, Tom pulled open his sleeping bag and burrowed inside for warmth. He huddled close to the ground trying to escape the brutally cold, biting wind. Then sleep, the irresistible drug, pulled him down into its dull heaviness. He tried to sit up and face the night, but the soporific grip of cold and exhaustion were too powerful.

In the deepest part of that event-filled night, Tom had a dream – a long and surreal dream about a wild and otherworldly celebration taking place after some kind of ceremonial meal. At first everything was disorder and chaos, homeless people living fringe lives. Then, turning a corner, Tom saw everyone dancing – a gentle swaying hula – all in natural and perfect synchronization, one effortless, seamless, moving, smiling whole. And there was his daughter with a goofy smile on her face, which seemed to say, "See, Dad. It's okay. Dance to the music. It doesn't matter where you are. It's everywhere." Nearby the wolf from his earlier dream watched, swaying imperceptibly in communion, a subtle wolf grin on his face, blessing the dance; Tom's spirit guide, he had been here all the time.

The dream was followed by another more disturbing one in which Tom learned from a physician friend that a former patient of his, a man named Scott, had committed suicide by jabbing an ice pick into his brain through his ear. An attractive young man, his life had been irreversibly altered by an earlier head injury from a motorcycle accident. After that, he had nothing but problems – depression, learning difficulties, social isolation, feelings of failure and shame. Scott was too proud and too ashamed to stay in therapy, choosing instead to wrestle with his downward spiral by himself. His suicide seemed like a brutal and final act of self-hatred. *What on Earth is that dream about?!*

The night ended peacefully. The wind had quieted down during the night, Tom wasn't sure when. His bone-deep cold was finally thawing in the warm glow of sunrise and his spirits lightened in a crystal-clear morning.

Tom thought back on his two dreams. The dancing scene reminded him of scuba diving, the way everything – plants, fish, and swimmer – respond as one as ocean swells pass through. It was as if celestial music was creating a cosmic dance, a joyous and simple celebration of the unity of life, a symphony of synchronized motion: one dance, one unity, everything part of in the same flow. This dream, he realized, revealed the mystical nature of reality. All it took to experience was "turning the corner," a metaphor Tom immediately recognized to mean shifting awareness into the pure, thought-free, and intensely heightened alertness of mystical consciousness. He saw, too, that this unifying dance brings the "homeless" back home to the transcendental oneness of being from which we all come. *Spiritually, we are all exiled and homeless*, he thought, *on our winding journey back to the One.*

Why was this lovely scene followed by the gruesome dream about a man killing himself with an ice pick? Unable to join the joyous dance of life, Scott had turned against himself in hatred and self-loathing. Chronically ignored by his remote and passive father, and unseen by a mother burdened with too many children, too many financial problems, and her own dying marriage, Scott interpreted his parents' disinterest as evidence of his own unworthiness. With his later brain injury and multi-plying life failures, self-loathing had turned to a murderous self-hatred. He hated his impaired brain enough to destroy it and kill himself. And this reminded Tom of Paul Jensen. Deserted in death by his mother and in alcoholism by his father, Paul had interpreted this abandonment as a referendum on his own personhood. In turn, he abandoned himself.

But there was one more step to his dream analysis. Tom knew from training and experience that every dream is really about the dreamer, the figures in it representing parts of the dreamer's own psyche. Tom had to confront the likelihood that he, too, had turned against himself. Growing up in a large family with a distracted mother and alcoholic father, he, too, had felt "not worthy of their love." Tom unconsciously chose a career in psychology hoping to heal this deep and pervasive wound. Paul Jensen symbolized his own struggles, and his own self-rejection.

But what had changed Paul for the better? That dream! That dream of Jesus coming out of the black lake. Maybe Jesus represented Paul's forgotten and betrayed self. How could that be? It came to Tom first as reverie, then as a hypothesis, and finally as a full-fledged epiphany: *Since self and soul were two symbols for the same essence – who you really are inside, one from psychology and the other theology – and since Christianity centered on the idea that God gave birth to Himself in Jesus, perhaps Paul had reconnected with his divine self!* Tom's thoughts continued further down this path. *Sometimes we must "hit bottom," in other words, go into the lake, symbolizing humankind's collective unconscious where the religious psyche dwells, to uncover this connection to our divine nature. Pretty heady stuff*, Tom thought, *but I get it!*

A moment later he wondered aloud, "Oh my God! Could this happen to me, too?" Tom slammed the brakes on this line of thought; he was not ready to give up his normal life for some kind of religious transformation.

The sound of drumming from the group's distant base camp pulled Tom from his spinning reverie. It was the pre-arranged signal for questers across the valley to come home. The three-day solo fast was over. Tom packed up his possessions, gave thanks to his medicine wheel before disassembling it, and began the long hike back, lighter now by three empty one-gallon water jugs and something else, something lifted from his heart.

On his arrival at basecamp, Tom greeted Sam and Mel, who welcomed him with the purifying smoke of a smudge stick and a warm hug. All morning the questers straggled back into camp, each silently joining the others in a breakfast of tea and a small bowl of hot cereal, their first meal in three days. The remaining three days of the Vision Quest would be spent in ceremonial circle for questers to share their life-restoring visions.

Chapter 23

When his turn came, Tom recounted his story – for over two hours. He told it slowly and deliberately, searching each experience for its deeper significance. What had really happened out there? What had the desert taught him? And what did it mean for his life and his problems back home?

Tom concluded that the desert had gifted him a mystical experience, or at least, moments of mystical consciousness. He saw how much his awareness and perception had altered during his solo time. And he knew now, once and for all, that Paul wasn't psychotic, he was living from a purer state of consciousness, a mystical one. The awesome power of the elemental desert had similarly altered Tom's own consciousness, revealing a sacred dimension of experience he had overlooked for nearly half a century. He understood now what Paul was seeing.

For the next three days, before and after the ceremonial circle, Tom wandered the peaceful wilderness surrounding the camp. He was still filled with mystery and mysticism, and his awareness of the sacred steadily ripened. Just saying the word "God" awakened his perception to the whole mystical universe, and it responded by enveloping him in its loving Presence. Inwardly he talked to God all the time. *God, I know you are here. I feel your closeness. I sense you everywhere. I am so grateful to be near you. You are my life, my very being. I am bursting with joy, utterly complete in you. There is no more I could ask for but this.*

He sensed the divine Presence everywhere – in the spaces between things, in the things themselves, in those around him, in himself. One moment he felt divine consciousness in his body, the next moment he knew this consciousness was his own and that God was seeing through his eyes. Sometimes he took God for a walk through His paradise, sometimes God took him for a walk. Who was who? Who was in control? Sometimes God made him want to dance with joy.

On one of these "walkabouts" something came back to him, something from long ago. This joyously altered state reminded him of his early childhood: sunlight sparkling off dewdrops, willow trees dancing in gentle breezes, the smell of fall leaves, running barefoot over newly cut grass – the enchantment of some great mystery filling every colorful corner of the yard, every bird and squirrel his friend. But it was more than sensory memories, he recalled feelings of safety and peace, of being held in the arms of love, cherished simply for being, as if the Earth was his real mother and she loved him unconditionally. Did Eden exist in early childhood, he wondered, paradise lost, a vision of eternity always calling you back? *I have been here before*, he thought. *This is my true home.*

But one unanswered question kept turning over in his mind: *How do I live in the conventional human world from this expanded awareness? It's clearly not something I can share easily with others – Paul had tried and wound up in a psychiatric unit! And how do I make a living when making a living now feels like a charade, a pretense, an act? Why play by the rules of a culture that doesn't see the divine in every face, flower, and thing; doesn't feel the divine in every breath, heartbeat, and word; and doesn't experience the sacred in every fresh, timeless, and irreproducible moment? How can I ever talk again to people myopically committed to a life of struggle, addiction, suffering and survival, in the very midst of eternity? And how can I ever communicate this to my family without frightening or alienating them with this weird new vision of me?*

More central still was Tom's desire to surrender his life to God. *If all is God, what more can I want? Living, dying, wealth, poverty, success, failure, health, illness – these ideas create illusions superimposed on divine consciousness and being, on God living me and me living God. Does it matter how anything turns out if I am immersed in God? Separation, struggle, identity, effort, goals, problems, and future*

— ideas only! Now I understand: the very ground of being is the living, conscious, radiant energy of the divine. To simply be, not as someone or something, but as pure energetic being, is to merge with God. The more I lose "myself," the more I find God.

In everything he did during those three days, Tom kept seeing the world as the divine sees it, without the selfishness of a separate, ego-centered existence, and it was incredible. He didn't recognize himself any more, and what a relief to shed his old clothes of identity, time and story. *Just be*, he thought. For in pure being was a joy beyond anything he could ever acquire in the world of man: the joy of being saturated with divinity.

As these final days of discovery approached their end, Tom was struck by a thought about aging. *The fires of ambition and romance burn in the eyes of young people*, he thought, *and it should. In the spring and summer of life, we are driven to make a viable place in the world of adults. Older people, like some on this quest, especially those past midlife, no longer seem to have that fire in their eyes. It's as if their heroic drive has died.* Tom realized that no one really reaches the top, or if they do, it isn't what they thought it would be. And no one stays at the top anyway. Whatever the scenario, the hero complex eventually dies. And when the hero dies, the quest to be someone or something burns out. *What's left is simply the "isness" of being.* With time running out in life, with only the present left, an aging person begins to value the moment more profoundly than ever before, and for anyone seeking to awaken, this may be the doorway to the divine.

Tom remembered watching his 83-year-old grandmother sitting peacefully in her sunlit back yard near the end of her life, and it occurred to him that the yard had, for her, become the mythical Garden of Eden again. Not every moment perhaps, but in moments when thought was arrested by the beauty of sunlight sparkling off the water in the birdbath or fall leaves drifting effortlessly onto the lawn. In such timeless, thought-free moments, her consciousness may have "turned the corner" and found Eden all around her – in the birdsong, the translucent leaves, the sun's warmth on her dark dress. In relaxing into the imminent holiness of life, she was intuiting her journey home, for dying has always embodied the symbolism of homecoming. And it was the same for aging, too! The task of the second half of life was this return to the garden consciousness of early childhood, lost so many years ago, but understood now with the maturity of age. This is what Tom now knew wholly – and as holy. He had gone on a quest to understand Paul's mystical consciousness, and found his own, and marveled at the miracles it revealed.

The questers did not retrieve their watches until the vans were loaded and they began the long drive out of the desert. Tom sensed, ominously, that they were returning to machine time, that relentless chronometer of progress and production that removes humans from the sacred world. The drive to the Las Vegas airport, however, was friendly and playful. Even the two-hour delay when the old van broke down seemed special: more time to visit and play at the desert's edge. But as the highway became more congested with tense and harried drivers, as billboards increasingly obscured the scenery, as fast-food restaurants and gambling casinos buried the wilderness in cement, they knew they were returning to another world.

The terminal was raucous and noisy, filled with partiers still intent on one more drink, win, or thrill. Boarding and flight information blared from loudspeakers, piercing Tom's wide-open consciousness. He was exquisitely sensitive to noise, energy, and abrasive emotions like irritability, hostility and hatred that emitted from many of the revelers around him. Even so, Tom was awed by the fullness of the world. Perhaps because the desert had been so empty, a vacuum that sucked everything away, the airport felt just the opposite. The world was now alive and flooded with holiness; it shimmered just behind the edifice of civilization. An open, loving heart filled Tom to the brim. Nothing mattered but the splendor of life itself.

Ronnie, Laura, and Erik greeted Tom inside Sacramento International Airport – bundles of positive and loving energy, each a miracle, so many questions, such fun, followed by dinner at the little Mexican restaurant around the corner from home. Erik wanted to know if Tom was enlightened now. *How do you answer that question?* wondered Tom. He tried instead to talk about how elastic consciousness can be in the desert, one minute organized by thought, the next wide open, boundless as the sky. Remarkably, Erik compared Tom's description to his baseball experience, explaining that normally the ball whizzed toward the plate so fast you had to count on instinct and muscle memory to hit it, but when he was in the "zone," the ball floated as big as a grapefruit, stitches rotating slowing, and you could hit it a mile.

"Yes," Tom exclaimed, "that's exactly it."

Laura, on the other hand, who was more concerned about snakes, scorpions, and wolves, said she would never spend the night in that kind of place, and rolled her eyes at Erik's metaphysical opinions. Otherwise, Tom didn't talk much about specific details of the quest. Sam, the journey's leader, had advised the questers to "guard the medicine;" that is, to treat all the learning as holy to be shared with intentional consciousness in sacred space. Ronnie was quiet through dinner, enjoying the family's back-and-forth and the kids' excitement at having Dad home. She figured they would talk later in the sanctuary of their bed. As fatigue wound down the discussion, they agreed it was time to go back to real life and get ready for the next day.

Settling into bed that night, Ronnie asked, "So how was it, really? What did you learn?"

"It was one of those really big experiences," Tom replied. "I don't yet know how to put it into words or even what it all meant. I think it will have to percolate down into my unconscious for some time before coming back up as real insight." Because the big questions did not interest Ronnie much – that was Tom's bailiwick – she held tight to the love and security of their marriage, which had returned with her husband. Happy to be together once again, Tom and Ronnie fell asleep in each other's arms.

Tomorrow Tom would go back to work. He had not stopped by the office or called Maggie or his partner, Mark. He dropped quickly into a grateful and exhausted slumber, oblivious for one last night to Emma Jensen, Dr. Spence, the Board of Psychology, his consultation group, and his own unanswered question: *How do I live in a mystically altered consciousness?*

Chapter 24

To Tom's amazement (though why should he think otherwise?), the world into which he awoke was unchanged by the nine-day desert tempest that had torn open his psyche. Though the McLaughlin family was glad to have him home, their morning behavior displayed the same swirling frenzy as always. Tom likened it to jostling a hanging mobile, where each piece swings chaotically and affects each other piece. Caught up in this mania, Tom showered, dressed, brushed his teeth, wolfed down breakfast, and sailed out of the door at 7:30 am sharp.

Remnants of his high desert consciousness still swirled around him. One foot in mystic time, the other in the twentieth-century machine time. Driving to work, Tom watched these states side by side: the automatic mechanical movements of driving embedded in the unfathomable mystery of being. Scenes flashed back from his memory: the gathering dust storm, solitary hikes across dry river beds, high-flying hawks, and that wolf watching him from their sacred site. And then dread: what would he find when back at the office?

Again to his astonishment, Tom found nothing out of the ordinary. A handful of messages, some scheduling changes, a new client appointment. No messages from Paul, Emma, Dr. Spence, or the Board of Psychology. Whew! So far so good. Maggie welcomed him back with news from the previous week: a dead skunk that had stunk up the basement and a toilet leak upstairs had dripped through the ceiling. Maggie's colorful monologue was interrupted when the phone rang.

"It's for you, Tom. It's Dr. Spence. Are you in?"

With a little trepidation, Tom picked up. "Dr. McLaughlin here."

"Yes, Dr. McLaughlin. This is Dr. Spence calling from Sacramento Psychiatric Hospital. You recall I hospitalized your client Paul Jensen a couple weeks ago. I just wanted to follow up on that admission. Mr. Jensen was with us five days. During that time, three electroconvulsive treatments were administered. The patient's religious delusions cleared almost immediately and he was discharged to his wife's care. While he was here, Mr. Jensen did sign a formal release authorizing you and I to exchange clinical information. I encouraged them to return to you for follow-up but Mrs. Jensen was adamant that the church provided enough support. Anyway, I just wanted you to know how things turned out in case you hear from them again."

Tom appreciated the feedback but did not know what to think about the shock treatments or their supposedly salutary effects. It was too late, and probably futile, to argue diagnosis or treatment options, or discuss his concerns about Paul's mystic state with someone who obviously wouldn't see or believe it. Tom courteously thanked Dr. Spence and hung up.

By this time, Maggie had cornered Mark with a story about her husband's dim-witted aunt, leaving Tom alone with his thoughts. *What really happened? Did the shock treatments eradicate Paul's mystical consciousness? What could it do to such a state? How tragic it would be if such sublime mystical sensitivity were destroyed by memory-erasing voltage to the brain. Would Paul's depression return?* Wondering if he would ever know what really happened, Tom began dialing Paul's home phone number but stopped. Did he have any right interfering in this man's life? Certainly Emma didn't think so. She would probably file another complaint with the BOP accusing him of harassment, intimidation, or coercion, and he definitely didn't need this.

The intercom broke Tom's trance. "Your first client is here. It's Mrs. Torrence. She said she missed you terribly. It's five minutes after the hour. You're going to be running late if you don't get started."

"Send her in," Tom instructed, and his first day back began as if he had never been away. Hour after therapy hour went by.

Clients automatically fell back into the groove where they had left off and so did Tom. Except that his altered state never quite left. At lunch, Tom headed to Sutter's Fort, a restoration of the original walled settlement now the center of a park. Once outside the office, his awareness subtly expanded until he could again sense that Presence and the serene and timeless silence he'd known in the desert. Relief! In this peaceful and awakened consciousness, the world was again OK. More than that, it was perfect. Nothing needed fixing. Nothing even mattered. Divine reality – grass, sky, breeze, dancing leaves – was enough. He grinned and then laughed out loud. "Thank you," he said, and breathed a great sigh of contentment. After that, Tom's afternoon seemed to flow effortlessly. Whatever happened, he concluded, all was right with the universe.

That night, after the dinner dishes were loaded into the dishwasher, Tom stepped out onto the quiet porch. The night sky twinkled with stars. "You are here, God. I sense your Presence," Tom whispered. And it was true. It was all around him. The same joy he knew in the desert welled up in Tom's heart, as his own presence opened like a flower within the ecstasy of divine contact. From inside, he heard Laura yell at Erik to get out of the bathroom and Ronnie yell at Charlie to leave the cat's litter box alone. Life had returned to normal.

"What were you doing out there, honey?" Ronnie asked as Tom came into the kitchen through the patio door.

"I guess I was reflecting on what spirituality means for me," Tom replied carefully. "I can't quite remember how it happened, so much of the Vision Quest is now a blur, but in the desert I sensed God's Presence and I feel it still. It's as if this other consciousness is everywhere, filling space itself. I am aware of it and it is aware of me. I don't know what to do with this realization, but it's amazing."

"You can sense God?" Ronnie repeated. "Can people do that?"

"Isn't that what Paul was doing? Isn't that what people do in near-death experiences and death-bed visions?"

"I guess so. But that's different. Those are extreme states. You are just here." Tom noticed an edge in Ronnie's voice, as if she were feeling threatened by his words and what they might mean for their relationship.

Tom tried to explain. "But don't you see? *Here* is God. How can it be otherwise? The Presence is our own awakened consciousness. We can experience it anytime. What I can't figure out is how this Presence affects someone over time. Can it change a person's life?" What Tom wasn't saying but now thinking was this: *If I change too much, will my family stop loving me?* He knew this anxiety was irrational but he still felt it. As a young child in a rapidly growing family, he remembered the terrible angst he had experienced as little siblings took over his place in his mother's eyes. He had begun to feel expendable, rejected, and frightened of provoking further alienation. Tom had explored his early childhood in his training analysis, and recalled the panic he felt as his mother grew tired of his need for attention. *Will Ronnie, too, grow impatient with me? Will the kids think I'm too weird and push me away? Will my personality changes leave them feeling that I'm not the father they know?*

"Tom, that sounds really crazy to me," Ronnie continued. "It's not psychobabble, it's spiritual babble, and I don't like it. It scares me. Especially the part about changing your life. What's wrong with our life? Why would you want to change it? How are we going to pay the mortgage every month and put the kids through college if you're out being some hippie bliss-ninny loving stray cats and transients? I wish now that you hadn't gone on that damn Vision Quest!" With that, she slammed the kitchen door. "I'm going upstairs to check on the kids' homework. Go back outside and talk to God. But think it over. Do you want this life, this ordinary life with this ordinary family, or do you propose to leave us for some mystical path to who knows where?"

"Ronnie, I don't think you understand."

"I understand only too well. It's you that's changing. Ever since you met that weird patient, you've been drawn to his crazy ideas. Even your consultation group agrees. You're scaring me. This life happens to be my happiness and security," Ronnie said, tears filling her eyes, "and you're talking about wrecking it. How do you expect me to feel?" She didn't wait for an answer.

Ronnie's pain and confusion stung Tom. He wanted so much for her to understand, to feel the amazing divine Presence too, and even if she couldn't understand, to at least support him as he tentatively explored his mystical awareness. Tom also sensed what Ronnie wasn't saying: that her father had abandoned their family when she was ten – his midlife adventure with a company secretary that destroyed the family. Security was paramount to her and Tom's change talk was rocking the boat. As a psychologist, Tom understood their unspoken and interlocking struggles, but in his heart, this insight only increased the threat. *What a mess*, lamented Tom. *I wonder if this happens to everyone who experiences the mystical realm?*

Tom's question was met by a rich warm silence that seemed to fill the room. It didn't, however, answer his question. Then he thought, *Tomorrow I'll call Clarence for another spiritual chat.* Tom walked upstairs hoping to reassure Ronnie by acting as normally as he could. His behavior may have looked normal, but things were once again tense in the McLaughlin marriage.

Chapter 25

Arriving at the office the next morning, Tom deftly avoided Maggie's opening soliloquy by streaking into his office, closing the door, and picking up the phone so she would see his light on her intercom and leave him alone. It worked. Tom placed his call to Clarence and they agreed to meet for coffee Thursday after work. Moments after hanging up, the intercom buzzed. "Tom, you have a call from that weird guy who drove you into the desert. He's on line two. Do you want to take it?"

Without answering Maggie, Tom picked up the call. "Hello, this is Dr. McLaughlin. Is this Paul?"

"Yes. Can we meet again? I'd like to tell you what happened in the hospital."

"Are you OK?" Tom asked with concern.

"Maybe you should be the judge. You're the doctor. Can I come in?"

"Of course. Can you come in today? I don't have any open appointments but maybe we could have lunch in the park. How would that be?"

"I'll meet you at noon outside the front gate of Sutter's Fort," Paul said, and hung up.

Then the second call came in.

"Dr. McLaughlin? This is Larry Bennett with the Board of Psychology. Do you have a minute?"

Tom caught his breath. *Oh God, what now?* "Sure. What can I do for you?"

"I spoke to Dr. Spence about that man we discussed, your former patient." Tom thought he heard a degree of sarcasm dripping off the word 'former.' "It seems that he responded quite well to the ECT and was discharged home. The psychotic state and its religious delusions were fully resolved, confirming Dr. Spence's diagnosis. The patient's wife wishes to proceed with her charges and we are continuing our investigation. Again I would advise you to secure legal counsel. You'll be hearing from us shortly. Do you have any questions?"

Tom's mind was spinning wildly. Things were again happening too fast. First Ronnie, then Paul, now this BOP investigator was hot on his trail. Where was God now? "No. Not at the moment," Tom answered. All he wanted was to get off the phone. There was no gyroscope in his reeling mind. "Thank you for calling," he said lamely, and hung up.

The morning was a disaster. Tom couldn't concentrate and his patients knew it. One concerned woman asked, "Are you OK? You seem preoccupied and far away. Do you want me to leave?" Tom tried to minimize his distress and keep going. Doing therapy in this distracted state helped contain his escalating anxiety. He needed to keep working.

Noon arrived. Tom picked up some sandwiches from the nearby deli and met Paul in the park. The day was bright and sunny, heading toward the high 80s. Brightly dressed, excited school children swarmed through the front gate of the fort, shepherded by no-nonsense teachers. Tom made a few insipid attempts at preliminary conversation while they unwrapped their sandwiches, sounding trite and hollow even to himself.

When they had found a shaded bench off the grass-beaten paths and away from the commotion, Tom turned to Paul and asked, "So what happened in the hospital? Dr. Spence told me that you had three shock treatments. Did they affect your religious experience? Are you OK?"

Smiling peacefully, Paul answered, "I am OK. Nothing happened. Oh, I was forgetful for a while after each treatment. They temporarily affected my mind and my memory, but not my awareness of divine consciousness. I know now without a doubt that it is changeless, eternal, beyond cause and effect, beyond medicine. I told the doctor and Emma that I was feeling better and stopped talking about my experience of God. They were both so happy. Dr. Spence let me go home and I just don't talk about it with Emma now. She took me to see Pastor Hoeller and I agreed with everything he said. It made Emma so happy."

"Paul, why are you doing this? You shouldn't have to hide your spirituality."

"It's better this way. And it doesn't matter – don't you see? I don't need to convince anyone of anything. I even got more hours as church custodian and handyman. Emma is so proud. I sweep up, fix broken doorknobs, change light bulbs, and rake the yard. I love it. It is all God. I clean, fix, love, and beautify God. What more could I ever want? I touch God everywhere – in sunlight, in broken windows, tying a child's shoelaces, helping the widow up the stairs, walking to work each morning. I am in love with life for the first time."

As Paul spoke, Tom noticed several trees on the other side of the park swaying in the gentle breeze. They seemed to be dancing, sensually, in unison, insidiously seducing Tom back into mystical consciousness. The birds were singing just for him. A silken zephyr of air gently touched his face and his mind ceased its ruminations.

"You understand don't you?" Paul said; more an observation than a question.

"Yes. I guess I do. I've seen and felt what you describe and it's wonderful. It's amazing. It is the dance of God." Tom filled Paul in on his Vision Quest experience. "But I still don't know what to do with it. Is it real? Can you live in this state?" Treading well beyond normal professional boundaries, Tom confided, "My wife is very uncomfortable with this experience. She hates me talking about it. But more than that, I know I'm at a crossroads. If I fully enter this space, how will I live? How will I take care of my responsibilities? I can't talk to people about their problems when all I see is their beauty, when all I want to do is to tell them I love them. It's hard to concentrate on paying bills when I want to write love letters to God and dance under the willow in the back yard."

"Dr. McLaughlin, this is not a dream. This is reality. What you have been living is the dream, a bad dream filled with fears, doubts, and worries. Of course you are happy. You are touching the face of God. Why should you not be? Yes, you feel drunk with ecstasy, intoxicated with this spirit. But is that so bad? And yes, you can live from this state. It is what we are all meant to be and do. It is normal, just not in the way we usually think of normal."

"But I don't want to lose my family or my job," Tom said.

"That's why I did everything Emma and the doctors wanted. I didn't mind. But it's harder for you with your career and family duties. There's something more you'll have to do or understand. I don't know what it is. You'll have to find out. But whatever it is, you'll discover that it's not what you think."

Slipping back into more conventional reality, Tom asked, "Did you know the Board of Psychology is proceeding with charges against me brought by your wife? I could lose my license and this whole discussion would be moot."

"Dr. McLaughlin," Paul said kindly, "we are here. The flowers gift us sublime fragrances, the birds their song, the sun its warmth. The light of eternity brightens every single blade of grass. You are alive. We are conscious. This is the miracle. Come into the world as it truly is. There are so few who live here. Don't you see? Look around you. Those people aren't living in the divine world we see. They are ghosts haunted by imaginary worries in a purgatory of their own making. That is the tragedy. You don't have to go somewhere or get something to be happy. Happiness comes from *not* trying, *not* pursing, *not* hoping. It is discovered simply in the joy of being part of God's Being. This is it."

They ate in silence for the rest of the noon hour. Tom could have stayed all day. There was something about being near Paul's transcendent state that altered his own. *God, what am I to do?* he wondered.

Finally, Tom stood up saying, "I have to get back to the office. I don't know how I'm going to resolve this. I don't know if I'll ever see you again. You certainly don't need me. But thank you for sharing your experience with me. I will never forget you."

"You have a foot in each world, Dr. McLaughlin. It is a delicate balance. Take your time. Slide back into your old life, if you like. It changes nothing. The Garden is always here, waiting to be entered again. It will find you when you are ready. You will be OK. All beings come home eventually. You are closer than most. I wish you well."

They shook hands and in this brief physical contact Tom slipped again into the timeless moment. Then, intentionally, he shook it off. He turned and walked deliberately back to his office, squeezed into his therapist mind and pretended to be a psychologist for the rest of the day. He was more lost than ever.

Chapter 26

A tacit agreement not to talk about his newly found spirituality imitated normal life at home. Tom counted the hours until he would see Clarence. His questions kept multiplying; his answers didn't.

On Wednesday, however, Mark suggested lunch together. Friends as well as partners, Tom and Mark had shared much of their lives over the past 15 years: professional interests, challenging cases, practice objectives, kids, and marital life. Like most men, they had never talked seriously about religion or their spiritual nature. Tom feared that Mark, with his heavily scientific bias, would dismiss his desert experiences as merely the side-effects of prolonged sensory deprivation or subtle group suggestion. But they had not talked since his return and Mark was obviously curious – and concerned – about what the hell was going on with his partner.

They walked down K Street to a funky restaurant with outdoor seating. It was another beautiful late-spring day. Sunlight sparkled off the silverware and accentuated the amber tint of their iced teas. Muted conversations surrounded them like an auditory haze. For a moment, Tom found himself relaxing back into that Presence, the eternal calm that permeated all things. Knowing Mark was not in this space – and maybe couldn't be – Tom made an effort to focus his thoughts and enact his more tightly wound personality.

"So, hey," Mark began. "Tell me about this desert thing. And what was that bizarre religious demonstration outside the office before you left? Weird people. And Maggie tells me the Board of Psychology has been calling you about some patient. Sounds like your life has been interesting."

"Shit, Mark, it's been a nightmare," Tom lamented. "Here's the deal. I thought a new patient of mine was having a prolonged mystical experience. It was really fascinating and I still think that's the case. Except his fundamentalist wife and their pastor didn't like him seeing me – like I was going to corrupt his religious faith. She and the pastor organized that church demonstration. Then the woman complained to the Board of Psychology and now they're investigating me for negligence in failing to diagnose a psychotic state. Why? Because she took him to Sacramento Psychiatric where – get this! – he was judged psychotically depressed, hospitalized, and given shock treatments. The admitting psychiatrist wrote off his religious experience as psychotic delusions. The Board investigator has never heard of a mystical experience. Armed with these official psychiatric pronouncements, I'm being accused of misdiagnosis, misuse of influence, and negligence. On the day I left for the desert Vision Quest, I had reached my limit. I couldn't take any more and had to clear my head."

"So what happened out there on the Vision Quest? Isn't that some sort of Native American rite of passage where young men go into the desert alone in search of a sacred vision for their life?"

"Yes, you got it. It's also used with older folks, really anyone needing a new vision for life. I thought I was going there just to sort out my thoughts. Instead – and here's the strange part – I began to see what this man was talking about. I began to have similar experiences. Perhaps that's my vision. But there's more: I began to realize that if you took these experiences seriously, you might be drawn to make some pretty radical changes in your life. Well you can guess how Ronnie took that. It really freaked her out. So I'm totally confused. Every time I think I have things figured out, the world turns upside down."

"Gee," Mark said, as he began to dig voraciously into his Caesar salad. "Tell me more about this mystical stuff."

"In a sense – and this just now occurred to me – it's so ordinary and obvious. It's the way the world is when you really see it. Brighter, more colorful, more beautiful, sparkling, already perfect. Like this tablecloth or this spoon, or the speckled pattern of light and shadow on the ground from the sun shining through leaves. When I look at it as if for the first time, fresh, pristine, without the filtering lens of thought and familiarity, it's incredible."

"So what's the rub? That's like appreciating beauty. I can see what you mean."

"But, Mark, it's more. I know now that everything exists in a larger consciousness, out there, one that holds everything, as if every single thing were suspended in it and made of it. In other words, the world, the universe, the whole cosmos, is alive and conscious. And when I make contact with that reality, I sense a joy beyond any joy I have ever known. Does this sound crazy to you? You can tell me if it does."

Mark's response surprised Tom. "Sounds like *Satori* to me."

"Satori?"

"You know, Zen enlightenment, when everything is seen as one. It's like no mind, no self, no ego. The deathless, timeless, perfect state known when ego is transcended."

"How do you know about that?" Tom asked in amazement.

"I read all about that stuff in college. I was going to be a religion major until I realized you couldn't make a living at it. Even dropped acid a couple times to see if I could experience Satori."

"Did you?"

"What I experienced was pretty far out. Like I was outside time. Things happened sort of randomly, uncaused, totally in the moment, and sensory stimuli were intense, fragmented and sometimes pulsing. The beauty of the simplest things arrested my mind. I spent hours on a song lyric and a spider web. So maybe I did, a little bit."

"How come you never told me about this?"

"It's not something we ever talked about. People think you're nuts or some kind of acid-head. Your experience also reminds me of Pascal's experience."

"Pascal? The mathematician?"

"Yes. He had such an enlightenment experience one night. He wrote some of it on a piece of paper and carried it with him the rest of his life. That was his Satori."

"Mark, you amaze me. I thought your scientific bent would have dismissed such mystical experience."

"Nope. It's in every religion somewhere, but you only find it described by the mystics."

"Ok, but here's my question. Why don't we live from this knowledge? If all this is God, if we live and breathe God, what's the struggle about? No goals, ambitions, or any amount of money can buy what we can find right here, right now, in this living moment. Running after material things actually causes us to believe we are destitute, and so we work ever harder to accumulate more. It's like the sand in the desert. Sand is everywhere and people have as much as they could ever want, only no one wants it because they don't know what it is."

"Some people do live that life. Monks, mystics, recluses, even enlightened gardeners or garbage men. They just don't talk about it."

"Why don't you live it?" Tom asked, playing devil's advocate.

"I've got too many debts and I like the good life."

"See, that's just it. What could be better than this?"

Mark's mood shifted. He looked slightly irritated. "Not everybody can do it." He looked at this watch. "We need to be getting back. I'll get the check. Here's the question for you: What would you do at this very moment if you had no money?"

That is exactly the problem, Tom thought to himself. *What do you do in this society if you don't make money? There's no more living off the land, which is far more difficult than the average romantic ever imagines, and few are born into limitless wealth. So what do you do?* Once again, Tom had no answer. On the way back to the office, Mark complained about Maggie's incompetence on the computerized billing program he had just installed. Tom nodded and made appropriate comments. He was miles and miles away. Sadness and despair began to fill his soul. Paul had found a compromise, but he had no kids and few expenses. It wouldn't work for Tom. Maybe Clarence could help.

Chapter 27

Tom slept poorly that night. The evening had passed without incident – it was amazing how easily Ronnie could repress things once the world looked normal again. But he couldn't. Tom woke up repeatedly through the night. Maybe Mark's reality check had hit home. Maybe it was just not realistic to live in this mystical consciousness. "Give it up," he had advised himself. And he had tried, but the resulting sorrow brought to mind the gospel refrain, "Sometimes I feel like a motherless child, far, far from home."

Sometime early in the morning, long before light, he had the following dream: He was in his home office visiting with an old childhood family friend, a very religious woman. All of a sudden the phone rang. He answered. God was on the other end. The voice was definitive, authoritative and awesome. Much was said to Tom in that phone call that he forgot instantly, as if his mind were incapable of processing such vast and profound knowledge. The only part he remembered on awakening was this, "Man listens only to the word of man, not to the word of God." He did not go back to sleep.

Chapter 28

They met in the same coffee house downtown. Sixties soft rock played in the background, barely noticeable. A handful of customers perched among the hard, shiny, heavily shellacked tables, computers lit, coffee cups refilled periodically. Clarence immediately saw the strain on Tom's face, and asked, "What's the matter, Tom? You look so sad."

"I don't know – or maybe I do and can't face it. I feel confused, betrayed and defeated."

Tom filled Clarence in on his Vision Quest, meeting with Paul, conflict with Ronnie, BOP investigation, and the despair that had engulfed him following his lunch with Mark. "I don't know how to put all this together. I thought I'd found the Holy Grail, and now I've lost it."

Shifting his position and putting his coffee cup to one side, Clarence began slowly, choosing his words thoughtfully. "Tom. Quite unexpectedly, and with no preparation, you became a seeker of God – though that seeking was probably always part of your nature – and the struggle you are having is core to the very nature of the religious search. You stumbled into mystical consciousness through your patient, Paul, who became your 'John the Baptist,' awakening your mystical eyes. As you went further into this consciousness on the Vision Quest, you realized that it is bigger than you are and it is God's consciousness. The Hindu Upanishads, very ancient scriptures, say he who has found this pure consciousness has found his true self, his own nature. Zen Buddhists say when the awareness of mind and body cease during meditation, Buddha consciousness is revealed. Even many of your Jungian writers hypothesize that the next step in the individuation process is for God's consciousness to be present in each of us, as it was for Jesus. Pretty heady stuff."

"Yes, I guess so," replied Tom. "And when you put it so clearly, it's mind-blowing. I'm still trying to digest it. But I think it goes even further for me. You said last time that in this awakened consciousness the divine is the true reality of the world but people don't see it. They only see what they think. But I do see it now and it makes me feel crazy! How do I understand this?"

"Yes, the mystics from every era and religion tell us that mystical consciousness changes our perception of the world. You begin to see it as divinity – matter, space, trees, rocks, everything. Hindus call it 'sat-chit-ananda,' which roughly translates to the equation: existence=consciousness=bliss. And as Blake said, if the lens of perception were cleansed, man would see everything as it is: infinite. Mystical consciousness transforms our seeing. Jesus spoke of this in the Gnostic Gospel of Thomas. He said that when you look at the ordinary world in this consciousness, it becomes Heaven on Earth right before your eyes. This is one of the greatest secrets of the spiritual path."

"On the Vision Quest, I sensed divine consciousness seeing through my eyes, purifying whatever I saw, rendering it pristine, perfect, miraculous and sacred. Is that what you mean?"

"Yes, it is a form of mystical union. When 'your' consciousness opens to divine consciousness, then there is only one consciousness. 'You' disappear and only God remains. Your patient Paul experiences this union. You have touched it, too. But to live in this state of awakened awareness is another matter altogether. The road gets very bumpy from here. As the Buddha proclaimed, conventional beliefs and attachments disappear in this enlightened state, even our precious identity and self. But it's hard to function in the conventional world without an identity or self. Lao Tzu, the legendary founder of Taoism, said that the enlightened man lives simply, caring nothing about home or possessions. These are difficult precepts to follow."

"Clarence, that's why I feel so beaten down. The mystic path is so impractical as to be essentially impossible to me. I'm not ready to give up my family, work, and home."

"Tom, the good news is that the mystical path often follows life's developmental stages as well. The Hindu culture, for example, recognizes that there are stages of spiritual life. You're in the 'householder' stage, a time meant for marriage, raising a family, entering a profession, saving money, and serving the community. It's not a time to quit your responsibilities. That comes in the next two stages, the "hermit" and "wandering ascetic" stages, when people retire from family and professional life and progressively devote themselves to prayer and enlightenment. While the full demands of these later stages are too extreme for most elders in the modern world, they can still serve as a model for spiritual practice in aging."

"So I have to wait another twenty years to take this step?"

"Of course not, Tom. You can still integrate this consciousness into your everyday life. The mystics say that the present moment is holy. Every event, no matter how it is viewed from mortal consciousness, is the divine unfolding and you are part of that."

"OK, that all feels real for me and I like the fact that I can tune in to the Presence as I go through my day. But for me the sixty-four million dollar question is this: How do I live from this amazing consciousness while operating in the world of conventional duties and expectations? What I feel in the Presence is so often incompatible with what I am doing. I can't let myself wander out of the office in the midst of a psychotherapy session to merge with the divine dance, or tell a patient that their problems are a result of spiritual blindness, or hug every beautiful child I meet on the street. My practice would fall apart, I'd get arrested, and I don't want to fail my family."

"You're right," said Clarence. "Even those folks who undergo profound mystical experiences do not usually drop out. They go on with their normal lives but they don't abandon this divine consciousness. As the saying goes, 'Before enlightenment, chop wood, carry water. After enlightenment, chop wood, carry water.' Even your patient Paul chose to continue in his worldly roles."

"I guess that's my essential challenge. I have no idea how I'm going to do this."

"That's why you trust the divine to open your eyes to your own way. Be patient."

Tom sat back, overwhelmed. "There is so much to digest here, Clarence. I owe you, big time. I gotta go. I'll let you know how all this settles in me."

Clarence gave his beleaguered friend a warm and sympathetic hug, said a silent prayer, and sent Tom into the night.

Chapter 29

The consultation group met at its regular time. Though Tom wasn't due to present, everyone wanted to hear about his Vision Quest and what happened to "that religious patient." Tom wasn't sure he should talk frankly about his mystical experiences in the desert, so he gave them a watered-down version. Opinions were exchanged about Paul's final diagnosis and it was concluded that his delusions had probably cleared despite some residual religiosity. Only Barbara remained quiet. Later that day she called Tom.

"Tom, I didn't want to get into an academic debate about the nature of religious experience," she began. "But I do want you to know that I believe this patient's experience is more spiritual than psychological."

"Barbara, thank you for saying that. I can't agree with you more. I find this whole case totally fascinating. I just don't know how to talk about it, how to conceptualize it in ways other professionals can hear. And I wonder how I can talk about this to other clients. I think that Paul represents a higher potential of human consciousness that psychotherapy should aim toward once symptoms are resolved, a greater state of human being. Therapy is not just about relieving suffering, it should also be about discovering the spiritual nature and purpose of existence."

"Yes, but to speak of it too plainly is to invite persecution. This kind of talk is scary to many people, including mental-health professionals and the clergy. Your client's pastor couldn't accept it, nor will the Board of Psychology. What those in authority fear, they will prosecute. My advice is to keep all this to yourself. Save it for those who can understand. Let the potential for cosmic consciousness remain in the background of your psychotherapeutic work until your patient is truly ready to understand and experience it."

Tom thanked Barbara again. They agreed it was good to know a few fellow travelers on this "road less taken," and said goodbye.

Chapter 30

Life began to return to normal. Even the Board of Psychology's investigation finally went away. It turned out that Emma was so happy with Paul's "conversion" that she never returned Mr. Bennett's numerous phone calls. Paul, of course, was totally uninterested in testifying for the Board and, in his state of mind, would make a poor witness anyway. Although Dr. Spence viewed Tom's diagnosis as an obvious mistake, he saw no reason to conduct a witch-hunt and politely discouraged the investigator's persistent requests for his professional criticism. The case dried up.

Family life, too, had gone on as usual, for the developmental energies of life don't cease simply because Dad asks religious questions. Tom quit talking about consciousness and Ronnie forgot the whole thing. Still, as the days and weeks slid back into their familiar groove, Tom's mind did not. His questions and ruminations kept pulling loose threads from his life's well-woven fabric. *What about this other state of consciousness? Even some physicists are beginning to talk about the universe as an infinite and self-aware mind. What are the implications? Shouldn't we be living in greater awareness of this larger consciousness? Isn't that what religions are for? Why aren't more people exploring these spiritual possibilities?* These questions kept bringing Tom back to his dream about God and the telephone. *Isn't this what God meant when he said, "Men listen to the word of men, not to the word of God"?*

Tom considered these questions navigating traffic on the way to work (*men truly do live lives of quiet desperation as Thoreau said*), during therapy sessions (*isn't mystical consciousness relevant to this patient's emotional problems?*), in the shower (*hot water running over my skin stirs such exquisite divine energies*), at his son's baseball games (*does baseball itself represent a metaphor of spiritual practice: the devotion it takes, its "zone" of heightened awareness, the symbolic rounding of the bases of life in order to come "home"),* observing teenagers' budding sexuality (*libido: one of the ultimate and most ecstatic energies of the universe*). *Why isn't this on everyone's mind?* Tom wondered.

On the other hand, Tom's athlete-son was suddenly overflowing with "far-out" metaphysical reflections and they pursued equally far-reaching conversations. But most of all, Tom was haunted by his own recurring question: *How does a middle-aged family man with all the typical social, economic, and family attachments and obligations live the kind of mystical awareness exemplified by Paul's transformation?* More personally, Tom asked himself, *How do I live from within this divine consciousness? Doesn't our spiritual growth require more from a man – from me! – than merely lip service?*

Late one night, sitting at his computer long after the family was asleep, Tom began to "discuss" these questions with God. Tom asked the questions and let God "answer." Jung called such an exercise "active imagination;" others described it as visualization or creative use of fantasy, psychics go so far as to call it "channeling." Tom realized it didn't matter what you called this experiment, just follow the flow and see what you learn. The dialogue went like this:

Tom: God, where do I go with this? I sense you all around me. I feel your Presence, your mind, your awareness, so close. What do I do with all this consciousness?

God: Experience it. It is what you are made of. I am your consciousness, your body, your being.

Tom: I feel so much joy when I realize you are my truest nature, my deepest being.

God: I am your being and your being is joy, ecstasy, unlimited love.

Tom: But isn't my life more than working eight-to-five, paying the mortgage, being a good husband and father, keeping up the house, and planning for retirement?

God: Your life is already lived in, through, and as me. Don't you see? How can it be otherwise? You didn't create yourself. You didn't create the world. All this is my creation, my being. I am you in the form of Tom. I am the Earth and the cosmos. Reality is the blossoming creativity of my being.

Tom: What is my part in this incredible symphony of being? Should I be taking some responsibility? Shouldn't I be like Mother Teresa and devote my life to unselfishly helping others? Aren't I supposed to be doing good works like Jesus, acting compassionately like Buddha or social reformers like Confucius, or serving as a wise philosopher like Lao-Tzu?

God: You are exactly as I have created you, exactly as I am as you. I am in every particle, every moment, every manifest happening. All this is my unlimited being-consciousness-bliss awakening, unfolding, forming, evolving, becoming. You are me! Just feel that and be. That is enough.

Tom: What about spiritual growth? Aren't I supposed to be in a religious organization devoting myself to daily spiritual practice?

God: You are growing spiritually right now, in this moment, by being in this consciousness. You don't need to go anywhere else. If it's in your nature to join something, you will, but it's not required. Nothing is required but conscious being. Reality, including you, is not something to be fixed, corrected, or improved. It is to be loved unconditionally. Not for my sake, but because love opens you to me and we become one.

Tom: I resisted that idea in the past. I questioned why a loving and generous God would make anyone worship him. It made you seem like a big narcissist.

God: Tom, you assume I am driven by ego like you. It is man's desire for personal power or fame that is confused with my nature. Let go of that. You already have everything. I have even given you my self as yours.

Tom: How do I live this gift of life?

God: Open your awareness to my moment-by-moment unfolding. I am developing as you, as others, as this day, this event, this movement, this feeling. Existence is my being and becoming, my eternal revelation – this moment is holy. Nothing is separate from me. There is only me forming as all beings. Make a conscious choice to be present to our moment-to-moment unfolding together.

Tom: Then why have I felt so separate, so forgotten, so alone, so mortal in the past?

God: Because you separated yourself from me, from your divine nature.

Tom: How?

God: By all your thinking. You created a self-idea and then believed it. Worse you compared it with everyone else's self-concept and then envisioned life as a contest. Your self-idea, its history and issues, is only an illusion.

That last comment struck Tom like a truck laden with bricks. Of course! That's how it works! Thinking, conceptualizing, abstracting, interpreting, analyzing, concluding – these mental operations create a false world of thought that separates humans from the direct experience of divinity. Thinking about God reduces this infinite cosmic consciousness to theological concepts. We invent ideas about God and then blame God for not living up to them! Even in our prayers, we try to control God. And religious beliefs turn into a formula for how we are supposed to live, and that formula replaces divine consciousness. And while it seems reasonable and normal to have plans, goals, future hopes and dreams, they end up taking over consciousness. We lose God in all that planning, figuring, scheming, and manipulating.

Tom's fingers began typing again and the screen filled with words.

God: I am here now in all things, in you. Open to me. As you do, I become you and you become me. Can you feel the joy of my consciousness spreading through you? I am living your life. Release who you think you are and know that you are my consciousness. I am you becoming me.

"Where does this stuff come from?" Tom wondered aloud, as he sat back from the screen. "I am awed. This is not taught in church. Isn't this some kind of blasphemy, as the Pastor Hoeller would certainly contend?"

Tom remembered his discussion with Clarence about all we must give up to know God. He realized that this really meant giving up what we think we know, including who we think we are and who we think God is, for even our idea of God separates us from God. *This, here, now, is God. It is this realization that brings us home.*

Tom resumed typing.

Tom: Then what about evil? What is my obligation to confront brutality, cruelty, hatred, poverty, hunger, and suffering?

God: Those who perpetrate harm, those who suffer, those who stand by, and those who are too busy and turn away, have all forgotten their home in me. Cruelty and suffering are symptoms of the pain of separation and homelessness.

Tom: The sorrow, rage, and confusion of spiritual homelessness?

God: Of leaving the Garden only to seek a false self and what you take as wealth or knowledge. Seeking something other than me leads to suffering. Yet I am here, always. I am your life energy and being. Find me in the experience of your own being and you are home.

Tom: What is my obligation when I see the terrible pain and suffering?

God: First, wake up. Open into mystical consciousness, the consciousness of consciousness itself, that takes you directly into me. Then you will see with pure vision unclouded by beliefs, points of view, reactivity, or your own agenda. Centered in me, you will know exactly what to do. It is humankind that makes the world ugly with ideas of good and evil. It is man that thinks he must solve these "mistakes" in Creation, as if I had left the world like a parent abandons his children. Come into my Presence, see the world exactly as it is, and then you will know what to do and the doing will come naturally. If anyone, sufferer or tyrant alike, truly knew who and where they really were, this experience of suffering would be transformed.

Tom: That is an amazing revelation. I can do that. I can't wait to see what unfolds.

God: One last thing. You cannot do this by more thinking. You have to live my consciousness and allow my nature to become all that is and what you are. One day all beings will know my consciousness and being as their own.

Tom was dumbfounded by this unexpected conversation. Where had it come from? *Another consciousness does indeed live in and through us,* Tom thought. *My God, this is so profound.*

Chapter 31

The days passed calmly. Summer moved into fall, the leaves began changing. The scent of fireplace smoke was again in the air. Families made their annual pilgrimage to Apple Hill to see the colors and eat apple pie *a la mode*. On his bike ride up the American River one day, Tom felt the power of brisk winds, saw the changing color spectrum of autumn, and felt the divine moving through his body as he pumped the pedals in this wild and precious dance of existence. He sensed the consciousness of every leaf, tree trunk, open space, and fellow biker. *This world, this consciousness, this being is so amazing, awesome, awake, alive, and wonderful, and I am awakening as God's pure, expanding, transparent, silent, deathless Presence. Thank you, God, for this opportunity to be and know what you are. What more could anyone want? What more was there? I am complete,* he thought, *I am what is.*

Tom practiced his mystical awareness everywhere, bringing consciousness into the experience of Presence that permeated the world. He noticed how incredibly still, peaceful and loving it was, how it changed him. Each day he merged more deeply into the One. He worked, walked in the park, and loved his family in the spacious and serene awareness of divine being. He told no one, realizing that none of this would make sense to others. Some, like Paul and Clarence and Barbara understood, but he didn't need to "preach to the choir;" they already knew. And he realized more deeply that it was not about fixing things, improving oneself, or overcoming challenges. Those were ideas that implied that there was still something wrong, incomplete. Struggle with them and you only to get more entangled in the messy world of thought. He also noticed the countless distractions that could steal this consciousness, including gossip, emotional dramas, competing opinions, money worries, and all the reactivity that came with having a personality. How easy it was to lose mystical awareness amidst the social pressures to keep up the act of being a person. What he liked most, however, was the enormous relief he felt in the warmth of Presence – no one to be, nothing to achieve, only joy and love and freedom.

Late one afternoon, sitting in a pharmacy waiting to pick up a prescription, Tom noticed a little boy dragging his father all over the store, up and down isles, over to displays, in and out of the bathroom. His good-natured father played along and both were having fun. *This,* Tom thought, *is part of the magic.* Neither father nor son cared about what they *should* be doing; instead the divine mystery of joy was playing with them. Here was a down-to-earth example of divine being – the dance of life – and all watching smiled in pleasure. Here was the dance he dreamed of on his Vision Quest lived out in such pure fashion. *We go in and out of this state all the time,* he mused. *Amazing.*

The dance was everywhere. Quite by accident, he spotted Paul and Emma one day in a fabric store at Arden Fair Mall, one of the classier shopping centers in Sacramento. She was obviously in charge, searching for some sort of fabric for a quilt or dress she was making. Paul, on the other hand, had no needs, wishes, or agenda. He was just there, his happiness hidden behind an enigmatic (some might say beatific) smile. Clearly he made Emma happy, demonstrating the principle that higher consciousness in one person subtly creates peace and awakening in others. *Perhaps this is what's meant by a state of grace,* Tom thought. Anyway, she was happier and probably attributed her improved life to God, though not quite as she imagined. They were part of the dance, too.

That night, Tom had found himself once again typing an on-screen dialogue with God. This time, however, God stopped talking and would no longer respond. Tom was completely flummoxed. The feeling of Presence was unchanged, but no more dialogue. It was just silence, waiting, awareness. Then a new, unidentified voice came into the dialogue.

Voice: Tom, you are the divine speaking.

Tom: What does that mean?

Voice: You are the voice of cosmic consciousness. Speak. Start talking. Say it all. You have a much larger calling than what you are doing. Your work is to talk about the nature of God. Your awareness is the Presence.

Tom: Who are you?

Voice: I am your own voice. I am God as you. It's your turn now.

That stopped Tom cold. What did that mean? It certainly didn't mean what it sounded like. Tom wasn't God. Tom couldn't speak for God. It made no sense at all. This was craziness. This was inflation. Tom couldn't stop.

Tom: Why did God stop talking to me?

Voice: Because that idea located God outside and separate from you. You are typing God's words right now. God is the consciousness within your consciousness. Speak from that consciousness.

Tom: What do I do? Start preaching about sin and salvation in tent revivals like a Pentecostal preacher? A psychologist that speaks for God? Who's going to believe that?

Voice: God speaks in everyone. Only you have discovered your real voice. You speak now as God.

Tom: Wait a minute. You and I both know what happens to people who say they talk for God – shock treatments, ridicule, crucifixion. Or worse, crowds, adoration, and exploitation. There goes my peace and quiet, there goes my psychology license, my family and friends. No thanks; this is too big for me.

Voice: You are the prisoner of your limitations yet you hold the key that unlocks Heaven and Earth. What are you afraid of? There's no death. You breathe eternity. You are eternity. Don't hide from this greatest of human potentials. What can happen? The more they take away, the more you are the One. You are no longer everyday Tom, you are Tom opening to God, speaking as God. You've been coming to this realization all your life. That's what your telephone dream was about: God calling you, giving you the words to say. Now its time for you to say God's words as your own and not worry about who you are or what people think. It's as natural as breathing. Be who you really are.

This was too much. Tom turned off the computer. Its screen went dark. *Put it away,* he told himself. *Erase it. Forget it. That stuff's history! Boy, what a nutsy fantasy. Me speaking as God. My practice would be empty in no time, not to mention my credibility, my friends, and my income. My life would be a shambles. No way. I think I'll just stay with practicing the Presence. That's enough for me. I'm sorry, God, but I can't do that. Somebody else would do a better job.*

Chapter 32

Tom hadn't seen Clarence Kelly in nearly six months. After several days of unsuccessfully trying to forget his last computer dialogue, however, he knew it was time to chat with him again. This conversation with God had felt different, felt too far out, too crazy. Maybe it was the idea of speaking God's thoughts. It seemed unthinkable at best, and blasphemous at worst. Would Clarence be outraged, insulted, or disgusted by Tom's "spinout" on the spiritual path?

Once again Clarence graciously agreed to meet Tom for coffee after work. Actually, he couldn't wait to find out what Tom had so self-consciously described as his latest "spiritual spinout." He enjoyed their talks. It was rare to find someone so sincerely determined to understand the great religious tenets. Most people, he mused sadly, were content with the conventional, spoon-fed beliefs or pursued all sorts of ideas and practices with little or no skeptical thought – magical thinking and feel-good spirituality in place of genuine, hard-won, spiritual realization. But Tom was a careful thinker. What could be troubling him now?

The principle benefit to computer revelations over the old-fashioned biblical variety, Tom chuckled to himself on they way downtown, was that you could save them on your hard drive and then print them out. *I guess even I've been "saved."* He laughed. So when Clarence arrived, Tom presented him with a sheaf of his "dialogues-with-God" and briefly explained the process.

"Clarence, I have been conducting a sort of experiment. Or I was. Now it's more accurate to say, the experiment has taken over and has been conducting me! Anyway, I have been exploring my thoughts, and my own mystical awareness, by writing these dialogues with God as kind of an experiment in imagination. You'll see what happened."

Tom sat back nervously. He watched Clarence's expressions

range between perplexity, surprise, amusement, confusion, and finally thoughtful deliberation, as if he were checking what he read against some internal CD of religious thought and experience. The second time through, Clarence seemed a little more comfortable, for he was beginning to grasp both Tom's process and its rather startling culmination. He sat back quietly, letting an air of calm settle around his bemused smile, sipped his coffee, tasted a scone, and smiled like the Cheshire Cat.

Tom spoke first. "So, Clarence, am I crazy? Are you going to recommend that I be burned at the stake or have my cortex fried in the psychiatric hospital? I know I'm way out on a limb with this weird stuff, but I can't get it out of my head."

Clarence laughed kindly. "No, you're not crazy, though I wouldn't be showing this kind of stuff to your local psychological society or, for that matter, to any religious organizations. I think I see what you've been doing. You are tapping into the numinous core of the psyche, the deeply shrouded holy consciousness at its center."

"That part kind of makes sense. But what about this idea that I am supposed to 'speak for God'?" Tom asked.

Clarence's response, again spoken slowly and carefully, surprised Tom. "We all speak for God. Every creative act is God speaking: Michelangelo's paintings on the ceiling of the Sistine Chapel, Mozart's symphonies born almost fully completed as he heard them within, the sacred art of Buddhists, Hindus, Native Americans, a Sunday-school teacher telling a Bible story, the sacred dances of India or Southeast Asia, someone quietly writing a hymn, a grown man holding a dying parent – these can all be forms of God living and speaking through us. Because the ego is involved, they are not always perfect. But all are attempts to allow the divine to shine through our spontaneous creativity into something shared. I guess I even do so when I write a sermon for Sunday morning, seeking within for inspiration and creativity, and often not knowing what I'm really writing until it's come through."

"But a message directly from God? That's nuts. This isn't the Old Testament and I'm not a prophet!" Tom countered.

"Don't flake out on that. We all get messages from God, far more often than we realize. Dreams, intuitions, signs. It's just that we typically ignore or dismiss them. If the world is a sacred place, if everything is revelation, then we can listen to what God is saying. The world is God revealing divine life through us, and each must listen, hear, and express it."

"That makes lots of sense. But anyone saying they are speaking for God, or as God, is heading into some form of megalomania. I am not God!"

Clarence replied, "You are being asked to speak from God, to teach from the inner light. As you imply, one has to be careful not to get personally inflated. God is being Tom, speaking through Tom's consciousness, speaking as Tom, but Tom is not the totality of God. Do you see the difference? Tom is a construct, a fiction imposed on divine consciousness. The purpose of this fiction is to create a frame for bringing revelation into the world. But God is infinitely larger than any individual. God is you as well as every-thing else. When you feel that unity, you feel your oneness with the consciousness that lives in us all. Then, you can sense when your words are divinely inspired, coming, as in any creative act, from divine intuition."

"Why me?" Tom asked.

"Why not? Words are your gift. Using them to describe the nature of God is your calling, your vocation. All the great religious writers have had this gift. Don't be grandiose. You're not the only or the final writer to speak God's language. But don't shrink from this calling either."

"But aren't we supposed to be apologetic and self-effacing on the spiritual path, to overcome ego?"

"Yes, for by yourself, you are nothing. But don't hide your gold. God gives each of us something infinitely precious to do or share or be in Creation. Shrinking from what you are and betraying your gift, that is the sin."

The word "sin" immediately pulled Tom back to his Vision Quest dream of his client Scott killing himself with an ice pick, and the jolting realization arose – that self-hatred was the "original sin." In self-hatred, we betray the soul and the sacred gifts entrusted to us to bring into the world.

"What am I supposed to write?" Tom asked.

"Whatever comes to you. Let it flow. Which reminds me of Jelaluddin Rumi."

"Who?" Tom asked, struck by this most unconventional-sounding name.

Clarence explained, "Rumi was a thirteenth-century religion professor in Afghanistan. Sometime in his own midlife, he met a spiritually enlightened wanderer who told him to throw away all his books and live what he knew. As the story goes, Rumi was awakened by this man's enlightened state, gave up his formal teaching, and established the religious order later known as the 'Whirling Dervishes.' More to the point, after his awakening, Rumi recited some 50,000 verses of spontaneous mystical poetry that is still being translated today. Students had to follow him around writing down his spontaneous utterances. Rumi's poems speak ecstatically of his communion and union with the divine, which poured out of him like a sacred fountain. That's just one example of what it means to speak for God."

Tom was fascinated, lost in thought, and a long silence enfolded their meeting. He appreciated Clarence's broad range of religious knowledge and experience. More than that, he appreciated his lack of orthodoxy, his ability to normalize such seemingly bizarre and culturally forbidden ideas. After all, to say that God has asked you to speak on His behalf, through your computer no less, would shock even the most liberal religious professionals. Clarence had again put Tom's experience into perspective. The long silence was finally broken when the waitress announced closing time in ten minutes. The two hours spent in the coffee house had felt like minutes.

Tom concluded their evening by saying, "I tell you, this is so amazing. Each time I think I have completely wigged out, you show me that it's just another step on the path. Did you go through all this struggle?"

"I still do," Clarence said honestly. "Despite what some may claim, none of us have really traveled far along the spiritual path. We grow with every discovery and every disappointment, and especially with every defeat of the ego. We resist the true spiritual journey with our childish longing for security and our supposedly inviolate convictions about the world. I love your struggle, Tom. It is a good and honest struggle. In finding and honing your own understanding, you are finding your voice. Let that voice fill with the words and images God gives to it. A larger consciousness is speaking through you more and more. You know what it's saying. Open your voice and say it."

Tom was quiet for the entire drive home. There was nothing he could say. Something wanted possession of his mouth, tongue, and voice. It was too big to know or say yet. But the ecstasy welling up within made Tom want to run wild and naked through the starry night.

Chapter 33

The days, weeks, months and years followed their prescribed course as the Earth spun on its axis and moved around its star. Tom's spiritual work grew to be especially satisfying. He published a book about the place of spirituality in psychotherapy: why this integration was important, what its perils could be, and the contribution of the divine Presence in the consulting room. He began presenting at professional conferences. He and Barbara collaborated on a workshop entitled, "Life as a Sacred Journey." He joined the board of Clarence's retreat center teaching courses on spirituality. Tom was beginning to see what Clarence had meant. He was "speaking for God" now but in ways that felt appropriate and well-grounded. True, he often felt "a little used up" after long therapy days but saw no reason to cut back. To simplify his work life, however, Tom moved his practice to his home office that Ronnie also used for her small-but-growing therapy caseload.

One day, Tom found an old Chinese fortune cookie in the pocket of a flannel shirt he hadn't worn in a couple years. He had no recollection of seeing it before. It simply read:

We are living in eternity.

The time to be happy is today.

Part II

Chapter 34

Fifteen years later. The McLaughlin's had moved into new orbits.

In the years since his Vision Quest, Tom's children had achieved full-fledged adulthood and he marveled at their changes. Erik had pursued a more experimental route. After two years of junior college and numerous brief career turns, including sporting goods sales, real estate, pet grooming, and junior college baseball coach, he announced plans to move to Cody, Wyoming to be a cowboy and follow the rodeo. With a genuine love for horses, Erik learned to ride, rope and compete, and followed the rodeo circuit for nearly a decade with some notoriety. His friends called him the "cowboy philosopher" for the metaphysical pronouncements he uttered at the most unexpected times – "Namaste, Bull. Your karma has arrived." After accumulating a growing collection of breaks, sprains, and concussions, Erik finally returned to Sacramento, settled down with his very conventional girlfriend – opposites really do attract – and, to everyone's surprise, went to work for her employer, a workers comp insurance company, in account management, where his gregarious personality made him an instant success in the office and a likable adjuster in the field. Metaphysical proclamations continued, of course, only now they referenced insurance claims in Beatle-listic dialect, "All you need is love." Though a little late on the family-planning side, there was a rumor that he and his wife were about to begin.

Laura, always the more practical offspring, had taken the direct route, graduating from college in four years, completing a master's degree in genetics, and going to work for the University of California, Davis Medical Center as a genetics counselor for prospective parents. Like a homing pigeon, she knew exactly where she wanted to go and arrived as planned. As a favor to her father, Laura had collaborated with him on a pilot study of epigenetic changes associated with mystical experiences. While the results had been equivocal, she knew he had most enjoyed the time they spent working together. Laura married soon after college graduation to a truly wonderful man who taught English at the Sac State and worked on his novel in the rare moments between the endless sporting events of their twin boys.

Meanwhile, Ronnie had found her way as well. Her fruition, Tom realized, involved expressing her artistic side long shelved in the frenzy of family life. Her empty-nest was filled with quilting, painting and pottery. Professionally she had developed a small private therapy practice out of the home office they now shared. She also volunteered as a crisis mental-health worker with the Red Cross and periodically traveled to natural disasters across the country.

Tom and Ronnie's relationship had settled into a mostly peaceful pattern of work, date nights, simple meals, occasional trips, and lots of babysitting. They loved being grandparents, watching this vibrant new generation spring to life in the endless round of humanity's unfolding journey. Tom's spiritual evolution progressively opened his heart, and Ronnie felt this deeper and freer love through his patient attention to her needs and feelings, pleasure in her company and pride in her accomplishments. They took care of each other and, as aging couples sometimes do, the McLaughlin's increasingly – albeit tacitly – shared one consciousness that encompassed and shared them both; you could give it a name but it didn't need one. Their respective abandonment fears evaporated like puddles in love's warm sunshine – though the future still harbored its trials and challenges.

Reflecting again on his family's wondrous generativity, it came to Tom that the divine was like an infinitely growing tree, made of pure intelligence, ever creating anew, joy spreading through its into branches, twigs, and leaves. And he sensed that each soul represented a leaf of awareness that can ultimately know its existence as either the individual embodiment of sacred being or as the one loving consciousness steadily awakening the whole cosmos, or both. This tree wanted nothing more than to be known intimately, personally, perfectly, and everyone participated in its rich proliferation whether they understood it or not. Sadly, foolishness and violence often tore the tree's branches and gifts. In a way he would never understand, Pastor Hoeller was right – humanity's hubris and greed were the enemies of the Spirit; it just wasn't the Devil.

Paul showed up from time to time and Tom always found pleasure spending time in his mystical state of being. Paul's "solution" to living in mystical consciousness continued to work for him – he was happy wherever Emma wanted him. He also kept Tom abreast of Emma's growing importance to the church and Pastor Hoeller's ever-expanding religious zeal that seemed to originate from some kind of inner hellfire – apparently the war against Satan's influence was never done. Tom was grateful to be far removed from that worldview.

And there was one more thing on his mind. Tom had just begun to notice the physical changes that come with aging – increased aches and pains, less energy, and subtle declines in auditory and visual acuity, sexual drive, and stress tolerance. Now 65 and approaching retirement, he would soon learn that a long life is not meant to be easy and smooth, it's meant to expand your consciousness even more, as every potted tree must one day outgrow its container. No one retires in enlightenment.

Chapter 35

Tom loved the long and winding bike trail that snaked up the American River Parkway, especially in the fall. Three times a week he'd jump on his bike, cross the Arden bike bridge, and ride north toward Folsom Lake and the Gold Country. Pedaling hard and steadily gaining altitude, he traveled through stands of oak and cottonwood trees, smelled the crisp air, and reveled in the quiet beauty of nature. This was living.

Resting on the western shore of Folsom Lake, smiling at a couple of young children playing at the water's edge under the watchful eyes of their young mother, Tom felt the first drop of rain and looked up at the darkening skies. "Whoops," he said aloud, "time to head home."

Luckily, home was downriver and the ride would be fast and easy. Re-adjusting his bike helmet, Tom pushed off onto the trail. Picking up speed he felt the wind cool his forehead, still wet with sweat. He soon felt something else. A cold sweat. Was he getting sick? Then he couldn't seem to catch his breath. He tried to breathe deeper only to notice escalating nausea and indigestion. "A great time to come down with the flu," Tom muttered. But the pain in his left arm wasn't right, and now he felt the crushing grip of a heart attack. He knew the signs. He knew he was in trouble.

Tom coasted to a stop and stood still, hoping the symptoms would pass. They decreased some but did not go away. Tom got out his cell phone and called 911, giving the operator his best guess on the location of the closest street to the trail. Increasingly scared and beginning to shiver, he sat alone and wondered what else to do. *Oh yes,* he thought, *call Ronnie!* She did not pick up so he left the calmest message he could, describing his symptoms, 911 call, and the likely hospital he would be taken to. Then he waited.

In minutes, over the brim of the levee, Tom saw a couple guys looking like EMTs. He waved them over. One ran to his side while the other returned to get the gurney. It was bumpy climb up the levee to the ambulance. Once inside, Tom's heart attack was confirmed with EKG. He was given an aspirin to swallow and a nitroglycerin tablet to dissolve under his tongue. He breathed oxygen through a mask and an IV was inserted in his hand. With one EMT driving and the other monitoring Tom's condition, the ambulance raced to American River Hospital, arriving in just under six minutes. Tom was rolled into the E.R. where he was met by nursing staff, transferred to a bed, gowned, hooked up to monitors, and blood draws taken.

Things were hazy and rushed after that...coronary angiogram, chest x-rays, "clot buster" drugs, and Ronnie, who burst into his curtained E.R. with fierce tears in her eyes. A long half hour later, Dr. Reynolds stepped in to give them the verdict: minor heart attack, three blocked coronary vessels, and coronary artery bypass recommended in no uncertain terms, scheduled to begin within the hour. Any questions?

Chapter 36

Erik and Laura rushed to the hospital to join Ronnie. They huddled around Tom, bravely holding back tears and fears, and reassuring him that everything would be all right. Erik advised Tom that "spirit guides" would protect him – Tom had no idea what Erik meant – and Laura's hands trembled steadily in the waning minutes. Then it was time.

An attendant moved Tom's gurney, with Ronnie attached, through hospital corridors into surgical prep where they were greeted by the surgeon, anesthesiologist, and nurses. Ronnie was politely but firmly exiled to the waiting room while Tom was transferred onto the operating table. Everyone was friendly, busy, focused on individual tasks. The room was cold, the lights bright, a blanket warmed him. "You won't feel a thing," they said. "We'll take good care of you." The anesthesiologist did something behind him and then everything went black. Nothing.

More nothing. Then something. What were those faraway sounds in the blackness? Beeping machines, suction noises, murmuring voices talking about blood-pressure readings, anesthesia levels, surgical instruments. People gossiping, telling stories and jokes. *Should I be hearing this? Am I dreaming? Is it over already?* Tom wondered silently. *It's so cold. I can't open my eyes.* Waiting. More darkness and distant noises. *What's happening?* Tom felt the surgeon's scalpel cutting through the wall of his chest. Precise, firm, deliberate. With rising horror, he thought, *Oh my God, I shouldn't be feeling this. Stop!* But no words came out. He could not move. Indescribable pain. Terror. More pain. *How can this be happening? There's something in my throat blocking my breathing. I can't talk. I am paralyzed. No one is paying attention to me. They think I'm unconscious. I've got to find a way to communicate.* Tom tried desperately to move his face, a finger, even his toes. He screamed but no words come out. Nothing worked. *They don't know! How long will this last? I'm going to die.* Tom begged God for help.

Tom blacked out only to wake up again. The surgery had progressed. There were fingers moving inside his body. He could feel them poking, prodding, pulling, cutting, tugging. Air touching his insides created sharp, prickly pain. No one talked to him. No comforting touch, personal reassurance, no tenderness. Tom was merely an inert body to his surgical team. *This can't be happening*, he thought again. Physical sensations of pressure, pulling, stretching, scraping. *Why don't they know I'm awake? Help me!*

Tom passed out. Woke up again. Passed out again. It went on and on. He prayed helplessly. He heard them talking about their kids and the music playing on the radio. It was a living nightmare. Suddenly, he found himself at the foot of the cross bearing Jesus's limp body. He could see his gaunt face, his head crowned with thorns. He cried, "Jesus, Help me. Save me." Then, strangely, the thief on his right side lifted his head and answered, "Be still. You will be okay." Blackness.

Awake again, Tom realized, they were stitching him back together. He could feel every stab of the needle, how the surgeon's arm pulled the stitch tight, and the way his body moved with the pressure. Unbearable pain again. Then, he was outside his body, looking down on the surgeon sewing up his wounded chest, chatting about golf to the anesthesiologist. He heard and saw everything. *How could this be?* Once again, everything went black.

Tom woke up in the ICU and started crying hysterically. "I was awake. I was awake. I was awake in the surgery! I saw what you were doing, all of you." People look startled. A nurse ordered a shot. "You'll be okay. It's just a drug-induced dream. Hush." Back to sleep.

Time passed. Waking again. Lying in the recovery room. Fully alert now, he couldn't stop thinking about what happened.

Flashes of the surgery experience ripped through his mind. He couldn't stop crying. He was inconsolable. Ronnie sat by his side, worried, soothing; nurses with anxious worried faces came and went. That night he was afraid to go to sleep, terrified of surgical flashbacks. Lying flat in bed reminded him of being supine and paralyzed on the operating table. Everything recalled the surgery. It was a long and horrible night.

The surgeon stopped by first thing in the morning. Tom broke down describing his experience. Dr. Reynolds looked shocked, stricken, said he'd check the records, and left. The anesthesiologist visited and seemed especially uncomfortable and perplexed with Tom's distress. He mumbled some technical details about medications and dosages, said he was very sorry, and left as soon as he could. Later, a hospital psychiatrist stopped by, listened to his story, and described a condition called *Anesthesia Awareness*, said it would pass, and left.

After three more days in the hospital, Tom was given recovery instructions, discharged, and sent home with Ronnie.

Despite his steady physical improvement, Tom's mental state worsened by the day. Crying spells, flashbacks, insomnia, nightmares, exhaustion, irritability, depression, panic, fear of death and doctors.

"The doctor said you can have medication for sleep or for your nerves if you want it," Ronnie offered.

Nothing helped. Tom's emotional breakdown continued. *Will it never end? What is wrong with me?*

Tom's whole family was alarmed now. "Something has happened to Dad. He's not himself," they whispered behind his back. No one knew what to do. Finally, at the urging of Mark, Tom's partner, Ronnie suggested consulting a therapist and getting on psychiatric medications.

Chapter 37

Tom remained off work for a month. Prozac, Ativan, Ambien. Restless pacing, insomnia, crying spells. He saw his therapist weekly. In the beginning, Tom would just come in and sob. He was inconsolable. His therapist gave him full support to come apart as much as he needed to during their sessions. Again and again Tom relived flashbacks of being cut open, hands working inside his heart, sutures going in, and the profound loneliness and abandonment he felt while paralyzed in the operation. "I'm dying," he would cry. "They are killing me!" he would shout. "Make it stop," he begged. And as usual, no one responded in these flashbacks because no one knew he was awake. Only his therapist listened and it was a long, long journey from this "conscious autopsy" to a life restored. Even as he slowly healed, Tom felt as if his chest were still open – a horrific terror that caused him to sleep every night with his left hand over his heart as if to keep the surgical wound closed. He felt crazy. He felt broken. He felt dead. No one could gauge the depth of his descent into this nightmarish suffering.

Mark was amazingly supportive. In his own wise way, he reassured Tom that breakdowns were sometimes breakthroughs and should be treated as opportunities for major personal or life changes. He asked Tom, "What if your heart 'broke' for a reason? Maybe you've grown weary of those long days in the consulting room. Perhaps you are being called to different kind of journey. Try not to judge this experience, just go deeply into it. Let it bring you its message. Remember that nightmare with the Board of Psychology. It turned out to be an invaluable turning point in your life. As the Chinese symbol for crisis implies, this situation is both a disaster and an invitation."

Spilling tears of gratitude, Tom hugged his old friend and partner. He knew Mark was right and it felt good for someone to see the value of his collapse. Deep in the ashes of his life, Tom sensed the early stirrings of a rising phoenix.

Despite Mark's advice, and feeling the need to do something constructive, Tom set a return-to-work date for two months out. When the time came, he began seeing clients on a half-time basis. It was unbelievably difficult. He couldn't think straight, had trouble focusing, and apologized constantly for misunderstood or forgotten details. Some clients worried more about him than themselves. At times he felt crazy – flashbacks of being back on the table, chest open, followed by post-op numbness in his chest. No way could he continue like this.

Functioning on sheer "guts and fumes," Tom's return to work lasted a little over a year. Then he gave up. He knew instinctively that he would never recover unless he put all his energy into healing, and Mark's words still echoed in his mind, pointing toward a new kind of life. With profoundly mixed feelings of relief and regret, Tom closed his practice. It felt like the end of his life.

Very slowly, time and therapy relieved Tom's most intense distress. Working through the surgical trauma detail after detail, emotion after emotion, he faced what he had already understood – he had suffered a severe Post-Traumatic Stress Disorder. His healing journey led him through a seemingly endless parade of flashbacks, nightmares, and nearly unbearable grief. It went on and on and on for 18 months. Finally, at long last, he began sleeping through the night, tolerated some exercising, and began wondering what to do from here. Though he was better, Tom understood deep down that he had lost the ability to do psychotherapy – the pain of others was too hard, too much to bear. His disability carrier sent him to their "expert" who opined that Tom just didn't want to work anymore, and his benefits were terminated.

Furious with this disingenuous, self-serving conclusion, Tom reviewed the research on anesthesia awareness. He learned that it happened when anesthesia levels dropped too low to suppress awareness but neuromuscular blocking agents – those curare-like drugs that prevent movement during surgery – literally paralyzed the patient: a perfect storm for abject terror. Add excruciating pain, fear of dying, terrifying helplessness, lack of communication, and feelings of medical abandonment and betrayal, and you had a recipe for soul-shattering terror. Tom's attorney advised that a legal battle in California courts could go on for years, with expensive experts warring over findings and no guarantee of victory. He settled for pennies on the dollar.

For over a year, Tom explored possible "next steps" but none were realistic – full-time writing would never support him, he still lacked the energy for teaching, and he definitely could not face sales. Ronnie's employment was only half-time. On long hot summer days, with nothing to do, Tom sweltered under a tree in the park trying to think through this dilemma. He could not go back to being a practicing psychologist. Lacking the emotional strength to carry the load, his career was over. A credit line gave them some breathing room, but it could not be a permanent solution.

From time to time, Tom wondered about his surgical vision – finding himself at the feet of the crucified Jesus, listening to the thief's reassurance. *What kind of craziness was that? A dream? A Near-Death Experience? A psychotic break? And what might its symbolism mean?* He could not shake this vision. And how could this level of suffering exist in a loving and conscious universe? Was there a spiritual dimension to this sudden and unexpected life change? Tom felt like a house of cards blown away in a gale. Lost in a wilderness with neither compass nor a destination, he was walking in circles.

Chapter 38

The kids were gone, his career was gone, and his community of therapists was gone. Everyone went on with business as usual except Tom. But he was not totally bereft of friendship. In addition to Ronnie's steady support and Clarence's spiritual friendship, the other bright light in Tom's life was his friend Rich – an 85-year-old retired psychologist. Thinning white hair, stubbly goatee, and short stature "like a gnome," he joked, Rich sported a silver cane for balance and moved his arthritic joints carefully. Typically sanguine, he spoke with a vaguely Massachusetts accent and always a twinkle in his eyes. Rich was a delight to know and he had come to love his younger protégé. They met every week for coffee and talked about their lives. Their conversations combatted the professional black hole sucking the light from Tom's world.

Not only a wise and senior psychotherapist, Rich had long ago disclosed his own profound mystical experience. It happened six decades earlier during a very difficult time in his life – graduate school, a young and difficult marriage, a new child; the stress was overwhelming. Late one night, overflowing with anger and frustration, his wife asleep in the other room with their baby, Rich had confronted himself in the bathroom mirror. The rage he saw on his own face shocked him – "Like a wolf," he recalled. Then, feeling acutely remorseful and harshly self-critical, Rich asked his reflection, "Is this all there is?" An image arose in his mind of a black cloud, as if symbolizing his hateful countenance. Suddenly light surrounded the blackness, creating a beautiful nimbus. What happened next was breathtaking. "I felt my whole being swept up into this light. It was ecstatic. It felt like a trillion synapses going off in my brain all at the same time. I was in touch with all knowledge. I kept saying 'I know, I know, I know.' I don't recall how long I was in the light, but I came down from it as if re-entering my self as an 'ego'd' personality again, with my familiar history, inadequacies and aspirations." Noting that the word ecstatic means "outside oneself," he now understood its real spiritual meaning.

The impact of Rich's mystical experience, however, was monumental. "I knew most of all that this light was infinite love. Existing behind any and all darkness, it was the source of all the energy in the cosmos. It was God." Following his mystical experience, Rich's consciousness had also altered. Love saturated his personality, spilling out everywhere, and the world was now luminous and fascinating. He remembered watching water drip from a kitchen faucet into a cereal bowl as if in slow motion, each drop creating perfect concentric circles in the standing water, the most beautiful thing he had ever seen. Still vivid and profound in his memory, Rich's mystical experience was as fresh as the day it happened.

"God, Rich. I feel so lost," Tom began one Wednesday morning over coffee. The smell of French roast permeated the small café, its counters full of colorful pastries, its clerks friendly and efficient, but the cheeriness of the scene failed to penetrate Tom's dark mood. "I feel like I am disappearing…my identity, my roles in family and community, my place in the world. Who am I now? I feel like I don't exist."

Rich smiled sympathetically, wiped a crumb from his goatee, sat up straighter in his seat, and said, "Tom, though you started earlier than most, what you're describing is the aging experience. I've been living its changing landscapes for two decades. You, see, Tom, with retirement, your world empties of the structure and connections that made up your middle years, like work, professional friendships, kids' activities. You fall into a desert of time with vast stretches and nothing to do. This void secretly terrifies most men and many women so they keep working as long as they can or desperately try to keep busy in retirement. You didn't get to choose, but here you are anyway. But understand that this life change, what some jokingly call 'men-on-pause,' eventually affects almost everyone."

"But why did this horrible trauma happen to me? I didn't just retire, I was blasted out of my life. I keep thinking it must have some kind of spiritual meaning or significance."

"Well, I agree that you were blasted out rather unceremoniously, but your heart attack and career loss are still part of the larger process that comes with aging. You have entered a new stage of the life journey, a part where the familiar 'you' gets taken apart and gradually – or suddenly – dissolves. It was going to happen sooner or later. In the aging process, we give up who and what we were. But I believe aging also represents a purposeful stage of life, inviting us into an entirely new dimension of consciousness, especially now with our increased longevity."

This remark caught Tom's attention. He knew people were living considerably longer than ever before, one to two decades longer. And he knew that difficult things happened in the aging experience – health crises, retirement losses, the deaths of parents, friends and loved ones, grown children with little time for parents, and eventually your own physical decline. What if these losses were part of something bigger? He was stunned. Then, vaguely, he began to sense that this crisis might indeed be part of something larger as Mark had intuited, something to do with the next expansion of mystical consciousness.

"OK, that helps, but still, who am I now? I feel as if I have died. I'm still here, but I'm not. I feel like awareness without an ego."

"One of the most profound experiences of aging," Rich resumed, "is this loss of the familiar self – the identity you've maintained for years. It took me years to come to terms with it. Who you think you are no longer exists – Dr. McLaughlin, breadwinner, professional, father of small children. Even your body is different and God knows we don't look anything like we used to – have you seen a photo of yourself lately? They still freak me out. Who is that old man in the picture? Yet I don't feel old, until I stand up and walk, but even still, I am the same inside. Consciousness doesn't change; it's ageless, only its contents change. They steadily fall away like leaves in autumn."

Tom sat still. He stroked his beard. He took a bite of his muffin and a sip of coffee. This was huge. *What does it mean to "not exist"?* He remembered his earlier conversations with God. What had he understood? Yes, that consciousness does not belong to "you;" rather "you" are in it. More to the point, the familiar "you" mostly consists of a complex of thoughts, essentially a fiction.

"So," Tom stumbled onward, looking for some kind of solid ground, "when identity disappears, what's left? Consciousness?"

"Of course," said Rich, "or more accurately, divine consciousness. This is the next step in the evolution of human consciousness. Age itself cooperates by dismantling the whole 'project of you.' This is 'Mystical Consciousness 2.0," he laughed, comparing it to a new computer operating system. "What you experienced in the desert intensifies greatly in aging, removing the filters of identity and belief like smudges on a car windshield. 'You' disappear into the infinite consciousness of divinity. The task of aging is to transform everything in this amazing consciousness."

"Wow. I remember the mystics describing this as part of enlightenment but how do you live without a self?"

"Tom, you already function without a self in lots of ways. When you garden, paint trim, dance, watch a movie, you're not aware of a 'you.' You forget yourself. We don't really need the self-idea most of the time. In fact, it leads to endless problems. People worry about the worth, success, and appearance of this imagined self. The idea of self is useful in organizing a complex society, determining where each person fits – butcher, baker, Indian chief, and the parts they play, but beyond that, it's problematic."

"Rich, how do you cope with this disappearing self?"

"I have learned to let it go and live in the sea of consciousness that's left. I am back in touch with the light, the divine consciousness I felt so many years ago. That consciousness was blocked and shrouded by my identity. Now its absence thrills me with joy. Especially learning to silence thought. What a relief! And inviting this living consciousness into my body fills me up like a helium balloon – I feel light, airy, energetic, joyous. The losses that come with aging are really meant to erase identity and belief, opening you even further to the transforming consciousness of the divine."

A strange question arose for Tom. "Does this fit somehow with my vision of Jesus on the cross during my surgery?"

"Jesus was an experience of the divine self, your larger consciousness, showing you the great act of self-release that is enlightenment. 'Let the body-mind go,' the dream is saying, but you were too terrified to understand. Just like Paul's Jesus-from-the-pond, this is the divine-self revealing its arrival in your consciousness."

"How did you learn all this?"

"Same as you will, through conscious aging, which I see now is so like my mystical experience. I've come to believe that aging is enlightenment in slow motion, full of spiritual insights and realizations. Little by little, as the contents of mind fade away, the space take up by 'you' fills instead with the consciousness of divinity. It was always there but the mind was too preoccupied with the self-idea and its goals, beliefs and worries to notice. You see, we are born into this consciousness in early childhood but the beliefs and rules of society eventually crowd it from awareness. As a result, we leave the radiant 'Garden consciousness' of early childhood and get caught up in the rat race of society. In aging, we get the chance to come back home to our original pristine awareness. It seems to be one of the great secrets of aging." His soliloquy complete, Rich settled down in his seat like a deflating balloon, eyes still twinkling.

Tom felt as if his world had once again turned on a dime. *How do I live from this empty-yet-spacious consciousness? What do I do with my time, with practical issues like bills and doctor's appointments?* His old questions had resurfaced. Still, this realization thrilled him. *Maybe the whole heart attack/retirement thing represents this kind of emptying. Maybe the pain and horror I felt was the price of being too tightly identified with my body and identity in the first place. What if I had been centered in this larger consciousness during the surgery instead of my body? Is that even possible?*

Tom sipped his coffee thoughtfully. There was so much to understand. "Rich, this is quite frankly amazing. I suddenly feel so liberated. Maybe I don't have to be anybody anymore. It's astonishing."

"It can be wonderful, Tom. It's a kind of enlightenment associated with the aging experience. (Buddha gave up everything; aging asks us to do the same.) Picking up steam and brimming again with energy, Rich added, "And this gift of divine consciousness further opens the heart. When the body fills with divine consciousness, love pours forth like a dam break. All our lives we men hold ourselves like weapons, tense, ready for anything. If you let that body armor dissolve and feel instead the timeless unity of consciousness and being, you begin to love everything, almost indiscriminately, as I did following my mystical experience. This is where humanity may be heading if we can transcend the instinctive habit of responding with fear and aggression to every real or imagined threat. Tom, this is the life that awaits you."

As if this wasn't enough, Rich continued, "And there's one last piece to navigating these unfamiliar waters. Sooner or later, Tom, you will realize that aging is ultimately about facing death. In fact, the central archetype of aging is death and rebirth. In your heart attack, surgery, and especially with your surgical awareness, you came face to face with dying, *your* dying, and this core experience always awakens something deep inside. This realization, that the end of your life will arrive one day in the not-too-distant future, begins a natural process of letting go of all you will eventually surrender at death, especially ego, identity, and all attachment to material things."

Rich elaborated. "You notice feelings of generosity. Suddenly you want to give everything away to improve the lives of others because you can't take it with you. Death is the final defeat of the ego, so selfishness evaporates. The realization of personal death also prompts the psyche to begin its inner preparations for crossing over to the other side. An intuition stirs inside about what that crossing will involve, almost like a memory. This whole process is subtle, and many suppress their awareness of it, but it's real, and the more you can feel it and surrender to it, the more loving, prepared and conscious you'll be when death occurs." Rich leaned back in this chair, took a deep breath, and sat quietly for several minutes as Tom let his words sink in.

A gentle breeze rustled the azaleas in the planter outside the coffee shop as Tom and Rich exited. The doorbell chimed, cars raced down the Fair Oaks Boulevard racetrack, sun glanced off dirty puddles from careless overwatering, but neither paid much attention, moving easily into the flow of the afternoon. After a warm and grateful hug, they parted ways, promising to meet again the next week.

Chapter 39

Tom's residual PTSD symptoms didn't disappear with these revelations, but he seemed to care about them less. Each time he reminded himself, "I don't exist, I am not this," he felt a sudden exhilaration of freedom and relief that came with releasing the self-idea and its complex of beliefs, goals and problems. He realized he'd been telling himself stories about this fictional self all his life. If he didn't exist, the stories simply fell apart. This was liberation. Tom felt as if prison gates had opened. But this freedom required vigilance. Each time he slid back into ruminating about his surgery and retirement, the suffering returned.

An adjustment to this state of pure consciousness came gradually but steadily. The act of letting go, he realized, was not a suppression of pain and suffering, like someone stuffing it into the unconscious to avoid feeling it. It was more like letting go of something no longer necessary. In its place, Tom found himself back in the "sea of love," loving the world more and more, especially children, animals and those in pain. He spent endless hours playing with his growing gaggle of grandchildren, made larger donations than usual to charities, but mostly treated everyone with sensitivity and kindness. Tom wished others could experience this liberation, but after failing to convince anyone else to give up their self – an act he found difficult to explain anyway – he gave up. *One day I'll figure out a way to help others see,* he thought, for he trusted this new state of consciousness to reveal his path one step at a time.

Chapter 40

"Clarence! It's Tom. We need to talk. You got some time this week?"

"Sure, Tom. Let's do Wednesday – same time, same place."

It was a windy weekday evening; the first scattered rains of winter had recently materialized. Dark already. Most folks were home from work. Blustery west winds bent trees and limbs shed their leaves. Tom was glad to be inside, out of the rain, with a hot cup of Joe warming his hands. Clarence, for his part, was unruffled as usual, though his unruly hair confessed its defeat in the storm. Bathed in the smell of freshly brewed coffee, however, he looked settled and content. The twinkle in his eyes said he couldn't wait for the next installment of the Tom McLaughlin spiritual saga.

"So, what's up, Tom? You look good, so it can't be another crisis. And you always have such interesting 'problems.' Talk to me!"

For the next half hour, Tom shared Rich's thesis on the spiritual purpose of aging. He wanted now to delve into its spiritual nature more deeply, particularly its implications for enlightened elders – what might their role be in the world? At the end of his monologue, both walked over to refill their coffee cups in silence before digging into this extraordinary information.

"Tom, I agree with your friend Rich's description of aging. Our older priests sometimes talk like that, too. I know one guy in particular. His name is Art. He's blind, arthritic and 90 years old, but he's totally at peace with his coming death. Indeed he brims with joy. He told me recently that he believes that the first half of life was all preparation for the coming of the fullness of life's second half, which offers a destiny and goal utterly beyond our human conception. Divine life sustains him now, he says, and he approaches each new day, issue, or physical symptom with a joyful, 'Yes, my Creator.' He is a teacher now of the highest order, teaching simply from his illumined Presence and steady kindness. I see him as an embodiment of Christ. He is a fulfillment of aging's ultimate transformation."

"He sounds like a sage," Tom observed. "The kind of person we may aspire to be someday. How is that different from the mystical consciousness Paul embodies?"

"It's not different. It only looks different coming from a different person, especially someone older whose spiritual maturity now reflects the ripening of divine consciousness. What's especially important is that this level of mystical consciousness has the power to awaken others. Because of your own awakened awareness you are encountering it more often. People in mystical consciousness are drawn to each other like magnets."

"Such a lovely state of mind. But here's my question: what can these quiet selfless people offer a world torn by violence, selfishness and so many conflicted beliefs and identities?"

"They offer peace."

"But who does this peace touch when they have solitary lives like your priest friend?"

"I believe Art is a beacon and a harbinger," Clarence said. "He radiates joy like a searchlight and I believe he exemplifies the state of consciousness waiting for us all in the aging process. Art is virtually an enlightened sage."

"Yes, but only you guys see him," countered Tom. "How can he make a difference to the world?"

"For that, you need an understanding of consciousness in its larger context. In pure consciousness, in other words, consciousness free of thought, identity and belief, there are no divisions between people or things. It's all one consciousness being refracted like light through different personality prisms. From this unity, your state of mind ripples everywhere like waves, throughout the cosmos, affecting everything. People don't necessarily have to perceive it benefit from it. That's why groups of meditators, all meditating at the same time, can reduce the crime rate in a city – they're spreading peace consciousness."

"But can one man, or a handful of enlightened elders, spread enough love to change the nightmarish world humans still create?"

"Hindus and Buddhists tell us that world does not exist as we believe, that it appears as a projection from a confused and roiling state of mind. It's imagination superimposed on divinity. A peaceful and loving consciousness works naturally to settle the collective chaos and dissolve negative thought forms. The more people reach this peace, the more the calm. This process appears slow at the present time in history, but its power is expanding. And when we look past our projections, we find again the imminent and ever-present divine world, the reality of Heaven on Earth, which is the ultimate state of peace and tranquility."

"So, work on your own transformation?"

"As they say in the pre-flight announcements..." Clarence chuckled, "...put on your own oxygen mask first before you try to help anyone else."

A long silence followed. Then Tom said, "We are in Heaven right now. All the mystics tell us that. But more to the point, we can experience this effortlessly when our conceptual world dissolves in mystical consciousness. I see it. So does Paul, my former patient. So does your friend Art. Do you?"

"Yes," Clarence replied quietly. "I see it, too."

"And I'm especially fascinated by the possibility that mystical consciousness expands when we're together. It really is contagious. But what now? You don't retire in enlightenment, or do you?"

"I think the answer to your question may lie with our two senior mystics, Rich and Art. As enlightened elders for many years, they know this new stage better than anyone else. Let's invite them to lunch at the retreat center and see what they think about life in enlightened consciousness."

"Agreed! I'll talk to Rich, you call Art, and we'll find a time to meet. This is really exciting!"

Chapter 41

The lunch meeting took place on a lazy Tuesday – no scheduled retreats, staff working quietly, nothing to interfere with this groundbreaking discussion. They met in the retreat cafeteria, fixing sandwiches and iced tea together, and then moved outside to sit on a patio sheltered between the office and the main conference room. The sun was high in the sky but filtered by a hazy cloud cover – warm but not hot. Bird calls were everywhere, punctuated by the insistent chips of squirrels hoping to join their lunch.

Clarence and Tom introduced Rich and Art to each other and welcomed them warmly. All had been prepped on the purpose of the meeting and an air of excited anticipation embraced the group. This was going to be something special, Tom thought.

After small talk about the weather, their professional backgrounds and current lives, Clarence set the stage with his first question.

"Tom and I have been working on the idea that mystical consciousness – that kind of heightened, thought-free consciousness the mystics associate with the experience of the divine Presence – somehow ripens in the aging process, offering to change elders into sages. Obviously it doesn't happen to the majority of older people who have paid little or no attention to their spiritual development, but to those who have, and who genuinely seek a transformative experience of aging, amazing things might happen in this awakened state of consciousness. But let's start with what's happened for you in the aging experience."

A long silence followed this introduction, partly polite, each guest waiting for the other to respond, but also a sign of the depth of reflection Rich and Art were bringing to Clarence's question. Tom and Clarence were in no hurry and waited almost reverently for these two sages to respond. Finally Rich offered to begin.

"As a psychologist and psychotherapist, I have long been a student of the human life cycle. I worked with kids, teens, young adults, and then, later in my career, with older folks like myself. It's clear to me that the human psyche is a living system that grows and develops through identifiable stages over the life span. It doesn't just stop evolving with the attainment of adulthood. The first half of life is about the emergence, formation and strengthening of the ego as the quarterback of the personality. It's about the development of the individual life in family, career and society. You develop a persona and a place in the world that lets you function within the defined norms and roles of the culture.

"For virtually all of human history, personal growth was limited by a very short lifespan. Children born of hunters and gatherers, if they survived very high infant mortality rates, maybe lived into their thirties, though under extremely fortunate and benevolent conditions, it could be longer. But even as late as 1900, the average lifespan in America was around forty-five. With the advances of agriculture, science, nutrition and medicine, things have changed tremendously. Now we live well into our seventies, and if you get that far, the majority will live into their eighties and nineties. I just turned eighty-five! So what does this mean? It means we have a new developmental stage. Yes it has been here for thousands of years, but only for a very small minority.

"So we now have this new kind of aging, but what is it for? I believe something very different happens in the second half of life and especially in our maturity. At this time, the ego – the personal "I" – turns from issues of survival, competition, identity, and achievement, to personal and spiritual growth, even transformation. And this shift, I believe, is inborn. The psyche seeks to return to the mystical awareness that was prevalent in our early ancestors and known to us temporarily in childhood. But the consciously aging individual is more mature and can understand this state in a new way. This awakened consciousness is the breakthrough of our time. It's natural to the aging process, though our culture, always behind the curve, doesn't understand this development yet and tends to deny, ignore or disparage it. This shift happened to me, and I can't wait to hear how Art understands it."

"Rich, how would you describe this new consciousness?" Clarence asked.

"Well, first we need to distinguish between four states of consciousness. I call them 'The Lands of the Religious Psyche.' We are most familiar with the World of Man. It's the regular consciousness we're in most of the time, filled with ideas, beliefs, expectations, assumptions, rules and roles, and it's all focused on personal identity – who you think you are, what you think you should be, on and on. I also call it the world of scary thoughts because it continually generates feelings of fear and unworthiness. In this state, divine consciousness is so masked by thought that we completely lose touch with the Presence and its consciousness."

"Darkness is the second land of the religious psyche. Since the ideas and beliefs of the World of Man tell us what we should think and believe, everything outside this system of thought is either unknown or unconscious. In other words, it sits in the dark. What also sits in the dark are aspects of the true self – who we were born to be – that we suppress growing up when we believe they were wrong or bad or unacceptable. All our unacceptable feelings and needs are hidden there in the unconscious. That's what psychotherapy is all about – finding and healing the true self we rejected long ago."

Tom, Clarence and Art were listening carefully now, often nodding in agreement or amazement with the simplicity of Rich's model.

"What's the next state?" prompted Tom.

"The next state is pure consciousness, which is itself Divinity. When you stop thinking, sharpen awareness, and focus on consciousness itself, you are literally experiencing God's consciousness. People call this state by countless names – God, Yahweh, Great Spirit, Jesus, Buddha, Emptiness, Divinity, Cosmic Consciousness, the Holy Ghost, etc. When we stop thinking, what's left is this consciousness. It's that simple, but few stop thinking long enough to even notice that God is always here as your very own consciousness.

"Now the fourth state is Creation. Here God has become the world, the ground of being, and everything is a sacred. The divine world is always here but, lost in our thoughts, we just don't see it. We see what we think, but not what is. This is a very important distinction. Take a deep, penetrating, and thought-free look at anything, and you'll be amazed at its beauty. You suddenly realize that you don't really know what anything is – you just have names for things and think you understand them as a result. This final realm is also known as Heaven on Earth. The mystics have described it from the dawn of time. It's always here, we're just too busy to notice.

"Most people live in the fear-driven World of Man where the ego constantly struggles to survive and succeed. Much of the true self, and the pain of all the compromises the ego made to succeed in the world, gets buried in the darkness of the unconscious. The deep work in midlife is to heal this true self. The true self is that part of God we are each given to express in the divine world. It's filled with our gifts and talents. Embracing the self naturally brings us closer to divinity, though we may not realize it at first. Our second work is to come into our divine self and let it transform us further. That's what aging is for. That's why you are experiencing all these new energies of consciousness, Tom. God is found everywhere now, including in you. Then when you start seeing the world through God's consciousness, in other words, in mystical awareness, it literally becomes the divine world, radiant with love and light and beauty."

After a moment of silence, Tom jumped in. "Rich! Wow! Yes! That puts it all in perspective for me. I see what you are saying. Thank you. Now my question, and it's a very personal and very old one, is how do you live in this awakened state? If you no longer believe in the thought world of identities, stereotypes, norms, roles and governing systems, what do you do?"

"Tom, that's why I described the four states. You learn to move between them. Yes, the World of Man appears as a tragic illusion to awakened consciousness, but it keeps everything in order – time, calendar, schedules, names, Social Security Numbers, addresses, occupations, money, farming, banking, medicine. In its own way, it's absolutely brilliant, though obviously unfair to so many people. It's just not the whole thing, but you can shift any time to the divine world by coming into mystical consciousness. And you keep working on yourself, because we all still have personal issues – old wounds or beliefs – buried in the darkness that pull us back into the conflict-ridden World of Man. So you see, it's a continuous work but as soon as you experience divinity directly, and see Heaven on Earth, the transformation accelerates – it's just too cool to ignore.

"One last thing," Rich said. "I believe that the process of aging itself expands consciousness. As the older person surrenders ego and identity, slows down, stops to 'smell the roses,' and values the remaining years more and more, he or she replaces head with heart, ambition with love, thinking with consciousness. Aging is a journey into a new consciousness, a journey home to the divine in this life. We knew the divine world once as children, we left it to be warriors in the World of Man, and with retirement, we finally hear the call to come home. Aging is enlightenment. All we need to do is pay attention and our mystical consciousness will blossom."

"Yes. Yes. Yes!" Tom exclaimed. "And I have one more

question. What do *you* do personally in this awakened state?"

"I love. I live simply. Things flow by themselves. I enjoy my friends, my grandkids, my wife. I spread this love that I am made of everywhere I go. And 'I,' the fictional me, don't exist much anymore. There's no Rich – just this consciousness. I am what God is, not in some grandiose way but in the joy and love released in conscious being. This is where we are all going in aging. If enough of us can free our consciousness from the prison of beliefs, we can change the world."

Once again silence pervaded the conversation, silence now pregnant with Presence. In this timeless moment, only consciousness remained and the beauty of the faces smiling at one another and the experience of the world as infinitely beautiful, precious and perfect. No one needed to talk at all.

Finally, Clarence turned to Art, cleared his throat, and said gently, "Art, how would you describe a life in mystical consciousness?"

It seemed to take a while for Art to find his voice, as if he had left his body and needed to return and get it started again.

"I lost my sight several years ago from macular degeneration. Prior to becoming a priest, I had been an architect and loved the visual world of forms and structures. Now I know only darkness. But it's the richest kind of darkness. It's not like the unconscious you call darkness, though I understand what you mean; mine is a visual darkness that is full of Presence – my own and God's. I live in that consciousness. Yes, I have learned to navigate the world of objects and tasks, and I do it fairly well in my small surroundings, but it's the dark face of God that I melt into daily. I wake up, think for a moment that there is something 'I' should be doing, then I lay still and feel the Presence envelop me with joy and love. It's like sinking into hot bath water. Yes, I miss the visual splendor of the world, but now I seem to know its inner splendor, because it's in me, too. And in a similar way, I 'see' divinity in everything I encounter, including other people. I hear your voice, feel your proximity, sense your presence, and then it seems as if we combine, like two gasses mixing, and I feel you and know you and love you in ways you can never know. So you see, I have lost the outer sight but gained something astonishing, something that I believe is preparing me for crossing over. I am ninety. Because I see nothing, I feel the next world already mixing with mine. I am waiting to be taken across. I am so excited. I have felt the touch of the divine hand. I am ready, but in no hurry. Either place is okay now."

"Do you believe you are somehow assisting others in this consciousness you describe?" asked Clarence.

"There is only consciousness. In silence, emptiness, and thought-free awareness, the conceptual World of Man goes away. Then, I am in the heart and mind of the universe, of the divine one. I know this helps the world because the love coursing through me is the love the world needs. When I hear of something terrible, I take it into this vast, loving, fathomless interior, and bathe it in God. I can feel it making a difference. I am more than content with this role in the world. I am grateful every day for this experience of divine life.

"Is this a new development, as Rich suggests? I think it is. I believe we are all capable of opening to this consciousness. It's always here. We are lost and alone only if we think we are. Behind, within, everywhere, and holding everything, is Presence. Mystical consciousness melts the walls between people and divinity. And as the individual matures and enters this consciousness, he or she is steadily transformed. We are seeing into the future of our species."

Quiet descended on the group again. The men nibbled at their sandwiches, sipped their tea, and silently shared their gratitude for the meeting. When Art said he was tired, the group bid each other goodbye and each left, lost in wonder.

Chapter 42

For Tom, the present moment opened ever more fully now into the experience of eternity. Identity, time, opinion, personal goals all evaporated in its thoughtless space, though he returned to World of Man when needed to deal with everyday tasks. Tom compared his life to his first trip to Disneyland as a child – always something new and exciting around every corner, and he understood why so many adults loved that imagined version of Heaven on Earth. He walked along the American River, watching turkeys, buzzards, hawks, and secretive coyotes live their unique lives. Sometimes he meditated in the woods by the river, losing himself in its thrumming sound and rapid movement. The frenetic world racing around him had almost no impact on his awakened state. When he wasn't dwelling in the mystical awareness of nature, he was writing, trying to put this new clarity into words that others might understand.

But what kind of life was this? Where was it going? How does one contribute from a state of mystical consciousness? While Tom recognized that these questions were merely thoughts disrupting the crystal-pure silence within, they kept returning as if there was some kind of work yet to do. What was his work now? He did not wish to compete, perform, or prove anything anymore, but he knew that the mystic's journey involved a movement back into the conventional world again, for the work of the enlightened being was to offer his or her illumination for the transformation of society. Tom was a reluctant Bodhisattva and shy prophet, too sensitive for the great battles for power, authority and wealth waged by competing egos in religion, science, politics, and business. But before he could even conceive a course of enlightened action appropriate to his own gentle nature, he needed to consider whether this new stage of consciousness might itself be working through humanity. *Is there such a thing as spiritual evolution?* he wondered. *Will the changes I'm experiencing one day spread more widely?* So Tom did what he always did with big questions in his life, he studied the problem.

Where was humanity going? Where had it come from? Was it still evolving? Was there some cosmic design in this unfolding experiment in consciousness? Tom dug first into recent discoveries in human evolution. He read voraciously in anthropology, archeology and evolutionary biology. On a whim, he Googled the UC Davis anthropology department and telephoned an interesting-sounding professor in the evolutionary wing. Dr. Dianne Powell, an archeologist, had spent an academic lifetime integrating archeology, behavioral ecology, molecular anthropology, paleoanthropology, and biology to study the history and evolution of human beings. She was polite but rushed in their initial phone conversations, answering Tom's questions in a clipped professorial manner and obvious impatience with the naiveté of his queries. Finally, perhaps from accumulating exasperation, she agreed to meet with him on campus. Maybe a half-hour session would get this bothersome psychologist off her back.

In preparation for his first meeting with Dr. Powell, Tom summarized what he had learned so far about human evolution. Apparently the human lineage branched off from its common chimpanzee ancestors some five to seven million years ago. Bipedal australopithecines appeared some four million years ago followed by stone-tool usage 2.6 million years ago, achieving the posthumous designation genus *homo* as a reward. Humans began migrating out of Africa 100,000 years ago in repeated pulses across now nonexistent land bridges, started using fire some 800,000 years ago, and became genetically Homo Sapiens 200,000 years ago, reaching our "modern" genome 40,000 to 50,000 years ago. At that time, there were actually other human-like subspecies including European Neanderthals (who may have settled there one to two million years earlier), Denisovans in

Russia, and a short (3.5 foot) hobbit-like race in Southeast Asia who were precursors to Australian Aborigines. While there is evidence of interaction and interbreeding, all but Homo sapiens disappeared.

Around 40,000 or 50,000 years ago, something very interesting happened that archeologists coined "The Great Leap Forward" or the "Big Bang" of human evolution involving a rapid acceleration in the evolution of both intelligence and culture. It was evidenced in the development of jewelry, symbolic sculptures, tools, improved hunting techniques, trade networks, rituals, clothing, buttons, fishhooks, bone needles, and remarkably beautiful cave paintings. The technological advances inherent in this "Great Leap" apparently freed humans from the evolutionary pressure of natural selection, allowing culture to replace mutations as a survival mechanism in our journey to modernity. Some believed this acceleration was related to increased adaptation pressure caused by catastrophic Earth events, such as volcanic eruptions (the Mount Toba Super Volcano erupted 70,000 years ago in Indonesia producing a global winter lasting six to ten years and reducing human population almost to the point of extinction) or the last ice age 13,000 years ago which buried most of Europe under two miles of ice (when the glaciers melted coastal settlements were wiped out worldwide, an event recorded as the *Great Flood* throughout the world's religious literature). In other words, humans adapted quickly, leading to the next great advance: settlements.

Ten thousand years ago, we began settling down, moving from hunters and gatherers to farmers, initiating the agricultural revolution and the husbanding of plants and animals that further changed the human world. From this development, small farming settlements evolved to hamlets, towns and villages, then cities and city-states, on to empires, and finally nations. In 10,000 short years, less than one tenth of one percent of our entire evolution, and just over 300 generations, we moved from being small, short-lived bands of hunters and gatherers to vast and complex civilizations involving billions of people, their survival now dependent on writing, electricity, mass production, television, automobiles, cell phones, air travel, science, agriculture, medicine, computers, and social media! And our longevity has increased three-fold!

What does all this mean? Tom pondered. He summarized: humans were evolving very slowly over millions of years until roughly 40,000 years ago when artifacts reveal a remarkable explosion in intelligence, culture, and technology. Our social evolution rockets off again 10,000 years ago when hunters and gatherers rapidly evolved into modern humans with a remarkable string of brilliant achievements. While some genetic evolution has continued, and there is debate about just how much, the advances we're seeing now are primarily cultural, scientific and technological, and the rate of change is accelerating.

Then Tom realized something even more startling: the next stage of our evolution is already happening right before our eyes. Our children, so interactive with computers, social media, search engines, and the ever-growing Internet, are rewiring their brains. In fact, the Internet has become an extension of the human brain and mind. We use it all the time to solve problems, find information, keep up with the news, and communicate with one another. Tom could barely remember what it was like before the Internet age. But more importantly, he asked, will this new kind of intelligence, this global interconnectivity and informational explosion, change the way we think?

Dizzy with discovery, Tom arrived at yet another startling observation: we are now poised at the dawn of a revolution in conscious connectivity, one which will occur faster than all our previous changes put together. Indeed the curve of our computer-assisted mental development is rising at an ever-steeper slope, toward...what? Some kind of singularity?

Suddenly, Tom got it. *We are heading toward a global mind, a single global consciousness! What if this increasingly interconnected mind tapped into divinity's universal consciousness, providing everyone with access to its unity?* The implications of this futuristic hypothesis took Tom's breath away. *Wow!* He laughed. *This would be an entirely new kind of human, a human with an active awareness of its own divinity.*

As if his own mind were suddenly moving at the speed of light, Tom's reverie leapt next to the transformation of self and consciousness that he was now experiencing in the aging process. Through ninety-nine percent of recorded history, the vast majority of humans never even experienced the "Midlife Passage" much less a "Late Life Passage." He recalled that his own Midlife Passage had involved his discovery of mysticism, leading to a decade of amazing creativity. Now the Late Life Passage of aging was again transforming his life. Perhaps a consciousness revolution begins the second half of life and reaches its crescendo in the bloom of awakened aging. Moving from an ego-centered to a consciousness-centered orientation, enlightened elders could become the vanguards and wise stewards of a new stage of human evolution. With decreased biological drives and increased maturity, awareness and experience, perhaps enlightened elders were being called to step forward as true sages and social visionaries. And this next leap of human evolution was already happening! *We are evolving right now, this very minute.*

Chapter 43

Tom met Dr. Powell, who preferred being called Dianne, in the brightly lit student union on campus. She promised to wear a bright red shawl over a white blouse and he recognized her immediately. The cafeteria was noisy and crowded, so they took their lunches onto the far side of the patio. An acutely perceptive woman with graying hair tied back with a practical clip, she watched Tom with some curiosity. She was irritated with herself for agreeing to waste precious research time with a nutty psychologist. She wasn't even convinced that psychology was a legitimate science. *Oh well, let's get this over with,* she thought. As she watched Tom more closely she noticed her feelings softening some. He was cheerful, pleasantly dressed, not unattractive for an older guy, with a well-trimmed white beard and amazingly not-yet-gray brown hair. *Maybe this will be fun. Whatever.*

"So," Dianne began, "you said something in your last phone call about evolution and mysticism. How can these opposites possibly be connected?"

Tom did not know how to get into this, especially with an academic scientist. She would have no idea what he was talking about. Then he had an inspiration.

"Do you remember that neuroscientist back east who had a left-hemisphere stroke, and during her stroke noticed a profound shift in her consciousness? She described the boundaries of her self and body dissolving, and her consciousness opening to a timeless and ecstatic space. In the absence of her left-hemisphere language functions, particularly her normal chatter of judgments and opinions, the idea of herself no longer existed and she discovered a most blissful and loving state of awareness. While her recovery was as difficult as any stroke victim, her awakening had been a completely unexpected gift. She concluded that Nirvana, Buddhist enlightenment, exists in the consciousness of the right cerebral hemisphere, and that its deep peace is always available when we learn to silence the brain's chatter, as many learn to do in meditation." Tom hoped that recalling this neuroscientist's experience might lend credibility to his own explanations of mystical consciousness.

"I do recall something of that woman's account. And, you will undoubtedly be surprised to know, I am a serious meditator. In fact, I always do better work after meditating, though I've never had any mystical experiences."

"Perfect! Do you notice," Tom leaned forward, "that your sensory perception is more acute after meditating, as if the world were brighter and more beautiful than before, or that a sense of peace continues for some time reducing your emotional reactivity? Do you notice feelings of contentment or happiness in the minutes afterward?"

"Yes on all the above," Dianne replied. "But what does that have to do with your mystical evolution?"

"Imagine increasing the intensity of your experience ten-fold, what would you experience?"

"OK. I can imagine an amazing wonderland of light and color and beauty, especially if my left hemisphere were quiet...

"You know," she added, "I did have such an experience as a child. It was during a hard time – my parents were fighting, and I used to escape into the woods beyond the back fence to be alone. Well, I was sitting up in a tree, must have been seven or eight years old, and suddenly I felt as if the tree loved me and I was being held in a timeless embrace. Everything stopped and I knew I would be okay no matter what happened with my parents. And a voice in my head – God? – seemed to say, 'This is the my world. You are part of it and part of me.' I sat there for what seemed like hours, though it may have been only minutes. I was okay when I climbed down. I haven't shared that with anyone until now."

"Dianne, I have found that when I ask people to remember

experiences like that in classes and workshops, almost everyone can find one, though most at first don't recognize their experience as mystical. You just did. That's the consciousness I'm talking about."

"What does that have to do with anthropology?"

"Ah, that's the question I wanted to discuss with you. Are you up for it?"

"I am now."

Tom reviewed his admittedly superficial grasp of human evolution as briefly as possible, not wishing to embarrass himself with his ignorance. *It's funny how worried self-judging thoughts return when you're feeling anxious,* he noted to himself. On concluding, he asked, "Do you agree that the pace of cultural, technological, and scientific change is rapidly increasing? We have gone from hunters and gatherers to moon walkers in ten thousand years! What is happening and how is this accelerating pace of change affecting our consciousness? And what's coming next?"

Dianne sat back a little dumbfounded. She hadn't expected this kind of question. She was already off balance from their unexpected discussion of her own childhood mystical experience. How to respond? She bit her lip, eyebrows came together in a thoughtful frown, and after a moment, she began.

"When my mother was dying of cancer, I spent an entire week with her in the hospital, day after day, night after night. She slept a lot, so it was sometimes boring. But other times I would stay up half the night with her, becoming really sleep deprived. Over the course of the week, I began to feel as if the world outside didn't exist, that only our intense union existed. I don't know why I am saying this, but I think that's what you're talking about, a state beyond normal identities and roles. It's not evolution, or not in the scientific sense, but it is a state of consciousness that I came to feel was sacred. How that connects with the pace of change, I don't know, but I think it is related. This intense interconnectedness we are forging everywhere in the world as you described may become the kind of oneness that will hold us all, like the tree held me, if it infused with consciousness. I know it wasn't the tree itself that held me, it was something mysterious, beautiful and holy, an omnipresence of some kind. You know, Einstein said that the most beautiful thing we can experience is the mysterious, and that mystery is what you are describing."

"Yes, it's about the mystery that is revealed when thought ceases and the senses open to existence itself. But I return to my question. Where do you think this is going? You study human evolution, does this fit in somewhere?"

"This is far beyond my expertise, and my colleagues would embarrass me to death if they were listening this conversation. That said, I can only guess that the existence of our Earth, just the way it is, filled with such rich diversity of life and consciousness, is so unlikely a possibility in the vast, empty and inhospitable stretches of space that it's all a miracle, and that science is just one way of grasping that miracle. Since evolution is part of that miracle, I am happy to let it unfold and I will study it scientifically; what you mystic psychologists do is up to you. I know I didn't answer your question, but I do share your awe and wonder."

"Do you think that consciousness is contributing to cultural evolution?"

"Insofar as consciousness is somehow related to enlightenment, like that neuroscientist's experience, and insofar as human beings are becoming more consciousness, which I believe is a part of our cultural progression, then yes, it is, though I can't tell you exactly how. But I think certain kinds of people are drawn to this edge – you know the type: the sixties' boomers, serious meditators, spiritual seekers, folks ingesting mind-altering drugs, and so forth. You might say that we are all born with the hard-wired capacity for mystical consciousness but some people are more driven than others to finding it. Of course, this natural capacity for non-ordinary experience goes as far back as the earliest shamans but now we have so many more people exploring consciousness and sharing their discoveries, which in turn affects others. Who knows what might happen?"

As always, Tom was stunned. Though he was getting used to being surprised by these unexpected encounters with mystically oriented folks, he was always grateful. An hour had passed. Dianne looked at her watch in shock, apologized and took off for scheduled student conference, waving goodbye and offering to meet again if he were interested. Tom drove slowly back to Sacramento, loving the wide-open delta sky on either side of the Yolo Causeway. Feeling somehow validated, he still wasn't sure where the evolution of consciousness was going – it was indeed a mystery, but one he wanted to be part of.

Chapter 44

Sitting once again at his desk in his home office, Tom fiddled with a paper clip, straightening and bending it back over and over, as if he were trying to straighten out his thoughts. Reviewing his notes on the history of human evolution, he sensed a larger pattern operating, one that involved stages of growth and change, each accelerating in pace, with later stages transcending evolutionary principles altogether. He tried to put his thoughts in order.

Humanity's first six or seven million years of evolution were extremely slow and primarily biological in nature, driven by the standard evolutionary forces of mutation and natural selection. The pace quickened 40,000 years ago with the "Great Leap Forward" arising from astonishing intellectual and cultural gains. With the resulting growth of technology in the subsequent 10,000 years, racing from agriculture and animal husbandry to the industrial revolution, automobiles, science and the development of computers, Internet, and social media, humankind's rate of change had exploded, racing faster than anyone could have anticipated. The next stage, Tom believed, would somehow be found or created in mystical consciousness, though he still could not see how this would work.

If you drew a model of these stages, Tom thought, *it would be a pyramid with biology at the bottom and mysticism at the top.* The dramatic acceleration in the rate of change made sense now – biological changes would be the slowest, intellectual advances would come faster with technology-created positive feedback loops accelerating the pace of change even more, and finally, mystical realizations which could happen in a single moment and, to the extent they were contagious, might result in perceptions of the divine world breaking through in the most unlikely places, setting human consciousness on fire.

With all this in mind, Tom decided to devote himself once again to writing, teaching, blogging, and speaking – at the retreat center, churches, aging conferences, continuing-education seminars, and online sites. He wrote a book on the spirituality of aging and contributed chapters to other people's aging books. With no particular plan in mind, he simply wanted to bring people into this discussion. He was pushing hard to force a cultural breakthrough; he wanted to share the knowledge he could no longer keep inside.

After a year of frenzied productivity, Tom woke up one morning and realized he was exhausted. He had fallen back into his old, well-worn pattern of over-performance, relentlessly pushing himself to produce, but this time it didn't work. Instead of feeling happy and productive, he felt empty, tired and despondent. Worse, it was affecting his energy and mood. He felt like a collapsed house of cards. His hectic schedule had replaced his time with Rich in recent months as he begged off one date after another with so much on his plate. No longer wanting to continue this ego-driven productivity, Tom finally called Rich and they scheduled a visit. This time Tom couldn't wait to talk. He had run out of gas and sensed this dead-end had something to do with the miracle of aging.

They met at the same little coffee shop, greeted each other warmly, ordered their coffees and pastries, and settled at a table near the front window. A stormy winter day, the wind swirled the leaves, small lakes formed in every depression, and the weatherman prophesized more of the same.

"Tom, how are you? Catch me up. You've been so busy. I can't wait to hear all you've accomplished."

After a deep sigh, Tom responded, "I'm worn out. I feel tired all the time. I feel like a hamster on its wheel. I'm not having fun. To tell you the truth, I feel run down and depressed. I no longer look forward to writing or speaking. I feel like crap."

"Yes, you do look tired, Tom. You've got bags under your

eyes, your face is drawn, and your usual buoyancy is missing. I think you are making one of those all-too-common aging mistakes."

"Which is?"

"To pressure yourself with the goals and values normally associated with the middle years. I call it compulsive productivity. You are still acting like the compulsive warrior, driving yourself to succeed. You did that for four decades and you accomplished a lot, but that ego state does not work in this time of life. You are trying to push the river. The hero mentality is now a false self that will not save you or the world. That kind of striving actually takes you further and further from enlightened aging. This is a time of transformation, Tom. Youthful, ego-driven ambition dies so that the divine can flow into the elder's awakening consciousness. In fact, the spiritual work of aging is to intentionally stay in mystical consciousness in order to further empty yourself, quickening the inflow of divinity. Then the ego serves the soul. 'You' as an identity only exist now as a convenient fiction – what you really are is consciousness, divine consciousness. Your old false self is wearing you out. Let it go; don't try to resurrect it. Instead, simply try to merge pure consciousness with your own being. Then 'you' will dissolve into the natural flow of divine life. You don't have to do anything, just let it happen."

As Tom was listening, he was already letting go, shifting back into mystical consciousness. "Rich, that makes so much sense. I've been pushing myself for months. When I now drop back into mystical consciousness, and bring this consciousness into my own physical being and energy, it feels like sinking into a deep feather pillow." Tom took a deep breath, let his shoulders drop, and relaxed. "And I sense now in this moment that fatigue is itself an energy reconnecting me to the state of conscious being you describe. I can feel myself healing even as we talk, sensing this fatigue dissolving so that I can more naturally and spontaneously do whatever feels right. It's like Taoism's idea of 'effortless effort' – it just happens like the wind moves across the landscape or the way water runs downhill. This feels so much better! Thank you, Rich!"

Tom sat in the delicious descent into the pure energy of physical being. He could feel his tension draining away, like water going down the drain. In the silence of consciousness being, Tom sat quietly in wonder while Rich looked on in obvious pleasure, nibbling his croissant.

Abruptly, a new version of the question that had been nagging Tom for months popped into mind. *If change doesn't come from ego-driven work, like I tried to do, how does a new civilization arise from mystical consciousness? We've talked about oneness, but what about form, about the new forms culture will evolve from shared mystical awareness.* Tom found himself thinking back on the first time he read Thoreau's *Walden* in high school. Here was a man who found mystical consciousness by himself in the woods. He wrote a marvelous book but little happened from there. Tom then remembered reading psychologist B.F. Skinner's visionary sequel *Walden Two* in college. It was supposed to be a scientific approach to constructing a modern utopia but was never attempted. Tom doubted that Skinner's vision could work in its original form, missing as it did the both the dark side of humanity – the irrational unconscious was not so easily conditioned, and the profundity of the mystical dimension – which Skinner frankly denied. Tom was suddenly intrigued by the new possibility of a *Walden Three* forming spontaneously from mystical consciousness. But how might this work?

As if waking up from a dream, Tom suddenly realized that he had pursued this entire train of thought without sharing any of it with Rich, so he backtracked and together they reflected on how this new and divine world might come about.

"If conscious being is not about ambitious plans, active doing, or forcing things to happen," Tom resumed, "how does a new world happen?"

Rich sat back, ran his hand through his thinning white hair, looked off into space, and finally replied, "Well, first of all, it's part of the cosmic evolutionary mystery that Pierre de Chardin described as the universe's creative impulse toward greater and greater complexity – in other words, God. But it moves through the generations in different ways. We'll get to the younger generation in a moment, but for us, it's about aging, Tom. Ten thousand boomers turn sixty-five every day and they'll live longer than any previous generation in history. It's a tsunami of change. If even a fraction of these people move into mystical consciousness, imagine what could happen. If I am correct in my theory that aging is enlightenment in slow motion, mystical consciousness will change the world. The most important thing an elder can do is to notice this evolution of consciousness." Rich emphasized the word "notice," underscoring its power. "Then, as identity and persona dissolve, an elder will find that this new consciousness is everywhere, around and through him. This is non-heroic aging. It's not about overcoming obstacles or defeating enemies, but permitting the flow of divine creativity to move in your own interior to form a new center of awareness and action."

"You know," Tom responded, "this reminds me of a program Walt Disney did many years ago to explain a nuclear reaction. As I recall, he placed hundreds of mousetraps close together in a room, each with a ping-pong ball resting on its spring-loaded snap bar, and then tossed a single ping-pong ball into the center of the room. The ball hit one trap; it went off sending its ball to hit a couple more, and they hit even more, and the effect increased rapidly until the whole room was a sea of flying ping pong balls. Maybe elder consciousness will spread like this, only not quite so fast."

Something else was rattling around in Tom's thought processes. "Rich, consider this. The elder's transformation of self and consciousness that you've been describing is happening at the same time as the Internet revolution is rewiring human brains. As the globe gets wired into the Internet, citizens of this digital age will have almost instantaneous access to local and international news, all the scientific, technical, and historical information humanity has acquired, a digital library of all the books ever written, instant opinion surveys and crowd-sourced solutions to all manner of problems, social activism on all levels, participation in law enforcement and identification of political and corporate corruption, self-paced education for all, a new distribution of vocational opportunity and economic resources, incredible creativity in all the arts, new marketing tools, greatly increased voter participation in the democratic process, and language translation programs fostering communication between everyone on the planet, not to mention self-driving cars, artificial intelligence, robots, and new technological develop-ments every day. And that's just the beginning! Think about private-sector space travel and new energy sources. In other words, new cultural forms are emerging at a record pace!"

With a radiant smile, Rich jumped in. "Can you imagine the implications of these trends? People will no longer identify with country and state; they may refuse to join the military and partic-ipate in wars; many will move beyond money to barter goods and services; everyone who wants can self-publish, the changes go on and on. But there is the dark side as well – government Internet surveillance, rampant spying, hacking, scamming and stalking; crime pursued on the untraceable 'dark' Internet; and political extremists plotting disruption and violence. It is an incredible time in the human experience."

"So how does this vast cultural revolution intersect with aging's mystical consciousness?" Tom asked aloud. Then another idea came to mind. "I remember doing neuropsychological evaluations early in my professional practice. Brain-behavior relationships fascinated me and the ability of psychological tests to identify areas of brain dysfunction was amazing. I learned how bilateral the brain really was: left hemisphere for language and conceptual functions, right hemisphere for visual-spatial awareness, frontal lobes for planning and execution. But there was more. As that neuroscientist observed, mystical consciousness is housed in the right hemisphere. I think this brain specialization contributes both to our evolution and our mystical awakening."

"What do you mean?" Rich asked.

"My hunch is that early Homo sapiens, hunters and gatherers, were far more mystically inclined, using right-brain non-language awareness to survive, creating Earth-centered religions as a result. These early humans lived in a conscious world where boundaries between people, animals, and Earth processes were pretty porous – all things were understood as sentient beings, allowing a deep sense of interconnection with the resources necessary for survival. As language developed, the awesome power of communication and conceptual mapping offered tremendous new survival tools. Now humans could write, record discoveries, map their new territories, pass on complicated advances in agriculture and technology, and so forth. As a result, the left brain took over and we lost touch with our mystical consciousness. In this new aging, we are coming home to our original 'Garden consciousness' without having to give up our conceptual understanding of the universe. But my bigger question is how will this resurfacing mystical consciousness interact with the Internet revolution?

"The young are working with left-brain conceptual intelligence, making new products, inventing new forms of connectivity, and in the process, building a revolutionary new communication and participation structure. Sure, they use their right-brain imaginative and spatial talents, but mostly in the service of a left-brain order and technological invention. At the other end, enlightened elders are moving back into mystical consciousness and learning to live more authentically from the experience of conscious being grounded in divinity. How will the young and the old come together? We are looking for a new marriage of left and right hemispheres, science and mysticism, young and old, human and divine. Where will it come from?"

With a particularly thoughtful look on his face, Tom said, "Let me just talk this through and see where I end up. The Internet revolution is rewiring the world and our brains – it's an explosion of interconnectivity driven by the young. The young are focusing on changing the world – as they should, that's their job. And demographers tell us that the millennial generation, born between 1982 and 2002, will be the most civic-minded generation in decades. They want to work together to repair the damage done by previous generations. At the same time, the new aging and its expansion of mystical consciousness is creating a generation of enlightened elders. They want love to prevail – good will, kindness, inclusion, and joy. They want to support this creativity with wisdom and balance. Both processes are happening at the same time. How will they come together? I'm beginning to wonder if a larger divine intelligence is behind both, driving different functions for the young and the old."

Picking up the hypothetical thread, Rich mused, "Maybe the more elders wake up, the more the world will wake up. Awakened consciousness spreads as it did between you and your patient Paul, as it often does in meditation groups. As the aperture of awareness opens for one person, another's awareness expands as well. Maybe the next important question is: What is the critical mass or tipping point of mystically conscious elders that will change the culture and bring some kind of unified enlightenment? If that happens, the elders' mystical consciousness will spread throughout the interconnected world, not only calming and healing people but affecting the consciousness of the young who are doing this rewiring. The young may actually be contributing to this growth in consciousness by rewiring their own brains, an intermediary step before that rewiring absorbs consciousness and becomes a new kind of human."

Rich and Tom chewed on this bone for another hour before Rich signaled *his* exhaustion. "I've had it, Tom. Gotta get home and give myself a rest. This has been great fun. I love these conversations. Let me know when the next one needs to happen."

Chapter 45

Buzzing with energy, Tom looked forward to figuring out what to do next. If divine consciousness were driving evolution, cosmic intelligence becoming aware of itself through human consciousness, pushing individuals toward more awakened states, why should he pursue any other goals at all? Why not just watch, wait, and go with the flow, see what happens? But then it occurred to Tom that older people undergoing these expansions of consciousness might mistake them for a mental breakdown or even dementia. And if his hypothesis was correct, that aging created a natural flowering of enlightenment, shouldn't elders be informed about what they might experience and given instructions for supporting its unfolding power in their own lives? He needed a larger platform than the retreat center. Why not a newspaper article? Of course, the *Sacramento Bee*!

Founded in 1857, the *Sacramento Bee* is the major newspaper for Northern California and the Central Valley, long ago defeating its main competitor, the *Sacramento Union*, which closed its doors in 1994. Like most papers, "The Bee" reinvented itself during the web boom and now has both print and online editions. Located in midtown along a leafy boulevard, it is the voice of the state capital.

Tom Googled the *Bee's* religion editor and wrote him an email about his theory that aging was a kind of enlightenment in slow motion that was probably confusing or disturbing to elders who may need some spiritual guidance. Two days later, Tom's phone rang.

"Hello. Is this Dr. McLaughlin?"

"Yes it is."

"Hi, Dr. McLaughlin, this is Terry Kline, the religion editor at the *Bee*. I got your email and I have to confess I have never read anything like it, and I hear from a lot of strange people, not to imply you are one of them. At first I thought I would just ignore your message or say it didn't fit my parameters, but the more I thought about your thesis, the more curious I became. Do you have a few minutes to talk about this?"

"Of course, and call me Tom. I'm glad you called."

"Thank you, Tom. So tell me, what kinds of things might elders be noticing that represent enlightenment in disguise? What do you have in mind?"

"Great question. Let me go over a few. Consider the common aging experience of a fading identity, as if the 'you' you used to be isn't so real or solid anymore. And, related to this, is an unexpected relief that you feel when you don't have to be anyone anymore. No more putting on the costume of identity. Does that make sense?"

"I'm only fifty-five, so I'm not quite in the age range you're talking about, but I have been kind of realizing that I'm really not who I thought I was or wanted to be. Plus when I retire, who will I be then?"

"You've got it! Who you think you are has always been a fiction, an important one for establishing a place in the adult world, but fictional nonetheless. It's what the famous psychoanalyst Carl Jung called the persona – our social mask. And by the end of the middle years, it often feels old, tiresome, and increasingly phony."

"Well that fits, but how is that enlightenment or, what did you call it, 'enlightenment in slow motion?'"

"Central to enlightenment, Terry, is a consciousness free from the filter of concepts, beliefs, expectations and identity. Your self-idea begins to fade because it is just an idea and it's a boring one now. And along with its disappearance people often discover a lessening of the ambition that was part of that persona. You get tired of fighting the same old windmills. Aging is like an emptying of all that stuff. Now, instead of thinking you're 'somebody,' you discover that you're really just the consciousness in which that 'somebody idea' was formed.

"Now another part of this emptying is what happens with memory. Older people start reporting that they're forgetting things all the time. Well, much of what they forget is the endless minutia of names, facts, dates, places, even your own past. It's not senility, it's this letting go of all the detritus of middle age – schedules, words, names of people you rarely see, and all the useless facts accumulated since childhood. This forgetting further cleanses consciousness.

"Finally, older people, at least the ones who are still growing, increasingly lose interest in material things. They are no longer so attached to stuff. This too is part of the emptying of consciousness, because stuff for elders is mostly a distraction and responsibility they no longer want. Stuff only became important because of its importance to the ego – fancy homes, cars, possessions, art. When the self-idea dissolves, its attachment to stuff also dissolves."

"OK, Tom, but why is consciousness so important? I know from my education in religion that Buddhism and Hinduism tell you to wake up from these illusions, especially the illusion of self, but what happens then?"

"That's the million-dollar question, and here you have to let your old mindset go. Our customary reality assumptions, bequeathed from our everyday culture, tell us that God is separate from us and that consciousness is merely an epiphenomenon of brain functioning. But those folks who have had direct experiences of the divine say that consciousness *is* God, that this consciousness is everywhere, and that it's only the idea of 'me' that creates the illusions that I'm separate and that consciousness is 'mine.' In moments of thought-free silence, we also discover that this consciousness is actually a 'Presence' – more than that, it is divine, intelligent and loving.

"As thought dissolves into this consciousness," Tom continued, "the 'self' construct disappears, leaving this larger consciousness as our real self. The mystics from every religion tell us that we are all eventually destined to experience divinity as our own nature. Directly experiencing this consciousness produces a kind of transmutation – every part of you is transformed by this living, intelligent force. I think its purpose is the evolution of a new kind of human, one much more loving, sensitive, selfless, intelligent and wise, and a new humanity capable of finally ending poverty, war, and the degradation of Earth's life systems. My goal is to show elders how important their growth of consciousness can be for themselves, for their families, and for humanity at large.

"And not to overwhelm you further, but the mystics also tell us that this awakened awareness transforms our perception. We see not a world of problems and issues, but a world of radiance and beauty. You discover that the divine has become the world and the world is literally holy. I know it sounds crazy, but you see Heaven on Earth all around you."

"Tom, Tom, slow down, stop. I am swamped. Can we go over all that again? I'd like to take notes this time and then see if I can understand your theory and come up with an article for the Sunday religion section. At the very least, the idea that aging as a kind of spiritual transformation could give elders new hope and change the way we look at aging's difficulties. Is that OK with you?"

"Of course. I love that you are open to the possibilities of this new aging."

After repeating and extending his theory of aging, Tom hung up. *A great start,* he thought, *and from a credible* Bee *writer. At least the idea of enlightened aging will be out there in the public conversation.* Things were beginning to happen.

Chapter 46

In Sunday's Religion Section of the *Sacramento Bee* could be found this headline: "Spirituality, Aging and the New Humanity." Terry's article roughly summarized Tom's theory of aging as a process of subtle enlightenment. He quoted Tom liberally and had most of the points right. Tom wondered what traditionally religious people would make of his theory. The idea that aging was a new developmental stage meant for the transformation of humanity, well, that was pretty far out. *We'll see*, he thought, *we'll see*.

What did happen, however, was completely unexpected. Because of its novelty, optimism, and rather sensational thesis – that elders could experience God directly, Terry Kline's religion piece was picked up by the wire service and soon spread though the blogosphere. The tsunami built slowly at first. Reporters began calling Tom and articles appeared in niche or New Age publications. One interviewer asked Tom about the likely cultural impact of this elder-centered enlightenment and he prophesized a variety of changes. Enlightened elders would either leave organized religion, choosing direct mystical consciousness in place of institutional programs, or reinvent religion as a vehicle of more radical cultural change. Deeply committed to peace, social justice and equality, they might stand up against war and military solutions to world problems. Capitalism's preoccupation with material consumption might be replaced with the local exchange of goods and services, creating more fair and balanced communities and undermining the hold of advertisers and large corporations. Fame, fortune, and movie stars would hold little interest to them and violence in sports and cinema would be avoided. Personal security would be found in meaningful relationships and intentional communities rather than insurance companies, savings accounts or home alarms.

Above all, love would be the organizing motive behind their lives; how they expressed it, from social activism at one end of the continuum to mystical communion at the other, would be different and unique for each person. As the interviewer observed, these consciousness-driven changes could transform society as we know it.

Most of the interviews seemed a little too intellectual or tame for the average consumer, until the day a conservative Sacramento "shock-jock" radio personality picked up the thread and blasted Tom for betraying Christianity, patriotism, and the American Way. From there, the backlash grew rapidly. Tom's message was portrayed as the rantings of a cult lunatic or communist revolutionary. If his prognostications were correct, the whole financial and military fabric of the country would collapse. As soon as the first shock-jock grabbed the bone, others went after it, demanding that Tom be investigated for fomenting revolution, terrorism, and religious heresy. The rising vitriol was amazing and equally horrifying, and the wildfire of acerbic opinion continued to spread. Telephone calls became threatening, interviews more caustic, and the consensus among serious conservatives was that Tom needed to be stopped. He ceased answering the home phone, changed his cell number, and reported threats to the police.

Despite the rising cultural madness, Tom's equanimity held. He observed this crazed cacophony as if from the still center of a cyclone. Ronnie was far less relaxed and eventually decided to escape the hostile tidal wave by visiting their son's family in the Bay Area. As he had so many times before, Tom called Clarence. It was time for coffee.

Chapter 47

The coffee shop was more crowded than usual, causing Tom to worry about being recognized and hassled. He thought he noticed people looking at him, and the atmosphere felt tense, though he could not say why. Absently-mindedly swirling the cream in his coffee and speaking above the noise, Tom quickly reviewed all that had happened and concluded, "Clarence, it's been just crazy! I've had slanderous attacks from the media and scary telephone threats; and Ronnie left town to escape the circus. Why this backlash from such a simple and hopeful article?"

"Speaking of scary, how *do* you feel?"

"At the deepest level I feel completely at peace. There is a stillness inside me, an equanimity, a fathomless space, where God's consciousness flows in like a breath. From that place, the phenomenal world swirling around me is just that – temporary forms and stories that upset others but don't touch me. But at the upper emotional level of my personality, I do find fear and worry. What's going to happen? How do I fix this?"

"Tom, it's obvious that the popular culture is very threatened by your understanding of enlightenment. The vast majority of people build lives on culturally sanctioned hopes and fears, never realizing that they are illusions. But it's what people believe, and your words take away their security, pulling the rug out from under them. And remember, mystics in every religion have been persecuted as heretics or criminals because their personal liberation undermines the political and church author-ities. People in power do not want to surrender it."

Suddenly the restaurant's front window shattered. Glass flew everywhere. People screamed. Everyone fell to the floor. A fire began burning by the counter. The owner, with blood streaming down his face, stood up and began beating the fire with his wet towel. Tom called 911 on his cell phone, looked around, saw a man running down the street into the park, and then found a fire extinguisher behind the counter. In short order, the customers put the fire out, administered first aid, and insisted the owner lie down and wait for the paramedics. Some people left, most stayed to give reports. Sirens announced the arrival of the police and ambulance. Tom waved them in and the place was crawling with professionals. After two hours of waiting, questioning, and waiting some more, the patrons were allowed to go home. Tom called Ronnie, reassured her that he and Clarence were safe, and promised to consider joining her at their son's house.

As Tom and Clarence walked watchfully toward the parking lot behind the coffee shop, they reflected on what just happened.

Clarence began, "This is exactly what we were talking about. This is not a coincidence. This is what persecution looks like. It's not theoretical. You were the target, Tom. From here on, you have to be especially careful."

From his timeless consciousness, Tom replied, "I am not afraid, but this situation presents a dilemma. People who love me will picture this as a terrifying drama. I am not this drama. I am the consciousness it passes through; I am the love that flows from within that consciousness."

"Tom, get back on the reality channel. You're playing with fire. You can die. In the great spiritual scheme of things, this event may have no significance but in the temporal world of everyday people, your dying would be a terrible tragedy. A lot of people would be deeply hurt."

"So if I participate in the drama, I am reinforcing fearful illusions. If I don't, I risk hurting people. What's the answer?"

"Perhaps the answer continues to be what your patient Paul concluded: Keep it to yourself, act the expected part, and look for ways to gently lead others into wisdom and enlightenment. It is a slow transition from the World of Man to Heaven on Earth. If you handed people Heaven on a platter in their present state of mind, they would throw it away as useless. You've tried. This transition will take time."

Until there was a better way, Tom agreed. He stayed centered in consciousness, resting in its profound equanimity and eternity. Nothing could touch it. Nothing could pollute, modify or limit it. Deathless, timeless, silent, motionless, luminous, loving, forever, this Presence was becoming his real self. Or perhaps more accurately, his "normal" self was dissolving into divinity as his true nature. From this center, planning was unimportant for there was no future, no past, no problems, no one to be – just the moment-to-moment flow of conscious being. Acting like a "normal" person was necessary, being one was not. A vast new depth of consciousness had opened. He was now a transitional being, not yet final, but no longer who he was.

Chapter 48

When the police came to his house, Tom expected more questioning about the firebombing. He soon learned that was not their agenda.

"Dr. McLaughlin, I am Detective Hendricks and this is Detective Rodriguez. May we come in? We have some questions we need to ask you."

"Of course. Come in." Tom opened the front door and led them into the living room.

"Sir, you were firebombed last week. You have been the subject of some pretty negative press. And frankly, that *Sac Bee* interview you gave the religion editor was a little far out. We don't know how to put all this together. But we have learned that where there's smoke, there's fire – no pun intended, and the smoke is all around you. Are you engaged in any religious activities that might be related to these attacks? Do you know anyone in particular who might want to hurt you?"

When Tom finally closed his mouth, he could hardly find his voice. "Me? You think I am connected to these attacks?"

"Why would anyone want to hurt you? Why would you have enemies?"

"I don't have enemies. The *Bee* article just threatened the establishment, I guess."

"May we look around your house?"

"I guess so."

Detectives Hendricks and Rodrigues walked around the downstairs inspecting each room, then the upstairs, then the garage and patio, provoking Charlie to a frenzy of barking. Tom followed passively, dumbfounded, careful. In the garage, they found a can of gasoline and some rags. Tom wasn't sure he'd noticed the can before. The gas on the rags smelled fresh.

"What's this gas for?" Detective Hendricks asked, who now

seemed to have taken charge of the interrogation.

"I have no idea. It's probably Erik's, something he uses to clean his cleats. Or the gardener's. I don't know. Why is that important?"

"There was a similar firebombing at the First Christian Church of Mayhew. Someone torched the sanctuary one night last week. You had some problems with that church a while back, didn't you?"

"I had a patient whose wife was threatened by my treating him. She arranged a demonstration. It all blew over."

"But it's a little odd, don't you think, that two firebombings are connected through you."

"I didn't bomb anybody."

"Where were you last Tuesday between midnight and two in the morning?"

"I was asleep."

"Can your wife corroborate that?"

"She wasn't home. She went to stay with our son and his wife in the Bay Area after the threatening phone calls started. I've already reported them. She didn't feel safe here."

"So you have no alibi."

Just then, a call came in on Detective Rodriguez's radio. He stepped outside. When he returned, he whispered something to Detective Hendricks. They both looked at Tom. Detective Hendricks said, "We just learned that Emma Jensen was also attacked Tuesday night. The smoke is getting thicker. I think you need to come down to the station with us."

"You're kidding," Tom said. "Why would I do anything like that?"

"Exactly."

Tom was placed in the back of the patrol car and taken downtown. He was booked, fingerprinted, and placed in a bare and smelly interrogation room, worse than any he had seen on television. Tom could not believe this was happening. How could they possibly connect any of this with him?

After nearly forty minutes, Detectives Hendricks and Rodriguez came into the room. "Thank you for being so patient. We have some more questions for you." Before beginning, they read Tom his Miranda Rights.

The interrogation went on for three and a half hours. Same questions over and over again. Where he had been, who were his enemies, why did he have the gasoline, when did he get it, when was he last at the Mayhew church? On and on. None of it made sense. It was exhausting. At the end of the questioning, Detective Hendricks said, "Dr. McLaughlin, you are under arrest for the assault of Emma Jensen and the firebombing of the First Christian Church of Mayhew."

Tom was placed in jail garb, fingerprinted, photographed, and a DNA sample taken. His arraignment was scheduled for the next day and he finally got to call Ronnie to get her searching for a bail bondsman and a criminal attorney. He was led to a cell.

That night, in the thick heavy darkness before dawn, Tom remembered the mystical experience of the great Indian mystic Sri Aurobindo. Arrested for his anti-British revolutionary activities at the dawn of the twentieth century, he was jailed and had one of the greatest mystical experiences on record. The walls, bars, blankets, other prisoners, and jailors, all became versions of the divine. For him, God had literally and concretely become the world. As Tom recalled Aurobindo's experience, and as he descended into his self-aware consciousness, he, too, began to see that everything was infused with – no composed of – divinity. In this timeless moment, deep from the silence within, he saw that only God existed, conscious and aware and fully present. Tom let himself melt into this experience of divine being. The room filled with light. His body filled with light. The light of consciousness spread throughout his being. Tom did not sleep that night. He was in what some have called the "unvarying Presence of the numinous."

Chapter 49

The press had been tipped off that Dr. McLaughlin was in jail, accused of assault and firebombing. His arraignment sparked a media frenzy about "that crazy cult psychologist" assaulting a former patient and bombing her church – it made for sensational headlines. Ronnie posted bail, hired a criminal attorney and notified the kids. Watching her world fall apart before her eyes, she was becoming increasingly frazzled. What kind of husband was this who could cause so much trouble? She huddled with Laura and Erik in legal planning sessions as if they were criminal defendants themselves. What a nightmare.

The day of Tom's arraignment, the courtroom was packed with press, the curious, and friends. The charges were read, pleas of "not guilty" recorded, and Tom was released on bail in the company of his family and attorney.

In spite of the surrounding clamor, Tom was still detached, drenched in a serenity that puzzled family and friends. Why was he not more upset? Certainly everyone else was, no dearth of distress there. Tom steadfastly denied all the charges. His attorney hired a PI to investigate Emma's allegations and both firebombings, and a trial date was tentatively set the following month.

"Tom! What's going on here? How did this happen and why are you so friggin' calm about it all?" Ronnie began in the car on the ride home.

Tom picked his words carefully. "Ronnie, I'm OK. All this is police conjecture. I had nothing to do with that woman's assault or those firebombings. Hey – I was the object of one of the bombings, remember? Would I bomb myself? This is all crazy and I will be cleared. You have to trust and believe in me."

"But you seem so peaceful in this nightmare. Are you on drugs? I can't tell if you're the same man I married or not."

"Mom," Laura interjected, coming to the support her struggling parents, "Dad is fine. I don't pretend to understand his serenity, but I know he's OK. He has found an inner peace. I think he's onto an insight or psychological practice that could affect the mental health of future generations. I know you're freaked out, but give him a break. You guys probably just need some time together. Go away. Go to Santa Cruz for the weekend and chill out."

Exactly, Tom thought.

Chapter 50

The beach extended in a full half-moon before their favorite beach town, Rio Del Mar, just south of Santa Cruz. The day was cold, growing colder as the evening approached. The wind had picked up and the sky was overcast. Only a handful of people were out walking their dogs or picking up driftwood on the beach. Seagulls called and circled garbage cans and the parking lot was mostly empty.

Tom and Ronnie had arrived the night before. The moment they opened the car doors and smelled the cold, salt air, the magic happened as it always did at this beach – and they relaxed. The tension of the previous week that had filled the car on the drive down instantly began to melt away. What a relief. That night Ronnie slept with neither insomnia nor nightmares.

The following afternoon, with the steady, soporific sound of waves breaking on hard gray sand, Tom and Ronnie were lulled into the familiar intimacy of their long relationship. Bundled up warmly, they strolled along the tide line for an hour and were now heading back to the little coffee shop across the parking lot.

Settling at one of the many empty tables, hands warming around cups of hot chocolate, the relationship's mood had indeed returned to normal. They fantasized about staying here forever, moving to the coast for their retirement years, letting go of the crazy high-paced Sacramento life. Eventually, however, the conversation meandered back to the legal charges and the trial, but there was little new to discuss and the topic was really a downer for Ronnie.

"Let's put this aside," Ronnie suggested. "Tell me about your newfound peace. I know you've been exploring mysticism in your classes at the retreat center, but I don't really understand what you're doing and how it's changing you. It's a little disconcerting to me, you know? What's going on?"

"OK. You know me better than anyone else in the world. You know I have always been drawn to experiences of personal growth and psychological transformation, like that desert Vision Quest I went on in Nevada. And you know how sensitive I've always been to spiritual energies, like the enlightened consciousness of that patient I had seen around the same time. You remember Paul. Well, my interest in transformation lit up further in my experience of aging. I've been noticing subtle changes in consciousness that I think are signs of emerging enlightenment, signs that aging is somehow intended to transform human nature. My friend Rich, who is well into his eighties, and an elderly priest-friend of Clarence's, also confirmed age-related mystical changes."

"Tom, enough history," Ronnie said, slightly exasperated. "What are you talking about?"

"OK. I have been going deeper into my own mystical consciousness and, as a result, understanding the process better and better. Before I explain what I understand, we need to talk about the power and problem of language. What we call things makes a huge difference in how we understand and experience them, and we definitely need a fresh vocabulary in religion.

"Here's an important example," Tom continued. "We say we are 'conscious.' We assume that means that consciousness belongs to me and is connected to my brain. But what if we redefine consciousness as God? It would mean that God is not far away or separate from us, but that God's consciousness is in us. And it would mean that when we intentionally focus on pure consciousness, consciousness freed from thought and belief, we are experiencing God directly. That realization is incredibly powerful. And here's the final kicker – that experience changes us. Pure, divine consciousness, calms, heals, and inspires us, and it stimulates a deep welling up of love, joy and spiritual under-standing. The more you dwell in this state of conscious being, and the more you feel it in your body, the more you are transformed. It's a kind of alchemy transmuting all it touches, turning matter into spirit, turning our everyday experience of consciousness and physical being into *divine* consciousness and being. The experience of pure consciousness reveals that God is what we are made of."

Tom could see the puzzled, skeptical, distrusting look on Ronnie's face. "What's bothering you so far about this?"

"It's just so 'woo-woo.' Nobody talks like this. I don't get it. It's too far out."

"Let me say it differently then, because there is nothing 'woo-woo' about it. It all comes down to observing your own consciousness without any assumptions, expectations or beliefs. Let's be empirical. We'll take it in steps. First, are you conscious? Can you tell that you are conscious?"

"Of course. We wouldn't be having this conversation if I were unconscious."

"OK. For a moment, stop thinking about this and focus your awareness on consciousness. No thinking, no analyzing, just tune in to consciousness itself."

Ronnie stared off into space as she focused her awareness.

"There's nothing there."

"How does the 'nothing' feel?"

"A little scary. Like a big empty space of nothing, like I'm not there anywhere."

"Let that be OK for a moment. You can always start thinking again and recover your normal sense of self. Go back to focusing on pure consciousness and sense it as if it were God's consciousness. What do you notice now?"

"It's actually peaceful, and quite full. It's my thoughts that scared me. I was afraid that I was nothing without thought, that I was empty."

"Good! Keep focusing. What do you notice now?"

"Strangely enough, I start noticing things around me in a new way. It makes the world seem clearer, more distinct, brighter and even more colorful."

"Yes! That's part of the mystical experience. Sensory awareness heightens. Now focus this pure consciousness into your body, your physical being. Don't interpret the sensations as 'feelings' or symptoms but just focus awareness on the body's pure energy. What do you notice?"

"It feels nice. I like it. It kind of makes me feel happy, I don't why. It also makes me love you. Wow, this is interesting. All this just from focusing on consciousness?"

"Yes. And now imagine that you do this kind of focusing a lot, intensifying the experience you're having right now."

"Oh my God. That's what you've been doing."

"Yes. Do you see now how simple it is? It's really a matter of suspending thought, sharpening and focusing awareness, and experiencing divinity directly. 'Your' consciousness is actually God's consciousness in and around you. Do you see how powerful this shift in language is? Calling consciousness God and then feeling how it changes you! And this experience steadily grows, not making you someone else, but making you the best version of 'you' possible. We get stuck in our limited, contracted and fearful identities and beliefs, but when we intentionally merge consciousness with being, we discover everything is different than we thought, including us. This is how the divine transforms us. And the love that comes from this divine self is like a magic spring, always present and flowing. I have never loved so completely and fully in my life."

"You know, Tom, I think I get it, but I would describe it much more simply. It's just releasing your learned fears and getting in touch with your innate goodness. It's not always easy, but it's the path that leads to real maturity and love."

"Works for me," Tom replied. "I do go for more flowery language, but the point is the same. Here is the practice in a nutshell. First, stop thinking, even just for a moment. Focusing on something close by helps because direct sensory perception stops thought all by itself, so pick something to look at, like your hand or pants. Sharpen your perception a much as you can. Notice everything about it – color, texture, pattern. Then heighten this awareness even more, become as awake and aware as you can, as if you've heard something outside your window at night and suddenly listen intently for more sounds. Now you are shifting into a heightened consciousness. Finally, become conscious of consciousness itself, recognizing consciousness as God's Presence. Feel this Presence all around and through your body noticing what happens. I teach these simple steps as a spiritual practice for people. It's a way of entering conscious being and that leads to transformation. This is the cutting edge of change. I believe we are on the verge of a new kind of human and a new kind of humanity."

"OK, now you're getting flowery again. But you don't scare me so much anymore. Let's go home and get conscious and experience you-know-what, wink wink."

Tom broke out laughing, distracting the manager's attention for a moment, and they left hand-in-hand, snuggling as they walked.

Chapter 51

Though Ronnie intended to bring this peace home with her, it unraveled by the time they reached Highway 680 and evaporated as they drove across the Yolo Causeway through Davis and into Sacramento. Though Tom could feel the deep calm at his core, he too found himself worrying. *We live on many levels*, he thought, and silently dissolved his thinking into the timeless Presence; happiness filled his being. They were silent for most of the drive home.

The next Friday night, Tom and Ronnie came home from their weekly "date" and opened the front door. Glancing into his office, Tom was shocked. It was a mess! Papers everywhere, his locked file cabinet wrenched open, and the contents of desk drawers thrown all over the floor. Someone had broken into the house. The dining room, living room, and bedrooms had been left in a similar mess. Their beagle Charlie, now also aging but not particularly enlightened, failed completely in her watchdog duties. Tom called the police, an investigator came out, asked questions, looked for fingerprints with messy black powder, and left with little to offer – there were no identifiable suspects. The detective guessed it was someone looking for valuables or prescription medications to support a drug habit.

Tom was disturbed by the burglary, and had a vague feeling that this was more than just a random break-in. Did someone have it in for him? Would they be back? Was this related to the firebombings? Should they get a security system with hidden cameras and police alerts? The only question they could answer for sure was the latter, with a resounding "no." They were not going to live in fear and paranoid fortification. Still, something was terribly amiss. After they cleaned up the house, Tom returned to his own deepening fusion of consciousness and being, his inner unity with the divinity that completely washed away the burglary's stain. Ronnie was not as sanguine; her fears were growing. Tom wrapped his arms around her convulsing sobs. Ronnie also called Laura and, through tears and muted crying, described the mounting terror she felt. Laura supported her as much as she could, and then she called Erik.

Ronnie went to work the next day; Tom stayed home. The trial was still several weeks off. A meeting with their attorney had been scheduled next week but until then, there was not much for Tom to do.

Across town, however, another sort of investigation had commenced. In Laura's warm bright kitchen – yellow walls, modern stainless appliances, and a sink full of family breakfast dishes – Tom's adult children met to conceive a plan of attack. Their dad, they agreed, was lost in some "mystical" other world and needed their help. But what to do?

"I've been thinking," Laura began, her hands around a steaming cup of coffee. "This whole series of events – the two bombings, that lady's alleged assault downtown, the robbery, the hate-filled tirade against Dad on those stupid talk radio shows – feels like it's more than coincidence. It happened so fast, right out of the blue, and it all seems connected somehow. I think someone has it in for Dad. The police are obviously on the wrong track but I'm sure they wouldn't listen to us."

"Yes," acknowledged Erik, his voice deep and severe, "I, too, feel a disturbance in the force. The Tao quivers. Evil lurks in the shadows of these events. We, superheroes of goodness and justice, must act to right the force."

Laura laughed out loud, that eruptive snort she has when her own mirth explodes unexpectedly even to her. "Are you nuts? This is not a job for Scooby-Doo. This is serious."

"I'm just kidding, Laura, chill! I'm just saying that maybe we can uncover the bastard stalking Dad. What do you think? What's our plan? How would Scooby-Doo and his friends uncover this dastardly villain?"

Erik and Laura brainstormed for over half an hour, generating a range of intelligent, insane, and unquestionably illegal sleuthing strategies, divided up the most appropriate, and left the house ready and charged for action.

Meanwhile, Tom, unable to sit still, and unwilling to waste his time fretting, returned to the theme that had been calling him for months – the transformation of civilization and the evolution of a new humanity. Glancing at world news, however, he frankly wondered if the world was evolving at all; maybe devolving was a more apt description, with its never-ending genocidal wars, wasteful political stunts, global epidemics, horrible poverty, rampant pollution, species extinctions, climate change – the list never seemed to change. If spiritual evolution were happening, it was darn hard to see. Then a light went on inside.

Tom made phone calls to Clarence, Paul, Art, and Rich. At the last minute, he also decided to call Barbara, the Jungian therapist in his former consultation group, and Mary, one of the most successful students from one of his mysticism classes at the retreat center, to join them. Barbara was so wise about the deep nature of the psyche and Mary, once a nun herself, had a practical and no-nonsense grasp of mystical consciousness. He asked them to meet him at the retreat center the following week. He was calling them to a mystical summit, a deep searching discussion of humanity's spiritual evolution and how human beings could actively participate in it. He knew that finding real answers was at best a long shot, and maybe nothing would happen, but Tom was excited – at the very least it would be a fascinating conversation.

The "Mysticism Summit" met in a side conference room in the main building late in the day. It was early in the week and the center was quiet; only some AA folks having a meeting in a building near the priests' quarters. The sound of keyboard tapping, muffled phone calls and vacuuming in guest rooms echoed through the halls, providing an insulating drone outside the door to the meeting room. You could tell that each participant was fascinated by this novel idea. Where would their discussions lead?

The group sat around an oval table set with a lovely runner, a pitcher of water, glasses, coffee cups and coffee, a large candle, and a small bouquet of flowers Tom had gathered from the retreat grounds. A plate of coffee cake, napkins, and small serving plates completed the welcoming refreshments. Tom dimmed the overhead lights and ceremoniously lit the candle to create a more intimate and spiritual ambiance.

Tom thanked the group for coming. He said he knew this idea was a bit crazy, but that it had risen powerfully inside him and he wanted to follow the lead of this divine inspiration. The mood was warm and respectful. All trusted Tom's judgment and each knew they were there for a reason. Moving into the convening topic, Tom spoke first.

"Each of us here now feels and lives increasingly from a state of divine consciousness. We've learned to stop thinking and dissolve into a luminous and timeless center of peace, joy and clarity. We feel this mystical core steadily transforming us, creating a profound experience conscious being. I am somebody quite different from who I thought I was. And the more I move through the world in this consciousness, the more powerful that change becomes. I think we would all agree that this experience is truly amazing. But we represent such a tiny minority in the world. So, here are the general questions for our summit: Can our awakening really make any difference to humanity as a whole, to the suffering and inequities humans impose on each other? Can enlightened elders contribute to humanity's spiritual evolution? Are we reaching some kind of spiritual tipping point that we can name and influence? I called us here to share our deep insights from this common center. As the mystics say, 'there is one river, but many wells.' Are you with me?" All nodded. "Good. Let us take a moment of silence to bring these questions into the depth of our inner wells. Go deep and then we'll talk."

Silence settled into the room and all relaxed into its hallowed source. Tom's questions had refocused each member's awareness from the preceding conversation to the luminous interior space of sacred being. Divine consciousness pervaded the room, space becoming alive, warm and loving. Five minutes went by; there was no rush. Finally, someone's cough brought the group's attention back to Tom's questions and the purpose of the summit.

Quietly, tentatively, slowly, Clarence began. "I sense that the blueprint of the future human is within us, in the core of every person, and already actualizing itself through people like us. We are but a vanguard. I sense divine consciousness transforming human perception, and as it does, more people will see that Heaven is already here, literally composed of the creator's divine being. In this new and direct perception of a pantheistic God, knowledge will be immediate, perception will be revelation, and love will source all action. I feel this happening already."

Art cleared his throat, announcing his intention to join in, and said softly, "With the loss of my vision, I have 'seen' (Art used the standard finger quotation marks sign) the unity of all substance, my own consciousness included. I have felt the oneness that makes us already divine. I am divine and I cannot fathom being any happier than I am in this holiness of being. If people only knew what they were made of and where they were, the world would be transformed in a heartbeat. It's already here."

Waiting until he was sure Art was done, Rich chimed in. "I completely agree. And I believe aging brings us this gift of awakening. With fewer distractions, less ambition, and expanding consciousness, perceptive elders recognize that most of their 'knowledge' is useless as a means of divine transformation. Beliefs and opinions won't save us. Identity and its assumptions are just words that disappear completely in this omnipresent, all-inclusive consciousness. In this sacred alchemy, the World of Man disappears entirely, replaced by the direct experience of Heaven on Earth. This is how we are changed, by waking up from thought. We are learning, as Meister Eckhart said, to 'live like the rose, to live without a why.' How to bring this discovery to the almost seven billion people alive today, however, is another matter."

"Whoa," Mary interjected playfully. "The moment you ask a question, you return to the thought world, don't you see? And the World of Man is not a problem to be solved, it is an idea structure. Its 'problems' are byproducts of this structure. Problems and questions disappear in mystical consciousness. Tragically, most people are caught in their personal labyrinths of imagined problems, racing hither and yon to fix something that they themselves have created. They worry about fashion, appearance, money, purpose, but all of this is mental. Racing on a treadmill of thought, they really go nowhere. If each would stop thinking and open to reality as it is, they would discover peace and love as their birthright."

"Let me piggyback on that," Tom said. "The mystical experience is not just something that happens to an individual, the mystical experience is the living sentience of the universe itself. Everything is conscious, infinite, alive and perfect. It's the veil of thought that makes the world ugly, wrong and scary. We live as if our thoughts were true, as if they accurately represent the reality. In the present human era, we have reached the zenith of thought – fifty thousand books published every year in America alone, talking heads on every channel and website, and three thousand years of philosophy and theology have not awakened mankind. Science and medicine may help eradicate illnesses and document the futility of warfare, and technology effectively organizes our lives, but humans are still driven by such primitive animal instincts and reactions. Our goal is conscious being. We know how to get there on an individual level, how do we achieve a collective conscious evolution for everyone?"

"I live in a world where there is only God," Paul said quietly. "Where there is nothing lacking. Where opinions run off my back like water on a duck. Where there are no requirements for salvation, no need to earn the unimaginable love of the universe. I agree with Mary: the world is not a problem, it is a flower opening spontaneously in the sunshine of consciousness. This is the 'new Heaven and new Earth.' Thought is not bad, it works fine for communicating directions and ideas, but it can also be deceiving and frightening, creating a Hell on Earth. But to be seated in the center of my own being, to be conscious of consciousness itself, moved by conscious being and one with all peoples, this is the new world that is obscured by thought. But I can feel it coming. This is a transitional time. Conscious awakening is spreading through all levels of awareness, with the more sensitive experiencing it soonest. It is happening."

Tom asked, "How many of your feel that divine consciousness is expanding? Raise your hands."

All raised their hands.

"Do you think that cosmic consciousness could permanently be blocked by human thoughts?" asked Mary. "How could that be? In fact, I notice that my own immersion in the divine affects others even without discussing it. It is contagious. Mystical awareness spreads like a sacred virus across the imagined boundaries between people, from one person's consciousness to the next. Of course, many people resist experiencing this mystical dimension because they don't know what it is, and fear losing control of their conventional life, so backlashes are likely. So I agree with Paul. I can sense it unfolding right now, and we don't have to do anything."

Now Barbara chimed in. "The archetypes of the collect unconscious do in fact encode this transformation and they always have, as if they've been waiting for humanity to achieve sufficient maturity to experience them. You find this blueprint of transformation hidden in stories, myths, and dreams, and in every religion. The central archetype of transformation is death and rebirth – the death of the old self and birth of a divine one. This archetype underlies the awakening we are all discussing. It is an inborn force now rising to the surface, constellating what it means to be alive. And I agree with Mary that humanity's resistance causes suffering and violence, particularly the belief that security resides in material wealth and personal superiority. It's like swimming upstream – exhausting, painful, and ultimately futile."

"If it's happening already, where can we see it?" Tom asked.

Mary replied, "I see it breaking through all over, in both subtle and obvious ways. It's happening, for example, in the rapid spread of social media. We are all becoming aware of each other's Presence, giving everyone a voice and access to a common awareness. You can already see the indirect results of this awakening everywhere – divisive beliefs are evaporating, new teachers are proclaiming the unity of spirit and matter, people are questioning the validity of war, religions are becoming more open and interfaith, even science and spirituality are in dialogue these days. Yes, people frightened of this 'modernity' will resist desperately, even violently, but this childish terrorism is a tragic phase, not a stable social order. So, while humanity stumbles a lot, for we are not yet used to this new collective experience of consciousness, the pace is fast and accelerating, especially when compared to our past evolutionary steps. The human world is becoming one consciousness with many interacting parts, and will one day include the sentience of animals, nature, and space itself. It's happening, Tom, it's here, we have only to wake up enough to see it."

"So we don't have to do anything?" Tom asked.

"We are there right now," Barbara responded. "Each person in this room can feel this unity of Presence. We are among the early responders. The long journey away from this consciousness that began in our early evolutionary shift from mystical awareness to belief systems is finally coming full circle – not losing the gains from science and technology, but making them part of the consciousness of this new organism. We are in it, it is in us; the boundaries and barriers are disappearing. We have arrived, though most don't yet know it."

"How will it change our behavior?" Tom wondered aloud. "How will the world be different?"

"When we experience unity," Art replied, "we will care for everything and everyone as part of our self. Here's a comparison. In the unity of your body, would you ever think of cutting off your hand so it couldn't steal your food or eating your leg when you're hungry? So too when we realize that the 'other' is me, we will love others as we love our self. It is a huge paradigm shift, a tipping point that will spontaneously change humanity forever and welcome us to the living divine universe. This insight is in every religion but humanity's spiritual development is only just on the cusp of being able to express it, to live it out."

Rich had one more thing to say. He wanted to talk again about the power of aging in this transformation. "I agree that everyone is being affected by this expanding consciousness, but in different ways. Elders, like Art and me, sense it because our consciousness is opening more each day as we age. The young, whose job it is to reinvent the world for their generation, express their awakening consciousness through creativity, technology, and concern for the world. Middle-aged folks, who often feel a need to hold society together, may resist change; that's their developmental role. The most conservative folks in the middle will even be part of the cultural backlash, resisting new views that they find particularly threatening to their identity, security and belief systems. Some of these people are probably responsible for your troubles, Tom. They attack what they fear most – the harbingers of change. So it is the elders that hold the lantern of consciousness to guide the world through this time of turmoil, darkness and despair. We need to take our places as conscious teachers, caretakers, prophets, sages and guides for a changing culture."

With that summary, the group again fell silent. Each had spoken what the others knew and all recognized these truths as self-evident proof of the new human. They were on the way to realizing it. What more needed to be said?

But Tom then posed another question. "How do we live in this new consciousness when so many others are stuck in the old one? Few understand our behavior or its cause. How do we teach and guide others in this extraordinary time in history? What are our goals? For example, I am going to trial in a couple weeks. The prosecuting attorney wants to convict me of arson and assault. His zeal is so misguided and irrelevant to the divine. How can I show people how wasteful this is? And how will frightened people deal with the unprecedented new forms of equality, freedom and self-expression created by the new consciousness?"

"Tom, you keep wanting to do something," teased Rich, emphasizing the word 'do'. "Goals come from the ego and merely produce more thought. They are inevitably goals after the wrong thing – more thought. Even if the thoughts seem laudatory, they are still thoughts. So, when you generate goals, you are slipping back into the World of Man. Remember, this consciousness expands naturally in love and joy and peace. It's our job to be true to our divine experience. People will value our transformation more when we don't try to explain it. Dwell in love, Tom, it's the best medicine society can have as we come over the tipping point. Relax into the flow, Tom, wherever it goes."

"Rich is absolutely right," Clarence said. "This new consciousness reveals what all the mystics have said: Heaven on Earth has already come, but we are just not awake enough to see it. Blake told us that when mystical consciousness wipes clean the doors of perception, we see the world as it truly is – infinitely beautiful, precious, conscious and loving. I see it every day. You do, too. It never left, we did. But to see it, you have to stop conceptualizing it."

"What about feeding the poor?" Tom insisted. "What's wrong with that concept? What about stopping global epidemics? Shouldn't we create programs with the goal of helping those in need?"

"We will do that naturally in this new consciousness," Mary replied softly. "We will do the right thing. But when you create a 'program,' it becomes an idea that inadvertently stimulates its opposite. It implies that there is a problem and that stirs fear and greed. People begin to hoard food, steal from the distribution centers, or sell medicines to rich dictators. When change comes from mystical consciousness, people use the same resources and creativity without trying to control things or bring about some conceptualized goal. We've witnessed the 'war on hunger,' 'the war on drugs,' and 'the war on poverty.' None of them succeeded. The word 'war' says it all – wars don't work. Conscious being results in conscious doing filled with joy. The joy is in the doing, not the program, the imagined results, or the ego's in charge."

Rich chimed in. "Tom, here's an example. Elders have long known that volunteering gives them as much pleasure as the recipient. I tutor kids in reading and I love doing it. It's so much fun. Though elders may not articulate it, they are in touch with a profound principle: the love that flows from conscious being is its own reward and it touches others in ways we can never know in advance."

Now Clarence jumped in. "I have a confession. I've begun reframing my Christian beliefs as both symbolic and prophetic of this great change. The church views its theology as unchanging dogma, but it can also be viewed as mythology, and mythology, as Joseph Campbell taught us, reflects the deep nature of human psyche, revealing its archetypal structure and what it suggests can happen. I guess Barbara's Jungian orientation has been influencing my theology." He laughed then continued. "I think the 'rapture' and 'end times' actually symbolize the joyful ending of the World of Man, the thought world, not the world itself. It is the end of time, for time is a concept, but not the end of Creation. Furthermore, this breakthrough of the divine consciousness in our own consciousness may represent the experience of incarnation – we are all capable of incarnating the divine. And the Pentecost, this down-pouring of the Holy Spirit, is just another way of saying it will touch everyone."

So there it was in a nutshell. The group's collective vision almost seemed anticlimactic to Tom. Or more accurately, it was all so obvious that he was amazed he hadn't seen it this clearly before. It was perfect. It was divine revelation of the first order, yet so simple and direct. *This is the gift of direct gnosis*, Tom thought – *you understand the nature of something immediately without endless analysis.* He had his answers.

Chapter 52

Ever since his Mysticism Summit, Tom had been feeling profoundly peaceful and relaxed. He was living in the divine mystery of conscious being. Even after their discussion in Santa Cruz, Ronnie could not understand why he was so calm and peaceful given their present legal circumstances and the unresolved danger that still lurked in the background. So, at Ronnie's urging, Tom called Detective Hendricks for an update. The return call came the next day.

"We're still investigating the firebombings. Obviously you didn't firebomb yourself, though you could have arranged it, but what about the church bombing and the assault on Emma? Do you have anything more to say about them? Don't think we are done with you, Dr. McLaughlin."

"Do whatever you feel is right, Detective Hendricks. Whatever happens will be alright."

"That is a really stupid comment."

"Yes, probably. Well, goodbye, Detective."

Within seconds the phone rang again.

"Hi, Dad, it's Laura. Erik and I have some interesting news to report. Are you free?"

"Of course. Want to come over now?"

"We're on the way."

Fifteen minutes later, Tom, Laura, Erik and Ronnie were settled in the family room. Tom had left NPR's classical music station playing in the background and seemed unbelievably relaxed under the circumstances. Erik liked this. He had begun to view his father as a "Ninja Guru Realized Being Rock Star" and loved it. With considerably more focus, Laura planned to do most of the talking. Still distracted, Ronnie listened quietly, assuming this discussion represented some soon-to-be-revealed family issue.

"Erik and I have been investigating your situation," Laura began. "Now don't start lecturing us about cooperating with the police. You are already their main 'Person-of-Interest' and the noose has only been getting tighter." Ronnie shivered when she heard this. "But the really good news is we figured this out."

This announcement was last thing Tom expected. "You did what?"

"Velma, Scooby-Doo and Shaggy sleuthed the villain."

Another explosive Laura snort, followed by her always infectious giggle. "What Erik is trying to say in cartoon language, Dad, is that we did an investigation of our own. But before we give you the results, we should explain our methods and discoveries."

"I'm all ears," Tom replied. Ronnie now sat upright.

"My first plan," Laura explained, "was to canvass the neighborhood and see if someone noticed anything strange the night of the home burglary. I went first to your neighbor with the horses on the other side of the private road. She told me that kids had been sneaking onto her property to taunt her horses so she put in a surveillance system with camera to see who approached the fence. She identified the kids. More importantly, she left the camera on 24/7 just to be safe. It's motion-activated so it has enough storage to record for several weeks. She pulled up the footage from the night of your robbery and there it was: a man skulking down that private road just past her horse corral and onto your property. She printed a picture – not great but clear enough."

"Wow," Tom exclaimed. "Let me see."

"Hold on, we're not done. I next went to see the neighbor at the top of the lane, you know, that crazy pathologist Ken who turned into a first-class paranoid after his wife left him. Comes home late from work, stays up half the night, and watches everything that happens in the neighborhood. But he's friendly and loves attention and was willing to talk. The night in question, he saw a strange car in front of his house, watched some guy lurking near it, and when the guy disappeared around the corner, Ken opened his car door, looked in his glove compartment, and got his name. Now we had a picture and an identity. But that's not all."

Seeing his opening, Erik jumped in. "Yes, and I had the idea of listening to the local talk radio show blaspheming your name and reputation – the host is a real nutcase. I called in, pretended to be one of the nuts in his can, and chatted up this guy. He told me that he'd read your article only after a fanatic listener called in to say the Devil was at work in the community, and that Devil was you. Though the radio guy wasn't too concerned about the Devil, he said the *Bee* article had given him some great material, crazy stuff like elders talking to God. You know, you are a little far out, Dad, even for me. But no matter. Then he told me the guy was a minister and gave me the name of his church."

"And…?"

"We're not done, Dad," said, Laura, taking the baton. "Turns out this guy's church has a website. I guess everyone is trying to get on the social-media bandwagon. And on his website was a photo that matched your neighbor's video print. And the car Ken sneaked into, that was the same guy."

"And he finally came on the talk radio show," Erik added. "You should have heard him! He was positively rabid in his accusations. Obviously you have become the target of some kind of satanic-warfare scenario he believes in. You should read the sermons on the church website. It's all there."

"And you know what else?" Laura chimed in. "In his very best cloak-and-dagger undercover disguise, Erik visited that guy's church pretending to be its insurance guy. He met a friendly janitor who showed him around. In the back storeroom, Erik spotted a can of industrial solvent. We bet it's the same combustible used in the firebombings."

"Oh my God," Tom exhaled, the implications crushing down

on him. "I can't believe it. This guy started the media backlash against me, firebombed a coffee shop I was in and his own church and then broke into my house to scare the crap out of us. He is certifiably insane."

"He is also certifiably criminal," Erik added.

Now Tom was bursting with curiosity. "OK, put me out of my misery. Who is this guy?" Ronnie waited, holding her breath.

"Are you ready?" Erik asked. "The guy's name is Jimmy Hoeller. He's the pastor of some church in South Sac."

"Oh my God," Tom exhaled. "That's the guy who picketed my office all those years ago because I was treating Paul, his handyman. He must have been after me all along. And his church was the site of the second firebombing! I thought that was a strange coincidence – it should have been a clue!"

"That's correcto, hombre." Erik chortled. "And on his website, he not-so-subtly suggests that maybe you did the deed."

"Me?" Tom replied in astonishment.

"A perfect cover," Erik replied. "You would never suspect a guy whose own church also got firebombed."

"Have you given this evidence to the police yet?" Tom asked.

"We wanted to tell you first. Dad, now you can prove your innocence."

Tears were streaming down Ronnie's face; tears of joy and gratitude. The kids gave her a long and healing hug.

Tom called Detective Hendricks and left a message with the telephone numbers of the "Scooby-Doo Detective Agency."

Chapter 53

"Tom, this is Detective Hendricks."

"Glad to hear from you," Tom replied.

"Thank you. Your kids have been busy. We don't approve of amateur investigations but we can't deny the results of this one. So I have a big apology for you. We confirmed that the bombings at the coffee shop and the First Christian Church of Mayhew involved the same accelerant. Cans and rags were hidden in a storage room in the church basement, as you know. We also examined your neighbor's video and matched the shadowy figure to the Pastor Hoeller in question. We started talking to him. He was incredibly defensive at first, got all high and mighty, threatened us with Hell and damnation. Finding his fingerprints on the can, however, was like pulling back the screen on the Wizard of Oz. So then he pulled out his Bible and started calling us all kinds of strange foreign-sounding names like Beelzebub and saying the Lord commanded His servants to destroy the pillars and alters of His enemies – I guess you were one of them. Apparently, he'd been watching your house and tailed you and your priest friend to that coffee shop, then tossed in the Molotov cocktail. You're incredibly fortunate that he didn't firebomb your house when he burglarized it. We think he ransacked your house to terrorize your family and look for evidence of Devil worship or something crazy like that. It's also my hunch that he's the kind of preacher who really likes personal adulation and felt this was a great opportunity to be famous. So you see, Tom, we were right to believe these bombings and robbery were the acts of a religious nutcase, we just had the wrong nut – just kidding."

"And Emma?"

"Yes. We also found out that Emma had been heavily medicated for back pain by her family doctor at the time of the alleged attack. Apparently she took too much, mixed it with cold remedies, became delusional and was found confused and wandering in Old Town. When the police picked her up, she thought she had been attacked. Later she forgot what happened but still believed she'd been assaulted. The only person she could think to blame was you. Pastor Hoeller probably realized that Emma's delusions were a perfect opportunity to cast further aspersions on your character. By the way, she was recently released from the hospital and seems to have recovered fully."

Tom had to laugh. "So I'm off the hook?"

"You're free to swim wherever you want. And I am truly sorry we put you through the wringer. Please accept our apologies. Sometimes we go down the wrong road."

The conversation ended amicably. This abrupt resolution also seemed anticlimactic, but it underscored for Tom the power and danger of prejudicial beliefs. At least it was over.

Tom called Ronnie, Laura and Erik to give them the news. They were ecstatic. He also called his Mysticism Summit friends to share the good cheer. Clarence asked, "What do you think was going on with Hoeller? Why was he stalking you?"

"I'm not entirely sure, but from the detective's descriptions of his mental state, it sounds like he harbors wildly dramatic fantasies of the final warfare between God and Satan on Earth, biblically rationalized fantasies that became frankly delusional. What a religious fanatic like him cannot understand is that these ideas refer not to the outer world of people and events, but to his own very disturbed inner world, and specifically to some horribly traumatic and unresolved childhood abuse and neglect. Unconsciously stuck in the past, a guy like this fights his inner demons by projecting them into the world and doing battle with them. And preachers like him love to get others onboard with their end-times scenarios. It confirms their delusions and justifies their actions. What all this also means, Clarence, is I think I dodged a bullet."

Clarence's question about Hoeller's motivation stayed with

Tom. He thought he understood what happened at the psychological level, but was there a larger meaning, a spiritual one? His mind wandered back to the Board of Psychology crisis 15 years ago and how it resolved so easily, almost by itself. How had that happened? Suddenly Tom got it. The real crisis at that time had been his own spiritual awakening, the breakthrough of mystical consciousness triggered by Paul's altered state. It had been, in effect, a spiritual crisis. His Vision Quest allowed this awakening to come through and be processed. As a natural consequence, the outer issues dissolved spontaneously. The inner and out issues had been connected, a phenomenon Jung had called synchronicity, in which separate events are related without an objective causal link – a reflection of the hidden oneness of being. But this stalking crisis felt different. It had only been resolved because of his children's clever sleuthing! What did that mean?

With his mind spinning in confusion, Tom decided to walk down to the river. Exercise and nature always seemed to clear out the cobwebs. At first he just let go of the whole question; it was not going to be solved logically. As sunshine warmed his back and delta breezes ruffled his hair, Tom meandered through the oaks to the river's edge and watched wood ducks feed in the swirling eddies. Here, free of human involvement, all was right with the world, a thought that sparked a new train of thought. *It is naïve to believe that mystical consciousness automatically protects you from the dangers of conventional reality, including human evil. It may reveal eternity but it does not necessarily affect embodied existence.* As Rich had explained earlier, humans moved among the four worlds: the *World of Man* – an intellectual realm of identity, time and story; *Darkness* – the unconscious with its repressed pain, and shadow motivations; *Divinity* – pure consciousness, joy, and union; and finally *Heaven on Earth* – the world as God's being including the evolution of a divine human. *As long as we're alive,* Tom thought, *our spiritual growth involves them all as the divine world gradually replaces the secular.*

Tom reclined on a flat, sun-warmed rock by the river, closed his eyes, and let the sound and energy of the water's current flow through him. *Thank God the kids took action when I was dithering about in transcendence,* he mused, and then released himself into grateful union with divinity – no boundaries, no separation, no one to be, just perfect fusion of consciousness and being. Such joy. *You don't have to solve the problem of duality, you just need to know the rules of where you are.*

Chapter 54

Another loose end wrapped up a week later.

"Tom! This is Dianne Powell calling. Got a second?"

"Hey! Good to hear from you."

"Thanks and good to hear your legal problems have settled down. I've been following the newspaper coverage of your case with interest and, I have to admit, trepidation. I knew you were innocent, but that and two-fifty will only get you a cup of coffee. The piece this morning said all the charges had been dropped and some wild preacher from the south area had been arrested."

"A long and dreary story, but well-summarized in the article. Thanks for your support."

"Your case notwithstanding, the reason I really called was about your interest in mystical consciousness and its place in human evolution. Our conversation on the patio that day stayed with me, stirring my own crazy wonderings – I'm not always the hard-nosed empiricist! I agree that our earliest ancestors probably had more reliance on right-hemisphere consciousness for their survival, before speech became so dominant. But what is the evolutionary value of this kind of consciousness returning to the foreground of our brain functioning at this time in history? Here's what I think. Mystical consciousness erases boundaries – between people, countries and beliefs, boundaries created by thoughts that in turn generate wars. When these boundaries disappear, it's like waking up from a bad dream – you realize that everything is okay; there is no enemy. The evolutionary value of this awakening would be incredible – no more wars. This also relates to how my consciousness changed with my mother when she was dying. We'd had a difficult relationship over the years, but the time we spent together in silent consciousness at the end opened a kind of love completely independent of thought. I saw her as a perfect being – not my mother, not my adversary, not my critic – but a being of beauty and light, as God changing form before my eyes. I don't yet know how to operationalize this hypothesis in a way that could be tested. We'd have to start with a definition and measure of consciousness that could be applied to warring peoples. You're a psychologist, can you think of a way?"

"There is a lot of work going right now in the intersection of psychology, religion and the neuroscience of consciousness. It's a very exciting time to be alive. We are watching the evolution of science before our eyes. Let me email you some references and see where they take you."

"Would you be interested in collaborating on a research project?" Dianne teased.

"Well, I don't know. You see my personal evolution has moved deeply into this field of inner divine consciousness. I don't feel a need to research it; I just want to live it. I would be happy to be a consultant for you, but me? I'm changing before my own eyes as well and don't want to be intellectually removed from this incredible transformation. I am different than I was. My ego-centered persona is collapsing into a consciousness full of joy and love, like that neuroscientist's but without the stroke. I feel myself becoming the original divine embodiment of me before I had to contrive another 'me' as a child to fit into the world. I know it sounds crazy – we still don't have a good vocabulary for it, but I am becoming a version of God as me. Not some omnipotent being, but a consciousness flowing from divinity filled with a gnosis that transforms my life, my vision, my very being. I guess that's a long-winded way of saying I am drawn elsewhere, but I love that you are on the trail and would be happy to help through more great conversations on the patio in the sunshine. You know what I mean?"

She did. Fascinated by his words, she promised to keep in touch. And they would definitely have another visit.

Now there was just one last loose end, at least in Tom's mind. He called Paul Jensen's house midday hoping Emma would be at work. Paul answered on the first ring.

"Hi, Paul! It's Tom McLaughlin. How are you?"

"I'm great. I thought I might hear from you. Been reading about you in the papers. Sounds like your problems are pretty much over, right?"

"Yes, thank God. It was craziness and it went all the way to Pastor Hoeller. A true scandal for the church. How did people react?"

"Oh, the usual way. Most don't believe it and accuse the press of trying to slander a man of God. He's out on bail basically preaching that message. But if he gets convicted, the church will have to find a new leader. And you know, Emma might just be the one to head the search committee. She is fully recovered now and in many ways, she *is* the church and will be the next preacher's right hand. The Pastor Hoeller scandal gives her more to do and more importance in the church. She sees herself doing God's work. So the church will survive and might even be stronger in the process."

"We have come a long way, Paul, from those first meetings in my office to that Summit of Mystics at the retreat center. Our relationship started off over fifteen years ago with me in the role of psychologist and you the patient, but over time that changed profoundly. You went on to assume the much more meaningful role of teacher. You taught me so much, Paul, not just by your explanations and your friendship, which have both been invaluable, but through your consciousness. Just being around you changed me and I will never forget you. I just wanted to tell you that and to see how you and Emma were."

"We are fine and I am fine. I am one with that deepest consciousness we are all given to find. All I see, all I touch, is transformed in it. That is enough. And I can sense you are moving into that same unity. Let's stay friends. It has been an honor to be your friend."

That, too, was enough.

Chapter 55

In the days and weeks after the legal storm blew over and calm returned to the McLaughlin household, Tom resumed his writing and teaching. Nothing big or heroic. Mystical consciousness simply led him there and he loved to share from this consciousness-centered state of being in the blog Erik had created for him, though he was never sure how many people read it. He also found himself thinking about death and how an elder's movement toward this final transition seemed to open up a subliminal connection with the other world. Tom could almost sense the thinness of the divide and experience the love pouring in from the other side. This, too, was a gift of conscious aging – to feel where you were going without fear. In fact, this "end point" began to feel like a goal that reorganized his perspective, further changed his way of living, and carried him along like a gentle river. Tom was in no hurry to go, but the passage was now a little closer and welcoming.

It next occurred to Tom that this might be a good time for another dialogue with God. He hadn't done one in a long time and wasn't even sure if they really were dialogues with God or himself, or both, but the information that came out had previously felt very meaningful. So, why not try again? He sat before his computer, composed his thoughts, and began.

Tom: God, humanity is racing into a future of virtually inconceivable possibilities – universal interconnectivity, instantaneous communication, artificial intelligence, nearly complete access to all known information, and absolute equality of all people. It's almost as if we are becoming one brain, with each individual a participating neuron grouped by interests or talents; or a kind of singularity, not the technological kind where invention races beyond human comprehension, but the spiritual kind, where the pace of spiritual transformation simply overtakes humankind's resistance. Is that happening? Where are we going?

God: *It's an intermediate step between individuality and spiritual unity. Technology provides the physical building blocks for the mind to realize its inherent oneness in consciousness. First you build the physical interconnectivity that in turn structures the brain, then you realize it was always here, always part of the mind's potential. All will flourish.*

Tom: *What is the endpoint?*

God: *To channel my mind into humanity and create a new order, a new kind of human being. One day in the future, when your individuality and my Presence completely merge, humans will be infinitely more intelligent and aware, and that means I will finally have a peer – another like me who can be my friend and equal. I want to share my thoughts with someone that can grasp the range and depth of my mind.*

Tom: *That is both tender and astounding. Where will this spiritual evolution lead?*

God: *Into the infinite present – no time, space or limits to obscure our relationship. It will lead to joy, play, creativity and love, and cosmic exchanges unlike any you can imagine.*

Tom: *What about our being one single consciousness? If you have an equal, then there are two beings here.*

God: *It will be fluid. You become Me, I become you, and the whole cosmos wakes up in a single yet infinitely differentiated chorus of consciousness, one great song, many singers, and some will reach equality and we will sing together as one in great celebration. The*

Heavens will ring out.

Tom: A uni-verse! It's so amazing. And what is death?

God: Just another transformation. We merge, you melt into bliss, then if you're still interested in more, you decide what you want to experience next, how you want to grow. Can you remember why you chose this present life?

Tom: No.

God: Let me show you. Close your eyes and 'see.'

Tom closed his eyes. He saw a whole string of previous lives. He recognized places, relationships, ordeals, joys, accomplishment, wounds. Teaching in a western town, being a surgeon in the army, a ballroom-dance instructor, a child who died of rheumatic fever. On and on. He began to understand that evolution is spiritual and it continues from lifetime to lifetime, involving whatever you want to experience. Tom had wanted to find God in this lifetime, in form, in being, in this round. And he had. He felt a surge of joy.

Tom: Why does this whole process exist?

God: Because it's what I am. Because I wish to experience myself in infinite ways, flooding the universe with love and consciousness, awakening everything in consciousness. The new humanity is simply the next stage of my becoming. Just as humans are wiring their brains through computer interconnectivity, I am wiring mine through you. It is fabulous. But not for any purposes you might conceive. This evolution is really no different than those little flowers growing on the top of that butte you beheld on your Vision Quest – they are growing there simply as expressions of me, just as you are.

Tom: What will this new world be like?

*God: It will be like the dance revealed in your Vision Quest dream —
one pulsing, flowing, differentiating unity, all parts dancing
together in the whole, the whole dancing the parts, all things infused
with me. It's already here; you are now just beginning to feel me
flowing like electricity through you, like blood moving through your
body. Don't be afraid. Trust this evolution. We are one. You
discovered this over a decade ago through Paul's mystical
experience. Now it's time to enter the dance. Let go; you cannot
reduce this to anything you can know or imagine.*

Tom: How do we enter this dance?

*God: Stop thinking, feel into the energy of your body, which is in
essence my joy and love, and then allow it to move through you.*

A song popped spontaneously into Tom's mind, complete with
melody and words. He began to sing…

The way is easier than you think.
It's coming closer now, don't look away, don't blink.

The power moves through everything you see.
Release yourself, come and dance with me.

Forget yourself and dance out on the floor.
Join the flow, it's timeless and ever more.
You are here to melt into my song.
Feel the love, you cannot do it wrong.

The song's chorus continued long after the verses stopped:

You who are free,
Come and waltz with me.
Open wide your heart,
Trust you already know your part.
Feel into the way, come and stay.

The music and words had replaced Tom's questions. Or more accurately, he was now in the rhythm, moving naturally, swaying, bodily joy erupting through his movements, as it had in the dream. This was the divine life before thought interrupted its flow. Now, in a mystical consciousness free from thought, tapping into the deepest level of being, Tom was there. He was in the new world.

One last time Tom asked himself, *How does one act with integrity in the world from this state of joy? Shouldn't we pursue social justice or great works?* Tom remembered Rich's teasing advice to "just be." Then the final piece of the puzzle fell into place. *As a portal for God's flow, enlightened elders bring divine love into the world right where they are, simply by being there, radiant with divine consciousness, shining like Chinese lanterns. In the light of consciousness, they respond organically to whatever situation exists around them, their Presence illuminating and transforming it with love. The moral? Love. If that means standing in front of a tank, fine. If that means planting a garden and sharing your bounty, fine. If that means tutoring the special-needs child next door, fine. If that means sitting on a park bench loving the world, fine. Whatever you do from this consciousness, fine. This is how the divine enters the world – all forms alive with divinity.* Anything else, he recognized, would be ego interfering with divine being.

Part III

Chapter 56

Tom was dying of multiple myeloma. It had been 17 years since he entered the dance, years that were rich and deep and joyful. He had moved with wonder and curiosity through the sub-stages of aging, from his sixties – the youth of old age, through the middle years of gradually declining energy, mobility and health, to this final stage of preparing to let go of his body. Touching others with his gentle radiance, simple wisdom and boundless love had become an effortless way of life for Tom; he had become a sage of sorts. The great questions that had driven his thinking had largely melted away, and he understood that they had been symptoms of his separation from divine consciousness – useful once but no longer important, for he had lived his way into the answer. And, having already given up so much of his separate persona, he, too, was ready to melt away into the shining divine.

Ronnie had aged along with Tom and together they marveled at the changes that age had wrought on their bodies, minds, and family relationships. Even the grandchildren had grown up to bring forth yet another beautiful generation! The mystery of aging now deepened for them, becoming a timeless flow of day and night, rain and sun, and ever-expanding consciousness. A sense of peace surrounded them, a peace so deep that family and friends visited often just to feel it. Tom could sense Heaven's presence all the time now as the boundaries between the worlds dissolved. Dreams brought visions of the coming reunions with loved ones who had previously made the passage. Paul had died 12 years earlier in a car accident; Rich had gone soon after from old age. Tom also felt unknown ancestors moving back and forth between the worlds, carrying love and wisdom in both directions. As rigid conceptual boundaries melted, Tom realized that here, there, past and future, were all one place with endless worlds and dimensions. What a journey!

In quiet moments, when he felt well enough to look back over the years, Tom began to see his own life and the evolving world on a larger canvas. Population demographics had continued to change the world, with countries becoming older, more democratic, and less violent. Education, social media, and gender equality had led to shrinking birth rates and a healthier balance between the old and young, and the world was finally taking responsibility for its earlier excesses – pollution, deforestation, and climate change – paying a large price in many areas. While space exploration had proceeded apace exciting many, others saw the immense value of exploring the inner world of spirit and consciousness, vast and immense in its dimensions, possibilities, and wisdom. He was witnessing the maturation of humanity, still stumbling but at least stumbling into divinity.

Looking back, Tom also began to understand how the events of his life had been driven by an invisible spiritual Presence pressing into the World of Man – meeting Paul introduced him to the mystical experience; a random workshop flyer brought him into the desert for his own awakening; a subsequent decade of spiritual creativity erupted from this new consciousness; his heart attack and loss of career introduced him to aging's further transformation of self and consciousness; and all along he had witnessed the recurring backlash from those threatened by change, people who could neither conceive nor accept the relativity of their beliefs and identities. But everything that happened, all the forward and backward stumbles, had contributed to the growing divinization of the world.

Looking into the future, Tom had visions of what lay ahead. There were still many areas of darkness in human nature. They sprang up repeatedly, like angry and spoiled children still unaware of their pervasive nature and purpose of love. But he also saw a world where all beings communicated with each other, celebrating the wonder of creation that had become Tom's world. Then, sometime eons into the future, when the world was completed in love, all this would disappear in God, making room for new worlds to form, like foaming bubbles riding on cosmic waves. Identifying now with this play of divine consciousness – he, too, had played like this as a child – Tom let go of any further need to "fix" or "improve" things.

Preparing for death, Tom asked his doctor to support a simple and natural passing with only "comfort care" to minimize pain – no heroic measures! He instructed his family to write his obituary any way they liked and provided instructions for a memorial service replete with selected music, personal stories, nostalgia and lots of laughter. Tom had been writing songs for years, songs about his grandchildren, his life, and his marriage, songs he accompanied with his acoustic guitar, recorded on his computer and shared with his ever-expanding family circle; he asked that these creations be played at his ceremony so that he might sing for them once again. He had also been writing "Grampa Stories" to share and explain his inner journey with his grandchildren and bound them in a small book with handwritten notes to each child to be delivered at the service. Finally, he asked that his body be cremated and the ashes be mixed with soil for a young apple tree to be planted nearby so family members would knew where to "find" him and share the renewal of life each year. *"Well done,"* he thought, *"well done."*

Tom was ready to go, ready to release his already-disintegrating body and fly through the tunnel into the next world. Did he want to stay on for another round or dissolve completely back into the light? Did he want to be God's equal or keep exploring God's nature? He had made no decisions yet. Creation was such an amazing and multifaceted experience, he might just decide to do more of it. He said a personal goodbye to each of his children, grandchildren, and great-grandchildren, along with his few remaining cohorts, and spent all the rest of his time with Ronnie, in intimate silence or reflecting on their long union and what they might find together in the next world.

Light filled his room. Light filled with consciousness. Welcoming smiles from those waiting, loving gratitude from those temporarily left behind. It was time.

Bibliography

To learn more about the ideas developed in Breakthrough, visit me at www.johnrobinson.org or refer to the following publications:

Robinson, John. (1997). *Death Of A Hero, Birth Of The Soul: Answering the Call of Midlife*, Council Oak Books, 1997.

Robinson, John. (1999). *But Where Is God? Psychotherapy and the Religious Search*, Nova Science Publishers, 1999.

Robinson, John. (2000). *Ordinary Enlightenment: Experiencing the Presence of God in Everyday Life*, Unity Books, 2000.

Robinson, John. (2005). *Living the Myth of Inanna*, Psychological Perspectives, C.G. Jung Institute of Los Angeles, Vol. 48: 110-120.

Robinson, John. (2008). *Heaven on Earth: Keys to the Garden*. Paradigm Shift, Issue 37, 5-7, 2008.

Robinson, John. (2008). A Theology of Resurrection and the Vision of Heaven on Earth. In Henry, Matt (Ed.). *Originally Blessed*.

Robinson, John. (2009). *Finding Heaven Here*. Winchester, UK: John Hunt Publishing (O-Books).

Robinson, John. (2009). Finding Heaven Here. *Science of Mind Magazine*, Vol. 82, No. 1, pp. 86-93.

Robinson, John, (2009). *Learning to Live in Heaven on Earth*. Unity Magazine, May/June, pp. 32-35.

Robinson, John. (2012). *The Three Secrets of Aging*. Winchester UK: John Hunt Publishing (O-Books).

Robinson, John. (2012). *Bedtime Stories for Elders: What Fairy Tales Can Teach Us About the New Aging*. Winchester, UK John Hunt Publishing (O-Books).

Robinson, John. (2013). *What Aging Men Want: The Odyssey as a Parable of Male Aging*. Winchester, UK: John Hunt Publishing

(O-Books).

Robinson, John. (2013). The Long Journey Home: The Odyssey as a Parable of Male Aging. In Bourk, Penelope, (Ed.). *Journeys Outward, Journeys Inward*. Chapel Hill: Second Journey Publications.

Robinson, John. (2013). Book Review. In Anthony, Bolton. (Ed.). *The Call of the Spirit in Later Life*. Chapel Hill: Second Journey Publications.

If you liked *Breakthrough*, please write an Amazon review and share with Facebook friends. Thanks!

At Roundfire we publish great stories. We lean towards the
spiritual and thought-provoking. But whether it's literary or
popular, a gentle tale or a pulsating thriller, the connecting
theme in all Roundfire fiction titles is that once you pick them
up you won't want to put them down.